OUR HEARTS + OUR JOURNEY = OUR DESTINY

(THE BLAKE FAMILY SERIES #3)

R.C. STERN

Cover Art by Daniela Colleo of StunningBookCovers.com
Formatting by Polgarus Studio

ISBN-13: 978-0-9965278-8-0 (paperback)
ISBN-13: 978-0-9965278-7-3 (ebook)

Dedicated to the first man who has loved me all my life…my hero, my father.
Love you always, Dad.
Gratias tibi

"Because what makes you a man is not the ability to make a child, it's the courage to raise one."
President Barack Obama

CHAPTER ONE

November

CARI

The sun is shining bright, and the ocean looks sparkly. Gramps is putting on more of that white stuff that keeps the sun from hurting our skin, and Grams is helping me fill up my sand bucket. Some of the other kids here are in the water with their parents, and some are building sandcastles together. I wish my mommy and daddy were with me so I can be just like the other kids.

"Grams?"

"Yes, sweetheart?"

"Do my mommy and daddy love me?"

"Of course."

"Then why isn't mommy and daddy here?"

She looks sad. I don't want to make Grams sad.

"Your mommy is with the angels in heaven."

"And is daddy with the angels too?"

"He wishes," Gramps says.

Grams looks at him, and then looks back at me. "No. Your daddy is not with the angels." She mumbles something about him being busy with his own life. "Why don't we go get some ice cream now?"

The flashback to that moment in time when I was five years old at the beach flits through my mind. For years, I longed to know who my father was, what he looked like, where he was, and what he did for a living. I wanted him there with me at school functions such as the father-daughter school dances. I wanted my father to be proud of my achievements like other parents were of their children, and do fun father-daughter activities on the weekends, but it never happened. My mother was gone and would never return; however, my father was somewhere and could have returned for me. He chose instead to abandon me, and now after all these years, he's here in front of me. A flurry of emotions swirls inside of me as I stand in the lobby shell-shocked by Max's revelation.

"I can see this comes as a shock to you," he says.

I'm flabbergasted. My brain makes an effort to process the news he just delivered while my mouth tries to form words. *Pull yourself together, Cari.* I force myself to acknowledge the jolting news. "Um, yeah. I'm at a total loss for words."

He nods his head. "Understandably so. I was shocked myself when I realized our connection," Max states.

"Cari."

The familiar voice calling my name causes me to pivot.

Deven approaches us. "It's you again?" He eyes Max suspiciously. "Max, right?"

"Yes, that's right. You have a good memory."

"I do. My memory serves me well." Deven looks back and forth between us and turns his attention to Max. "Why are you here?"

Oh, goodness. Deven is in protective mode and is intent on making Max feel uncomfortable.

"I had something I wanted to share with Cari."

One of Deven's eyebrows arches. "I wasn't aware you know Carilyn well enough to share anything with her." *Carilyn?* He rarely uses my given name. "I find it disturbing that you somehow managed to track her here. This *is* my building and I can have you escorted out of here."

I can't let him do that. I place my hand on Deven's arm and look at him with imploring eyes. "Deven, please don't. It really will not be necessary."

Max speaks up. "I understand how you feel, but let me assure you I mean Cari no harm. I only came to share some important news with her."

Deven scoffs and crosses his arms. "You don't know her. What news can you possibly have to share with her?"

2

Max looks back at me seeking my permission to tell Deven.

"Why don't I tell you later?" I ask Deven.

"Why don't you tell me now?" Deven retorts.

Ugh! I roll my eyes. The expression on his face indicates he wants his question answered now, but I am not going to divulge the information at this moment.

"Later please," I say beseeching him.

He reluctantly gives me a nod, uncrosses his arms, and turns his wrist to check the time on the Maurice Lacroix watch I gave him the first Christmas we spent together. I love knowing he still wears it often. "We need to get going. We have reservations."

I pull out my cell phone from my handbag. "Max, why don't you give me your phone number, and we can set up a meeting to chat more?"

"Cari, we're already fifteen minutes late," Deven impatiently says.

"This won't take long."

Max and I exchange numbers but before I can even save his information, Deven slips his hand into mine and shows Max the exit. *Sheesh.* There is no need for him to be brusque with Max. Once he is satisfied Max is out of sight, he pulls me outside and we get into the waiting Mercedes parked in front of the building.

"What did he share with you?" Deven asks cutting right to the chase.

Ha! I refuse to answer his question until I receive an answer to mine first. "Why were you being so rude?"

He has a stern look on his face. "*Rude?* This man whom you don't even know was able to pinpoint your location claiming he had something to share with you. What if he threatened your life and you had no protection? How do you think I would feel if he physically hurt you or tried to kidnap you for ransom?"

"That's ludicrous."

"Is it now?"

"It absolutely is. I trusted my instincts."

"*Your instincts?* Instincts are not always accurate. Your well-being and safety mean everything to me. If anything happens to you…"

3

Deven tends to be too overprotective of me and this time it has proven to obscure his brain. I take hold of his hand. "But nothing happened to me. *See?* I'm still in one piece." I give his hand a light squeeze. "The reason why he needed to find me is because he wanted to tell me that he's my father."

He looks skeptical, releases my hand, and shakes his head. "No. That's impossible. I don't believe him nor should you. He has a motive. He knows you're marrying me and wants something."

I am convinced he has completely lost his mind. "Why do you think that?"

"It's quite obvious that he is an imposter. Look at the timing of it. Where was your father when you wanted him in your life? All of a sudden, he magically appears after our engagement was made public last month. It's easy to deduce he has a motive. Besides, you don't look anything like him."

"That's because I look like my mother, but it doesn't disqualify him to be my father."

"He's Chinese."

"Why does that matter?"

"It matters because I find it hard to believe that he is your father."

"I don't know anything about my father and neither do you. How can you say that you don't believe he is my father?"

"Be sensible about this. You just said you know nothing about him; therefore, how can *you* be certain he is your father? The only way to confirm he is indeed your father is to have him do a paternity test."

"Absolutely not. I will not have my father subjected to such a test. He has no reason to lie to me." I'm beginning to feel vexed by Deven's reservations about Max.

"Stop being naïve about this. Of course, he has reason to lie. He's aware you will have full access to our money once we're married. He's seeing dollar signs everywhere."

I scoff at his absurd comment. "I disagree. I'd really like the opportunity to get to know him."

"I don't think it's a good idea. There is no evidence supporting his claim that he is your father. In addition, he could say anything he wants to say about your mother. There's no way to verify if he is being truthful about any of it."

"What if you're wrong?"

"What if I'm not?"

Hmmph. I don't bother responding to his question. I stare out the window allowing the awkward silence to linger between us. He is being obstinate and not even giving Max the benefit of the doubt.

He lets out a heavy sigh after some time. "Angel, I don't want to argue about this. I just don't want you to get your hopes high."

I shift my attention back to him and notice his expression has softened. I lay my hand over his. He looks down at our hands.

"I believe he's telling the truth." I prefer not explaining why I do believe Max, but I do. Perhaps it is my gut instinct. "I've always wanted to know who my father is, and now the chance has presented itself. I don't want to pass up this opportunity. You know who your parents are, but I never knew mine."

He takes his free hand and covers the top of my hand with it. "Fine. If that's what you want then I won't stop you."

"It's what I want. If something doesn't add up and it turns out he is not my father after all, then I will let it go."

"Fair enough," he says after some hesitation.

"However, if it does turn out that he really is my father, I would like for you to give him a chance and get to know him as well."

He removes his hand and scratches the back of his head. I can sense he does not want to get to know Max, but I hope he will agree to it for my sake.

"One step at a time, Cari."

It sounds like a compromise to me.

"Okay," I say and lean in to give him a kiss on his cheek.

~ * ~

Deven chooses not to return to the office and comes home with me after lunch. I go into the kitchen to pour myself a glass of merlot while Deven heads to his home office to finish up some work. I grab my phone and send Max a text requesting to meet with him. After taking a swig of the wine, I call Rodrigo. He answers after the second ring.

"Hi sweetie. What's up?"

"You're never going to believe what happened today."

"Oh, I am eager to know. Do tell."

"I met my father."

There is no immediate reaction from him.

"Rodrigo, are you still there?"

"Yeah, I'm still here. Did I hear you correctly? Did you say you met your father?"

"I did."

"Your father is alive?"

"He is."

"How did this happen? Start from the beginning."

"Do you remember that Asian man I had told you about the day we had lunch in Chinatown?"

"I do. You said he's the one who approached you and said he knew your mother."

"It turns out that he's my father."

"You're shitting me."

"Not at all." I fill him in on what transpired.

"Hmmph."

"What?"

"I'll be damned. Did you ask him where he has been all these years?"

"No. We didn't have the chance to speak much. Deven was rushing him out of the building."

"Does he believe this guy, Max, is your father?"

"No. He has doubts that Max is my father."

"I can't say I blame Deven."

"Not you as well."

"How can we not have doubts?"

"Why are you skeptical that he is my father?"

"Probably for the same reason why Deven is. Don't you find it peculiar that he has suddenly waltzed into your life? Where was he when you said your first word? When you graduated from high school and college? I think he's a con artist."

"You're judging him."

"Nope. I'm protecting you."

"Did Deven beat me and call you first?"

"No. Take the blindfold off. Now that it's official you and Deven are engaged, people will try to befriend you or claim that they are some long lost relative of yours. You're going to be worth a lot once you become Deven's wife. This man declaring himself to be your father knows it too."

"Rodrigo, you have known for a long time I have always wondered about my father."

"You also gave up hope that he would ever find you."

"I kind of did, but there has always been a part of me that never stopped giving up hope that one day I would meet him. You never had to wonder who your father was, or what he was doing, or where he was because he's always been there in your life. He's always been there for you."

"Your grandparents were always there for you. I don't remember them ever letting you down."

"I didn't say they let me down. They had always been there for me, but it's not the same."

"They didn't love you any less."

"I didn't say that either."

"What makes you think this man is being truthful with you?"

"He said I look like my mother. It doesn't make sense for him to say such a thing if he didn't know what my mother looked like."

"Well, I can't dispute that unless he went to great lengths and did his research on the internet."

"There is not much on the internet about my mother. She died very young."

"Hmm. You have a point. What's next then?"

"I asked for a meeting with him so we can talk."

"I'd love to hear where your father has been all these years and why he never came back for you. He has a lot of explaining to do."

"That he does."

"Hey, maybe you can do three way calling instead and ask him."

"I will not do that."

"I can stay on mute."

"I will not do it. I want him to look me in the eye and tell me everything."

He sighs. "Well, I expect to know everything he tells you just to make sure he has no other ulterior motive."

"I promise you will know everything."

"Remember who your family is."

"I always do."

Rodrigo and his family became my family years ago, and they will always be my family. They have done so much for my grandparents and I, and we have all shared many memories together. It's inevitable that the family ties will continue to grow once I marry Deven, and I am anticipating it will also grow once my relationship with my father flourishes.

CHAPTER TWO

CARI

It's Thanksgiving morning and I awaken like I do each morning…in the arms of the man I am deeply in love with. He's snoring lightly and I'm convinced it's due to exhaustion from our very passionate night. I must get up to make breakfast and start on the side dishes that I am bringing to dinner tonight. Gently releasing myself from his muscular arms, I try not to wake him as I get out of bed.

Before I begin work on my culinary creations, I send Rodrigo a text wishing him a Happy Thanksgiving. Rodrigo and Hunter are spending the Thanksgiving holiday in California with Hunter's family. I will miss celebrating this holiday with them, but we'll be together for Christmas and New Year's. With the phone still in my hand I quickly text a Thanksgiving greeting to Max. I'm eager to meet with him next week and finally have my questions answered.

I put my phone down on the counter and take out all the ingredients needed to make pumpkin pancakes. As the griddle heats up on the stovetop, I mix all the ingredients together. The smell of the batter brings back fond memories of Thanksgiving mornings with my grandparents. I drop ladles of the batter onto the hot griddle and wait for the bottom to set before flipping them over.

"Mmm. It smells delicious."

I turn to see a shirtless Deven running his hands through his unkempt hair. *He looks so yummy right now. I can pass on the pancakes and have him for breakfast instead.* He wraps his strong arms around my waist.

"Morning, angel." He layers kisses on my neck.

"Morning."

9

He tilts my head up and brushes his lips lightly over mine. Then he pulls back and holds my stare. "Happy Thanksgiving."

"Happy Thanksgiving to you. You're just in time for breakfast."

"I always am."

I laugh. "I'll bring it into the dining room."

"I'll set the table then." He grabs some silverware and makes his way into the dining room.

I shut off the burner and transfer the pumpkin pancakes onto the plates. I set the plates on the table and take my seat.

Deven cuts into his pancakes, pierces some of it with his fork, and takes a bite. "This is damn delicious, angel."

"Thanks. It's a family recipe."

"Was it your grandmother's recipe?"

"Actually, it was my great grandmother's recipe."

"Those are the best recipes. Folks back then made real good food."

"I agree. Grams would have been happy to know that you enjoy the pancakes."

"I do. I like the pancakes very much. Don't restrict this to just Thanksgiving morning."

"I'll try not to. Grams would make this for breakfast every Thanksgiving morning. It became a tradition for us Snows. After breakfast, my grandparents and I would sit in front of the television and watch the Macy's Thanksgiving Parade."

"I would like to keep the tradition of this delicious Thanksgiving breakfast for us and our kids."

Our kids. His mention of it puts a smile on my face. "That means a lot to me that you want to keep the tradition."

"You mean the world to me. Besides, why not keep the tradition going?"

He's right. There is no reason why the tradition should cease just because my grandparents are gone.

"Have you ever gone into New York to see the parade?"

"No. Grams was petrified someone would snatch me in the City. She was overprotective."

"She wasn't the only one."

"Was your father the same way?"

"No, but I know people who have the same protective instinct your grandmother had."

He's overprotective of me already and I wonder if he will be that way with our children. "Will you be an overprotective parent?"

"Most likely. Will you?"

"I may be a little overprotective."

His eyes dart to his empty plate. "It feels odd without Dad's presence this Thanksgiving."

I reach for his hand.

"Even though he was at the care facility, he was still alive."

"His memory will always be alive in your heart and your mind."

He nods. "Yeah. It will be for as long as I live."

~ * ~

We're delighted Jordan is joining us for Thanksgiving dinner. Before we can even get out of the car, May swings open the front door and comes over to us. Rockie runs out behind her and starts barking. Rockie is the newest family member. He is a German shepherd that Deven adopted for Leigh. She wanted a small dog, but when they went to the animal shelter and she saw Rockie curled up in the corner looking lonely and scared, she changed her mind. Rockie stole her heart.

May goes to give her brother a hug first. Then she hugs me as Deven bends down to pet Rockie.

"Happy Thanksgiving! It's about time you got here!"

"Happy Thanksgiving," Deven and I return at the same time.

Deven eyes his sister suspiciously. "May, are you in some kind of trouble with Mom?"

"Oh, come on. I'm not a little kid, and I am not in any trouble."

"Then why do you seem to be ebullient?"

"I always am, but I do have a special reason to be today."

"And what's the reason?"

"Brad is celebrating with us this year."

And there it is.

"*He is?* I thought he had plans to spend the holiday in Boston and left early this morning."

"He did plan on it, but I persuaded him last night to come to our house for Thanksgiving instead," she admits proudly.

Deven rolls his eyes. "Brad's parents look forward to having him there for the holiday. You could have extended the invitation to his family to come here, or go to Boston with him."

She scrunches up her face. "No way do I want to spend Thanksgiving with them. I would have had to bring Crystal there with me. I don't think his parents would have been pleased if I brought her along."

I don't know much about Crystal other than she is May's roommate at Princeton.

"Did you invite her to our Thanksgiving dinner?"

"I did."

Deven shakes his head and lets out an exasperated sigh. "Doesn't she have a family to spend Thanksgiving with?"

"That would be us."

"I meant *her* own family."

"Not really. I told you her parents are divorced."

"I'm cognizant of her parents' marital status, but couldn't she have spent the holiday with either one of them instead?"

"She would if she could, but she can't so she won't."

He is not making any effort to conceal his displeasure of May's roommate being here, but I interject before he can say anything.

"It was really thoughtful of you to invite her here so she wouldn't be alone."

He stares at me with wide eyes.

"Exactly what I thought! We think so alike. It's no wonder we're destined to be sisters."

Deven ignores May's comment and opens the trunk to take out the bags containing the side dishes I made for dinner.

12

As May and I near the house, Mauricio steps out. Deven and I no longer see Mauricio as often anymore. He spoke to Deven about semi-retiring after May left for college. Deven thought Mauricio should fully retire and enjoy his retirement, but Mauricio wanted to continue to serve the family in a limited capacity. He wasn't ready to hang up his hat quite yet so Deven hired Jordan to allow Mauricio to semi-retire.

We swap hellos and hugs with Mauricio. He helps Jordan and Deven bring in the food. I follow May into the kitchen where Leigh is busy preparing the rest of Thanksgiving dinner.

"Cari! Happy Thanksgiving!"

"Happy Thanksgiving, Leigh," I say embracing her.

"Smells delicious, Mom," Deven tells her as he goes to give her a hug.

"Thank you. Happy Thanksgiving to you."

"And Happy Thanksgiving to you."

"I hope everyone is hungry."

"Definitely. I brought my appetite with me," Deven responds.

"Good because there's plenty of food. Brad and Crystal are in the basement. Go down and see them."

"Let's go down." May is very excited to have Brad over.

"Come, Cari. Let's go see them." There is a hint of sarcasm in his voice as he entwines his fingers with mine and leads me downstairs.

We find them sitting on the oversized couch watching a reality show. Deven clears his throat to get their attention, and both of them turn their heads simultaneously.

"Hey." Brad stands up.

"Crystal, you know my brother."

"Hi Deven." She smiles at him while batting her eyes. *Is she flirting with him?*

"And this is my soon-to-be sister-in-law, Cari."

"Hi Crystal. It's nice to meet you."

Her smile diminishes. I really should be used to this by now. It's always the same reaction I get when they realize Deven is *my man*.

She observes me from top to bottom. "Hi."

"How are you, Crystal?" Deven asks forcing her to shift her eyes away from me.

"I'm good. Hey, thanks a lot for having me here." She grins at him again.

Deven sits down next to Brad and pulls me onto his lap. "You don't need to thank me. It was all May's idea."

May squeezes herself between her boyfriend and her roommate. The guys start to talk about work when I catch Crystal staring at me. She quickly looks away.

"Can't you guys talk about anything other than work? It's Thanksgiving for God's sake." May sounds exasperated.

"There's no better way to show our thanks than by talking about how the company is thriving," Brad replies.

"And we are quite thankful for that," Deven adds as they give each other a high five.

"There are plenty of other things to talk about."

"How about those Jets?" Deven asks changing the subject.

Crystal giggles.

May scowls at Deven. "No football talk."

"I like football," Crystal says.

"Thanksgiving is about giving thanks which we were doing, and it's about football -"

Mayleen abruptly cuts Deven off. "I said no football." She turns to me. "Cari, I'm so excited you have a dad! How come it took him this long to find you?"

She catches me off guard with her question. I am not prepared to discuss my father in front of Crystal.

"May, this is not the time to talk about it," Deven warns her. He knows this is a personal matter to me.

Comprehension dawns on her face. "Ah. You're right. I'm sorry, Cari."

"It's perfectly all right."

"Hey, did May tell you that we signed up for a cooking class together?" It's now Brad's turn to change the subject.

Deven raises an eyebrow. "Did you sign up to learn how to cook or did you sign up to sample the food?"

"Dude, of course, I signed up to sample the food."

His response makes us all laugh and food becomes the topic of our conversation.

~ * ~

It's past midnight when we finally get back to the penthouse. It was a good first Thanksgiving dinner for me with the Blakes and company. Leigh made an amazing and delicious Thanksgiving feast, and my side dishes were a hit.

After brushing our teeth, we climb into bed. Deven habitually picks up his phone to read and respond to some emails. I rest my head on his hard chest and watch an action movie. He sets the phone back down on the nightstand when he's done and draws me closer to him. He places his cheek on the top of my head.

"All caught up with your emails?"

"Yeah." He lets out a yawn.

"Deven?"

"Hmm?"

"I'd like to have Max and his family join us for Thanksgiving next year."

His chest rises up and down. "Well, thanks for the advance notice." He doesn't sound thrilled with my suggestion.

"I think Leigh and May will welcome them."

"They definitely will. They're very supportive of you."

"And what about you?"

"I'm your number one fan."

"I'm referring to my father."

"You don't know anything about him nor do I; therefore, I think it's premature to want to have him over for next Thanksgiving."

Deven is still not convinced Max is my father, but I am not backing down from where I stand with this. "He's going to be a part of my life now whether you like it or not. I don't plan to exclude him from spending any time with us."

"I don't expect you to exclude him *if* he is really your father, but it's not something we need to discuss this moment. I'd rather concentrate on you right now."

He tugs off his silk pajama bottoms and then works quickly to unbutton my pajama top. Within seconds, he has me on my back and pulls off my pajama bottoms as well. Lowering his face to mine, he kisses me tenderly as our tongues connect in the most intimate way. When he finally releases his mouth from mine, his mouth treks southward and stops to savor my breasts, one at a time. He gently sucks on each nipple sending jolts of electrified pleasure through my body and a tingling sensation between my legs.

After unlatching his mouth from my breast, his tongue skates down my body to the inside of my thighs. Burying his face there, he alternates between licking and sucking my wet delicate spot. My head is stuck in a cloud of ecstasy while a raging fire burns through my body. He raises himself over me and my legs instinctively wrap around his waist. Then my inner walls constrict around his shaft as he drives into me filling me to the hilt.

Like magnets, our lips come together for a deep kiss. The need and want between us is strong. Our tempo changes as our lips pull apart. Both of us are panting heavily as we move together in harmony.

"Cari…I need…*oh, God…*" He wrestles with completing his sentence as he thrusts into me.

It's erotic to watch as he starts to come undone. Releasing a growl, he picks up speed and thrusts even harder into me over and over until we reach the peak of the mountain of passion. We hold onto each other tight as he injects his hot liquid inside me.

Our bodies are clammy with perspiration as he lays his chest on mine trying not to crush me. He pushes back the loose hair that covers my sweat infused forehead and showers my lips with sweet kisses. Once our heart rates stabilize, he lies down beside me. We turn our heads and gaze into each other's eyes. *He's even more gorgeous after we have sex.* I roll onto my side and cuddle up against him.

"You're so perfect in every way, and I love that you're mine, Cari."

CHAPTER THREE

DEVEN

I woke up this morning not in the best of moods knowing Cari will be having lunch with Max. My suspicions of Max haven't let up. With a packed morning schedule, I left Cari sleeping in bed and headed into the office earlier than usual.

I have been traveling most of the morning to the different buildings my company owns to monitor the progress of the conversions and renovations. My presence at these projects also serve as a reminder to my staff that I am a CEO who is very involved with the work my company does, and nothing goes unnoticed by me.

By the time I return to the office, Cari has left for lunch. *Damn.* I haven't had a chance to see or speak to her since leaving the penthouse earlier. I look over at her desk wishing I had been invited to their lunch meeting. I, too, have questions for Max. The knock on my door tears me away from my thoughts.

"I'm stepping out to lunch. Is there anything else you need before I go?" Catrina asks me.

"Not at the moment. Have a good lunch."

"Thanks. See you later."

I open the bottom drawer of the file cabinet next to my desk and reach under the hanging file folders. I pull out a large manila clasp envelope and look over the papers inside which are the results of the background check I had run on Max. Cari will be upset if she ever finds out what I did, but I had good reasons to run a check on him. I flip through the papers again scanning over the information compiled. I let out a huff and lean back in my chair.

Against my hopes, the background check on him had come back clean. I place everything back in the envelope and bury it underneath the folders in my drawer.

"Hey."

I look up to find Brad standing in my office.

"What's up?"

"Want to grab something to eat?"

"Sure." I rise from my chair and walk over to the closet to get my coat.

"I'm in the mood for a burger."

"I could go for a burger," I say closing the door to my office.

I update Brad on the progress of the buildings as we wait for the elevator to arrive. A few of the administrative assistants emerge from the south wing. They don't have coats on which indicates to me they're going to have lunch at the café in the lobby. Brad and I greet them, and they greet us in return; however, they are obviously eyeing us. Brad is appreciatively admiring them while making small talk. I try my best to refrain from punching him in his gut. Sometimes he forgets who his girlfriend's brother is.

Ellie (the assistant to the Senior Project Manager) asks us where we are heading for lunch and I answer her. It turns out it's one of her favorite eateries and she asks me which burger I like best. Soon enough, the other admins partake in the conversation and it's all about burgers. I'm very relieved when the elevator reaches the lobby as Ellie did most of the talking on the ride down.

"Is Cari planning to come back to the office after lunch with her father?" Brad asks as we wait for the signal to change before crossing the street.

"That's the plan, but I may have her meet me for coffee first."

"She's fortunate her father is still alive. I never knew my birth father."

"Different circumstances."

"The circumstances may not be the same, but neither of us had our birth fathers present in our childhood years. Maybe this guy genuinely wants to reconnect with her."

I sneer at his opinionated comment of Max.

"You're still harboring doubts about him then?"

"Yeah. Why shouldn't I?"

"Because this isn't about you. Look, I understand how you must feel. You also need to understand how she feels. She's naturally excited and curious about him. I bet Cari harbors some doubts about him too and is being cautious herself. Maybe this lunch they are having will prove whether or not he really is her father. Don't underestimate her. She's smart as a whip, and if she suspects he is making a false claim she won't give him the benefit."

I concur with him that Cari is highly intelligent, but there's just something about Max that makes me doubtful of him. "Why is it at this moment you seem to sound reasonable?"

"That's because I haven't passed judgment on her father as being a con man."

Hmm. "Touché."

CHAPTER FOUR

CARI

Max and I made arrangements to meet for lunch in midtown Manhattan. Jordan has been assigned to chaperone me on my lunch appointment. I was quite perturbed when Deven made mention of this. He was insistent that I not go alone to meet my father leaving me no choice but to give my father an advance warning that Jordan would be accompanying us.

The day is overcast and colder than it should be for this time of year. Jordan and I are outside my favorite Thai restaurant waiting for Max to get here. I can't wait to talk to him.

"Cari?"

I turn to my left. "Hi Max. Thanks for coming."

"Thank you for inviting me."

We both smile and stand there in silence.

"Shall we go in and sit down?" Max asks breaking the silence between us.

"Yes. I made reservations for us."

He opens the door for me. "It was good you did. This place is always busy."

I approach the hostess to let her know we have reservations. Max, Jordan, and I are shown to our table. We take our seats and the hostess hands us the menus. I know what I want and just skim over the menu to allow Max and Jordan time to decide.

"Must he be at the table with us?" Max gestures his head towards Jordan as he lays his menu down on the table.

"Yes, but he won't pay us any attention."

The look on Max's face expresses his disapproval of this arrangement, but there is nothing that can be done about it. Jordan is loyal and will do whatever Deven asks of him.

The server comes to our table and sets three glasses of water down prior to taking our orders. When he is done memorizing our orders, we return the menus to him and he leaves.

"If I may, I would like to start off and say something," Max tells me glancing at Jordan to make sure he's not listening in on our conversation.

"Of course. Please do so."

"I'm sure you and Deven have some doubts about whether or not I am actually your father."

Deven does have his doubts, but I cannot share that with Max.

"I'm willing to take a paternity test if that's what it takes to prove that I am your father. I could tell that Deven is skeptical, and I want to put his mind at ease as well as yours. I would like to reassure you that I am not after anything other than wanting to do the right thing which is to be your father if you'll let me. I have done well for myself and can prove it."

Deven will be all for the paternity test, but my gut tells me that Max is being honest.

"You need not prove anything. I trust my instincts that you are my father."

Max leans back in his chair appearing relieved. He looks over at Jordan again and turns his attention back to me. Jordan is keeping himself busy with his phone. I am confident Jordan will not repeat our conversation to anyone if he is indeed eavesdropping.

"I appreciate your belief in me, but if it comes to it, I will oblige to take a paternity test."

"Thank you, but it will not be necessary."

"I've been looking forward to today. I feel so joyful and excited about our reunion. I promise you I'm not going to disappear again. Now, I want to know everything about you. I want you to tell me about yourself. Tell me everything like life when you were a child, your favorite shows, your educational background, your dreams, your fiancé…all the stuff a father should know had I been present in your life."

I begin by going back in time and share with him my life with my grandparents. It's imperative he is aware of how well Grams and Gramps took care of me and supported me. They were not just my grandparents. They became my parents when I had no parents. Then I fill him in on everything he wants to know about me. I also tell him about Rodrigo and the significance he has had and will always have in my life.

"You have been surrounded by a circle of good people. Not only did your grandparents take good care of you, but Rodrigo and his family as well."

"Yes, I have been."

"How did you and Deven meet?"

"Oh. Um, it's kind of a funny story."

"I'd love to hear it."

I tuck some of my hair behind my ear. "We first met at a club, but we really did not do a lot of talking." Max's eyebrows rise. I quickly clarify what actually happened. "We danced briefly. I was nervous and shy. And I ended up leaving the dance floor the first chance I got. The next time I saw him wasn't until a year later when I started working at his company. I was walking back to my desk with a cup of coffee in my hand when he accidentally bumped into me and the coffee landed on my dress."

"What are the odds that the two of you would actually meet again like that a year later?"

The odds were definitely very high, but fate had plans for us.

"I hope he offered to get your dress cleaned."

"He did."

"It must have been quite a shock to have run into each other again."

"It was. The connection between us was very strong from the beginning. I didn't think we would ever see each other again. And then a force, call it fate if you will, brought us back together. I had no inkling who he even was until the coffee incident." It feels strange yet comfortable sharing all this with my father.

"*You didn't know who he was?*" Max asks in disbelief.

I shake my head. I didn't know I would end up working for Dalton Blake's son instead of Dalton Blake.

"Didn't you do your homework before starting there?"

"His father was still the CEO when I accepted the position. I wasn't aware his son would be taking over the company."

"His father built that empire from the ground up, so it makes sense Deven would have wanted to follow in his father's footsteps."

"Only he didn't expect to be the CEO so soon."

The server comes to our table with the food. It smells delicious, and we dig right in.

"It seems you and Deven are meant to be. And that engagement ring he picked out for you is very impressive."

It definitely gets a lot of attention. "He had the ring custom designed for me."

"It's a beautiful ring. He seems like a good guy. He loves you, and I can see how protective he is of you."

"He's truly amazing. You'll get to know him and be able to see for yourself how amazing he is."

Max nods and then points to his food with his fork. "This is really good."

"The food here is excellent."

"How did he propose to you?"

I recount most of the details of the proposal from the romantic dinner in the courtyard to the candles on the beach. I hold back from disclosing the purchase of the private island along with our temporary break and the loss of the baby. Some things are better off not being shared.

"I wouldn't have pegged him to be a romantic guy. That was quite a proposal. How could you have refused him? Have you two decided on the date yet?"

"We have. The wedding will be on June eleventh which also happens to be Deven's birthday."

"The wedding is on his birthday? Why choose to have the wedding on his birthday?"

"It's the day he wants us to be married, and it falls on a Saturday."

"And you're fine with the chosen date?"

"I am absolutely fine with it."

"Have you thought about places for your reception?"

"We've decided to have our wedding in Newport."

"Newport, Rhode Island?"

"Yes."

He tilts his head. "Why did you two choose Newport?"

"Newport holds a special place in our hearts."

"It's a beautiful location."

"It is. Deven's family also has a house there."

"Ah, I see. The wedding will be held at the house then?"

I let him in on our plan and inform him a wedding planner has been hired to show us possible venues and help with arranging this event. I don't have much more to share with regards to the wedding, so we move on and discuss my career. I tell him what I wanted to do, and how things moved along when Deven gave me the opportunity to work on his company's website. As a result, I have been contracted for ten jobs. They are all businesses Deven works with, but it's a start.

"That's really incredible, Cari. I have no doubt you will be the most sought after web developer. You've grown into such a lovely lady. Your grandparents did an outstanding job raising you. I'm ashamed to be first learning all about you now when I should have been there from the moment you were born, but I am extremely proud of you."

He's proud of me. Those are words I had longed to hear when I was younger. Words a father says to his child had mine been around. *Better late than never.* "Thank you."

"I'm sorry I missed out on so much. I regret not being a part of your life. I never should have…" His voice trails off and there's a look of remorse on his face.

What occurred in the past cannot be altered. However, I do want to know about my mother, and I want him to tell me what he remembers of her. I shift my fork on the plate. "I never knew my mother. I've always wondered what she was like."

Max leans forward and folds his hands. He looks down at his folded hands and I cannot distinguish if he is praying or just staring at his hands. Slowly, he lifts his head and starts to speak. "Your mother was *different*. She was beautiful, but she never had a lot of friends."

Coincidentally, I don't have a lot of friends either. Like mother, like daughter.

"She would wander through the halls speaking or singing to herself which fellow students found to be odd."

I don't want to interrupt him, but I can't stop myself from asking him a question. "Did you find it to be odd as well?"

He purses his lips, but his hesitation reconfirms he did. "I did," he admits.

All I can do in response is shake my head and let him continue.

"She wasn't very coordinated and from what I remember, she was always one of the last to be selected to be on any team. And the few friends she had were exactly like her. We attended the same elementary and middle schools, but I never spoke to Charlotte until we were in high school."

"How did you end up speaking to her?"

He glances upwards towards the ceiling as if searching for an answer. "We didn't move in the same circles. The only class we ever had together was trigonometry. We spoke a couple of times mainly pertaining to the class. I had already heard rumors she liked me. Your mother really was beautiful. And after some time, I asked her out. We went on just one date, but you can guess what happened on that one date."

Max is a handsome man and my mother was beautiful from the pictures I have seen of her. I can see why there was an attraction between the two of them, but isn't that how it is in high school? It's more the beauty on the outside that attracts than the beauty on the inside.

"Did you force her to…" I can't quite finish the sentence. I'm afraid what he may admit to.

"No. I absolutely did not force her into anything. It was consensual."

I exhale a sigh of relief. A part of me is satisfied knowing he didn't rape my mother. "I was told you wanted her to abort the pregnancy and she refused. Why did you do it? Why did you turn away from her?"

He looks straight into my eyes. "I was an imbecile at the time…a coward. It wasn't possible to tell my parents. My parents would never have accepted such news. I had a very strict upbringing where education meant everything.

My parents had high expectations of me. If they knew, not only would it have complicated my college plans, but it would have disgraced the family. I couldn't disappoint them because I had chosen to be reckless, so I did the cowardly thing instead. I ran away from my responsibility."

Listening to my father admit that he is a coward makes me realize he's not the only one in the family. I was also a coward for not telling Deven about our baby. However, Deven would have handled it differently. He never would have run away.

"There has not been one day since then that I have not felt remorse for my actions. What happened to your mother was very tragic, and it's haunted me all these years. I should have done the right thing and dealt with the consequences, but I didn't. I should have been the one to raise you." He shakes his head. "I can't go back in reverse and change things, but I want you to know that not once did I stop thinking about you. I always thought you would look like your mother and *that* is the one thing I did get right."

"How come you never tried to find me?"

"I wanted to, but I had to keep moving forward with my life. As I mentioned, education was everything to my parents so I concentrated on getting through college. During my college years, I was also in a serious relationship with my wife who happened to be my girlfriend back then. I had thought of telling her about that part of my past. But I knew she wouldn't have been able to accept what I had done, so I chose to stay silent about it."

Such information might not be acceptable to some people. I think about how I would react if Deven was in such a predicament. Would I be able to accept that he had a child? I like to believe I would have been able to accept it.

I can't help wonder if his wife knows about my existence. "Does your wife know about me now?"

"She does."

"How did she take it?"

He inhales a deep breath and releases it. "Not too well. It's going to take some time for her to accept the fact that I have another daughter. I should have told her about you at the beginning of our relationship all those years ago. I regret not doing so, and I deeply regret not owning up to my responsibility of being a father to you."

He's carried this guilt with him for far too many years, and I don't want him to bear this guilt any longer. "The past is behind us and the future is what's ahead of us. Perhaps the present is your chance for redemption."

He nods. "You're incredible. You are wise beyond your years."

I shake my head disagreeing as I know I am not. One cannot undo the past, but one can learn from it and focus on what lies ahead.

"How long have you been married?"

"Seventeen years."

They've been together for a long time. They must have children together. "Do you have children?"

"We do. We have two daughters."

A surge of excitement sears through my heart as I learn I have two half-sisters. "What are their names, and how old are they?"

"Rylee is fifteen, and Harper is thirteen."

There is a wide gap between our ages and many years have passed between us already. We probably don't even have much in common other than the fact we share the same father. Nevertheless, I want to meet my half-sisters and form a relationship with them.

"Is Rylee in high school?"

"She is. She's a freshman."

"And Harper is in middle school?"

"Yes, that's right. She's in the seventh grade."

"What are they like?"

"They're both involved with sports, and very involved with school and church activities. Harper is very sweet whereas Rylee does have a sweet side, but you won't see much of it. She's tougher of the two."

There seems to be a subtle warning in what he just told me about Rylee.

"Are they aware they have a half-sister?"

"Not yet. It may be difficult for them to receive the news. I plan to tell them very soon. And once I do, I would very much like for them to meet you."

Rylee may not be too keen on knowing what her father had done years ago which resulted in an older half-sister. She will probably not be receptive towards me; therefore, I may have to work harder to win her over.

"I would certainly like to meet them. I always wanted siblings."

"And now you have them. I want nothing more than to have all three of my daughters know each other and have that bond."

"I'd like to meet them soon."

"And you will. Do you have plans for Christmas?"

"Yes, I do."

"Why don't you come over to meet them one weekend before the Christmas holiday if you're free?"

"Oh, it would be very nice to meet your family."

"And they also get to meet the newest member of our family." He smiles warmly. "Which weekend are you available?"

"It cannot be this weekend as we have to meet with the wedding planner."

"What about the following Saturday?" He seems anxious to get this arranged.

Deven and I are supposed to do our Christmas shopping that day, but we can push it off to the next day instead.

"Yes, that will work," I confirm.

"Great. We can figure out the time next week."

"Yes. We can work out the time then."

"And this Rodrigo fellow you told me about, invite him to come over as well. I'd like to meet him."

"I'm sure he'd be delighted to come. Can I invite his husband as well?"

He looks shocked. Perhaps I should have mentioned Rodrigo is gay. Maybe he's not open to Rodrigo's preference. "Certainly. Both of them are invited."

"I'll let them know. Thank you."

"Do your grandparents still live in West Nyack?"

I shake my head. "No. My grandparents have long passed."

"Oh. I'm very sorry to hear."

"Thank you."

Max is quiet and I am curious to know what he is thinking. *Was he hoping to meet them and apologize? Is he filled with more remorse now that he knows Grams and Gramps died?* I reach for my glass and take a couple of sips of water.

"Life can be so unfair sometimes."

"It can be."

"Even though the grandparents you've only ever known are gone, you still have living grandparents."

The latter part of his statement surprises me. After he explained to me earlier how he couldn't tell his parents that he impregnated my mother, I don't know how he is going to explain the existence of me to them.

"But they don't know about me, do they?"

"No. I haven't told them yet."

"Springing such news on them may not be a good idea. Wouldn't it disgrace the family?"

"Let me worry about that. I made a mistake and I need to make it right again even if it is many years later. You are my daughter and that will never change. They will come around."

"Do you think they will want to meet me?"

"Yes, of course. You're their granddaughter."

Their granddaughter that they are first finding out about. I hope he's right.

"I would very much like to meet them."

"I will arrange it and make sure you do meet them along with my sisters and their families."

Our time together passes by quickly. I wish I can talk to my father for the remainder of the day, but we both have to leave. He has to get back to work, and Deven is probably waiting impatiently for me to return to the office.

Max insists on paying for lunch. Once the transaction is complete, we put our coats on, and leave the restaurant. We're both on the sidewalk with Jordan only a couple of feet away.

"If it's okay with you, I would like to give my daughter a hug."

His daughter. I nod, and he opens his arms. I finally get to hug my father. It feels good to know that my father is alive and cares about me. Jordan clears his throat forcing us to break apart from the hug.

"You should get back to Deven. He's probably anxious for you to return to him," Max says and looks up at Jordan. "Does *he* live with you and Deven?"

"He lives in the apartment one floor down from us."

"At least you both have some privacy."

"Jordan never bothers us. Well, I better not keep Deven waiting. I look forward to meeting your family soon."

"You're my family as well, and nothing will ever change that. You are very much my daughter and part of my life." His words deeply resonate with me. "See you again next Saturday then."

I bid him farewell and start heading towards the office with Jordan right behind me.

"Ms. Snow."

I stop and look up at this six foot five giant. "Yes?"

"Mr. Blake would like for you to meet him at Starbucks."

I take out my phone and double check to make sure I didn't miss his call or text. "He didn't text or call me."

Jordan shows me the text message on his phone, and a sigh escapes my lips.

"Let's go to Starbucks then."

I walk the couple of blocks with my bodyguard to Starbucks. Deven's gorgeous face lights up when he sees me.

"Hi angel. I missed you all day." He kisses my cheek.

Jordan takes a seat at the next table. I sit down and there's a cinnamon dolce latte on the table for me.

"How did the meeting with your father go?"

"It went very well. I found out a lot."

"Yeah? Like what?"

"I have two half-sisters."

"I presume they are younger than you."

"They are. Rylee, the oldest, is fifteen. And Harper is the youngest. She's twelve." The latte is comforting. It's exactly what I need to warm up.

"Did your father fill in the blanks on his whereabouts all these years?"

"He did."

He sits back in his chair rubbing his chin with his thumb and forefinger. "Go ahead, Cari. I want to hear what he told you."

I apprise him of the conversation my father and I had. Even after sharing this with him, he doesn't let go of his suspicions. I was hoping he would have a change of heart about Max. Max is my family and part of my life now. Deven will have to find a way to deal with this and accept it. He just has to.

CHAPTER FIVE

December

CARI

It's a cold and dreary day in Newport. Rodrigo and Hunter are with us to meet Belle, the wedding planner. May and Brad were supposed to come as well but had to cancel at the last minute because May had to study for finals. We park a few blocks down the street from the wedding planner's office which is located in a historic Victorian house not far from Bellevue Avenue.

"What's her name again?" Rodrigo asks indignantly.

"It's Belle," I reply.

"And what's her last name? *Ding dong?*" Rodrigo chuckles wryly.

I shake my head as Deven rings the doorbell. An older lady opens the door and welcomes us in. One by one, we step into the foyer. She closes the door but doesn't introduce herself. She shows us into a room where there's a fire going in the fireplace. The house appears to be well-kept, and the furnishings of the house are reminiscent of the Victorian era.

Atop the credenza is a tray of assorted miniature desserts, coffee, and tea. The same lady tells us to help ourselves to the sweet treats. Rodrigo asks her for a bottle of water and she steps out of the room.

"Look at this place! It's no wonder why she can afford to have an office like this. She must charge her clients a fortune in order to maintain this house and feed her clients such fancy desserts. *Really, Deven.* You could have just hired me for free."

Deven ignores Rodrigo's comment. There's still some bitterness Rodrigo has towards Deven over the hiring of Belle even though Deven reassured

Rodrigo he will maintain a crucial role in the planning.

Hunter reaches for one of the fruit tarts. "Rodrigo, we agreed you wouldn't do this."

Rodrigo lets out a loud sigh. "I know we did, but I'm the bigger queen. I should have been asked first if a wedding planner was necessary."

"It's not our decision," Hunter reminds him before taking another bite of the tart.

The assistant comes back with a bottle of water for Rodrigo and right behind her must be Belle.

"Mr. Blake?"

Oh. Belle appears to be younger than I thought but not too much younger. She looks to be in her early thirties. Her hair is pulled back neatly into a bun. Her makeup is flawless. The suit she is wearing is perfectly pressed, and she smells like a walking floral bouquet with the perfume she has on. She is blatantly ogling Deven as she licks her upper lip with her tongue leaving me utterly appalled. *How brazen when we are here to discuss our wedding with her.*

"You must be Belle."

She puts her hand out and Deven shakes it. "I am. It's nice to finally meet you in person."

"Let me introduce you to my fiancée and her best friends."

Her hand is still gripping Deven's. He realizes it too and frees his hand. She eyes me from head to toe as Deven makes the formal introductions. Then she offers me her congratulations and shakes my hand nearly crushing my bones with her strong grip.

Rodrigo looks her up and down. "I'm the one who you will be working closely with," he informs her ensuring she's aware her interaction with Deven will be very limited.

She looks between Deven and Rodrigo and then turns to Deven. "Mr. Blake, I think it will be best if I work directly with you and Miss Snow."

"We will be involved but mostly indirectly."

"There may be decisions that he cannot possibly make on your behalf."

"Excuse me?" Rodrigo asks rolling his head. "I have plenty of experience planning events. I also happen to be best friends with the bride. She and the

groom trust me with decisions; therefore, *you will* be working directly with me."

I glance over at Deven first and then at Hunter. Deven's face is impassive. Hunter shoots Rodrigo a look of warning to not say another word.

"We have full trust in Rodrigo," Deven says confidently.

Rodrigo's face is smug.

"I see." Belle sounds disappointed. "Well then, I guess it's settled." She sits down. With her gaze fixed on Deven, she crosses her legs, smiles, and then opens up her leather planner. "I have your wedding date down as June eleventh."

"Yes, that's correct," Deven replies while I nod my head.

"I'd like to begin by knowing how many people you plan on inviting to your wedding."

"We approximate the number to be five hundred," Deven answers.

"*Five hundred?!* Since when did the guest list grow to that number?" Rodrigo is offended he wasn't told this sooner.

"Since *I* decided to invite a bunch of people I happen to know," Deven responds daring my best friend to challenge him on this.

Rodrigo is about to say something and I give him a shake of my head to let him know it's best to remain quiet. I had no idea either how many people Deven actually knows. Belle goes through a list of questions that Deven answers as if he had studied and prepared for an exam. After she has all of her questions answered, she announces a shuttle van will take us over to The Breakers first.

The Breakers is the grandest mansion in Newport. The mansion is decked out in holiday decor and open to visitors. There are already some visitors inside on the self-guided tour when we walk in. Belle leads us into the huge foyer better known as the Great Hall. Rodrigo can barely keep his mouth closed as he takes in the opulence of the famous summer home that once belonged to Cornelius Vanderbilt II.

It is a beautiful and impressive place to have a wedding. Belle guides us to the outdoor terrace to show us the lawn where the ceremony will take place. She suggests that we hold our cocktail hour, and dinner at other venues stating there wouldn't be enough time to transform the lawn from the ceremony to the cocktail hour and then turn it again for dinner. Rodrigo pulls me aside as Belle explains how the transition to the other venues will be handled.

"Wow! This place is really perfect," Rodrigo remarks. "I have the most fantastic idea for your wedding."

"What is it?"

"I think you and Deven should do something different." He points to the inside of the mansion. "Look at this place. Your wedding should be evocative of the era the house was built in but with a modern twist."

"Are you suggesting we have a themed wedding?"

"I am thinking of a wedding where the past and the present blend. How cool will it be if you and Deven have a fusion wedding inspired by the Gilded Age?"

"It's an interesting concept, but I can't be certain if Deven will agree to it. After all, he's paying for the entire wedding and it's only fitting to get his approval."

"Of course."

"I don't know if he's too keen on the fashion from that time period."

"Neither of you have to dress from that time period. Your wedding will be a fusion of past and present. Your guests can have the option to dress in the fashion from that time. Speak to him about it. He'll like my suggestion."

"You seem sure of it."

"I am sure. If you and Deven decide to go with this idea, I can handle all of it. You don't need that wedding planner."

"We do need Belle to handle a lot of this. She has connections here and her office is also located here. It just makes sense."

Rodrigo rolls his eyes. "Fine."

"You and Belle will be working together. She must go to you for approval. Deven and I will also need you to help with other things back home. I'm going to need you to help me with finding a dress and whatever else comes along. Let Belle handle what she is getting paid to handle."

"Okay. She can do what she's supposed to do, but Deven will agree to my idea."

"Don't be so sure of it yet."

"He will. Let's go back and join them before she gets too comfortable with your man."

We catch up to the others. Belle wants Deven to envision what the sprawling back lawn will look like set up. I am not sure what Deven is picturing, but I visualize it to be stunning as the guests are seated facing the Atlantic Ocean. The cold wind suddenly hits my face and disrupts my visualization. Thankfully, it will be much warmer in June.

CHAPTER SIX

CARI

Once we are done sighting the other two mansions as potential venues for the cocktail hour, and the dinner reception, the four of us leave Belle's office and have an early dinner at Deven's favorite restaurant in the downtown district. Over dinner, we unanimously agree that having the ceremony and receptions split between the three mansions is a brilliant plan. It will be up to Belle to secure permission to hold the events at the mansions before she can proceed with anything else.

Deven and I drop off Rodrigo and Hunter at the hotel on the way back to the house. Deven did invite them to stay with us, but they declined wanting to give us our privacy. The house is warm and toasty when we return. As I follow Deven into the hall, he abruptly stops and turns around. I almost crash into the back of him. He cradles my face in his hands. His head tilts and he lowers his face to mine. Our mouths clash and our tongues connect, wanting and demanding. My hands grip his ass as his hands slide off my face and land on my hips pulling me closer. I can feel his erection as I brush up against him.

He pulls back and presses his forehead to mine as he catches his breath. "I waited hours to do that. Let's go upstairs."

Speechless and trying to catch my own breath, I am only capable of nodding my head. With our hands clasped, he leads the way up the stairs to the bedroom. He dims the bedroom lights and turns on the gas fireplace. Then he presses a button and the shades roll down on the window and balcony door.

I sit on the bed finding it difficult to keep from drooling as I watch him strip off his shirt exposing his muscular chest. I remember the word Faith used

37

to describe him…*hunkalicious. He certainly is.* He quickly removes his pants and boxers letting his manhood spring free. What a magnificent physique he has. I could stare at him for hours.

"Like what you see?"

"Mmm-hmm."

"I'd like to see you naked."

Before I can react, he has me on my back. The tip of his nose skims down the side of my neck as his lips leave a trail of light kisses along the way. He slides a hand under my sweater and cups my left breast producing a low moan from me.

He gazes at me hungrily with those spellbinding blue eyes of his. "Cari, clothes off now."

I obey his command. I tug off my sweater and remove my bra. Then I wiggle out of my pants and panties, and toss all the articles of clothing onto the floor.

"Get on top of me, angel."

My legs surround his thighs as his hands grasp my hips. I position myself over him and slowly slide down on his erection.

"Look at me, Cari."

My eyes connect with his. Desire flows through my veins consuming me entirely. I need to feel him deep inside, but his hands are clutched tight on my hips. *Is he just going to have us remain in this position and torture me?* As if he could read my mind, he lifts his hips up and pushes in deep producing a scream out of me. Concupiscence is boiling over inside me and I take control. I rotate my hips against him watching as he tilts his head back and groans. He is perfect inside me…thick and long…filling me completely. He matches my rhythm and we rock together as one. Our pace quickens. I can sense he is getting close to going over the edge. He resumes control and thrusts his hips up slamming into me. *Oh, yes! Yes!* He does this repetitively until his body becomes rigid and then…*oh my God. Hmm.*

I am about to collapse on him when he manages to sit up while still inside me. As he does, I can tell he is aroused. *Can men actually be aroused again so quickly?* My legs wrap around his backside, and his hands cup my back cheeks giving each side a squeeze. He nuzzles his face in between my breasts. Then his mouth teases each nipple before completely taking what he can of one breast into his mouth. I throw my head back from the sensation of him sucking on my breasts. *He knows exactly how to make love to each breast with his expert mouth.*

He releases my breast and peers up at me. "Baby, get on your elbows and knees."

"But you're not soft yet."

"I know."

I gently pull myself away from him and get on my elbows and knees like he wants. He moves behind me and licks me *there* from front to back with his tongue. I whimper from the feeling it sends throughout my body. His fingers leisurely draw invisible circles on my clit hitting my G-spot and sending me spiraling into orbit. Then he easily slips a finger inside me and massages my inner walls.

"Like that, angel?"

"Hmm." I can barely form words as my orgasm surges.

He places the tip of his shaft in between my butt cheeks, and I gasp. His tip travels down and makes its way to the front. He glides completely into me going in as deep as he possibly can. The feeling of him inside me in this position is out of this world. I rock back and forth intensifying the pleasure for both of us. He growls and pulls slightly out of me. Tightening his grasp on my hips, he rams his elongated manhood into me. Fueled by his feral need, he pumps harder and faster while muttering words of love.

I'm nearing the peak of my orgasm. He continues to drive hard into me until his body shudders and he completely fills me again. He slips out of me and lies down on his back. My legs are trembling from the intensity of what just happened. We've had sex many times, but that was the most intense moment ever. I lie on my side and stare at him as we both try to steady our breathing and our heart rate.

"Come here, angel." His voice is hoarse.

I muster some energy and move closer to him laying my head on his chest and wrapping an arm around his waist.

"How do you feel?" Deven asks.

"That was so, um, intense."

"Never had such level of intensity with anyone."

"Never ever?"

He plants a kiss on the top of my head. "No, angel. Never ever."

His confession secretly pleases me. I'm feeling tired. I start to close my eyes when I remember Rodrigo's idea.

"Deven?"

"Hmm?"

"Rodrigo had a suggestion about our wedding."

Deven strokes his fingers up and down my back. "Did he?"

"Mmm-hmm."

"And what exactly did he suggest?"

I deposit a couple of kisses on his perfectly sculpted chest and a low groan escapes his lips. "He suggested we should have a wedding inspired by the Gilded Age where the past and present come together. He referred to it as a fusion wedding."

He's gone quiet and I'm not sure if he welcomes the idea.

"It's only a suggestion."

"How do you feel about it?"

"I like it."

He's quiet again and this time for a while. I have a sinking feeling he does not like Rodrigo's idea.

"So do I."

His response takes me by surprise.

"You do?"

"Yes, I do. I think it's a brilliant idea given the history of The Breakers and the other mansions."

"It's probably going to cost you more."

"Angel, I want you to have the wedding of your dreams. Money is not an issue."

I raise my head and look at him. I think it's more the wedding of *his* dream.

"Thank you." I smother him with kisses.

"Mmm. Your kisses are delicious like you. You're so addictive." He flips me onto my back and he's hard again. *Ooh.* "Let me show you how badly addicted I am to you."

I gaze into his smoldering eyes and within seconds he eases back inside me.

"My Cari. You are everything to me."

The connection between us is profound. It's a connection unlike anything else I have ever experienced. *I am forever his.*

CHAPTER SEVEN

CARI

According to the GPS, we are almost at my father's house in New Jersey. Rodrigo and Hunter are following behind in their own car. The road we have been traveling on offers a magnificent view of the Hudson River and part of the New York City skyline. My father and his family live in an exclusive suburban town called Alpine. The houses here remind me of the houses in Greenwich. They're ostentatious and most have prestigious cars like Jaguars, Mercedes, and Land Rovers in the driveway.

We have passed by many extravagant houses and I wonder what my father's house is like. I've been simultaneously nervous and excited all week about meeting my father's family. I want them to like me and accept me as part of their family. My father and half-sisters are the only blood relatives I have left.

I point to the white brick manor. "There it is."

The GPS instructs Deven to make a right turn into the semi-circular driveway. There's a BMW SUV parked to the side in front of the garage. I can barely take my eyes off of the large house. It's almost as big as the one Deven grew up in. Deven gets out of the car first and comes around to open the door for me. After he helps me out of the car, he opens the back door, and takes out the huge fresh fruit basket. We walk over to Rodrigo and Hunter. Rodrigo has a box of pastries that they bought from a Chinese bakery in Chinatown.

"Your father has some house," Rodrigo says gawking at it.

I agree with Rodrigo. "He does."

Deven turns to me. "You ready for this?"

I draw in a deep breath and release it. "Yeah. I'm ready."

Deven reaches for my hand. We climb up the few steps to the front door and I ring the doorbell. The door opens and my father greets us. He gives me a hug and shakes hands with Deven. I introduce him to Rodrigo and Hunter and they too exchange handshakes. He thanks us for the goods we brought with us and takes the fruit basket and pastries.

"I'm very happy to have you all here. Come on in." He opens the door wider and we step into the two story marble foyer. "Your sisters are excited to meet you, Cari."

"You mean her half-sisters," Deven corrects him.

I stand there with my mouth agape.

Max looks Deven squarely in the eyes. "We haven't known each other for more than five minutes, but I don't appreciate that comment. They *are* sisters."

Oh gosh. This is not a good beginning between my father and Deven. I must put a stop to this before it escalates.

"It makes no difference if they are referred to as my sisters or half-sisters. We're still family and I am excited to meet them. Are they home?"

"They are. They'll be down shortly. Why don't we go into the kitchen and I'll introduce you to my wife?"

We follow him inside. Their kitchen is modern and spacious and flows into the family room where there is a built-in fireplace. Behind the island must be my father's wife with her back turned to us.

"Aimee." She spins around. Aimee is a lovely petite Chinese lady with a stylish bob haircut. "I want you to meet Cari. This is her fiancé, Deven. And these are her best friends, Rodrigo and Hunter."

"Welcome to our home. It's very nice to meet you," she says not making any effort to embrace us or shake our hands. She has a much different welcome style than Deven's mother.

"Likewise," Deven replies for all of us not seemingly bothered by Aimee's lack of warmth.

Max offers us a seat on the sectional sofa in the adjoining family room. He settles for one of the chairs next to the sofa. Aimee brings over a tray with empty glasses, a pitcher of lemon water, and a small plate of pastries. She sets it down on the coffee table, pours water into each glass, and takes her place in the other chair next to my father.

"Please help yourself," Max tells us.

"Thank you," I reply.

Two young girls come into the family room. They look at us and then turn to their parents. Max makes the introductions. The oldest, Rylee, has a hard look on her face and I don't get a warm feeling from her either. Harper, on the other hand, is the opposite. She offers a smile and a wave.

They are both pretty and have long black hair. Rylee has blue eyes, but I suspect she has contacts on. She is also taller and thinner than Harper. Harper has dark brown eyes and sports a pair of light pink glasses. Harper takes a pastry and joins her sister at the end of the sectional. There are no hugs, no air kisses, nothing. My sisters have barely said anything to us. They don't seem elated to meet their older sister.

Deven leans forward placing his elbows on his knees and breaks the uncomfortable quietness in the room. "Rylee, I'm guessing you are the oldest."

A smile emerges on Rylee's face. *If only I could roll my eyes.* She's awestruck. No one is immune to Deven's charm or his looks.

"Yeah."

"And you enjoy playing tennis?"

"Yeah."

"That's a great sport to play."

"Do you play tennis?"

"Not anymore. I did for a short time when I was in school. I wouldn't say that I was good at playing tennis."

Well, that's surprising. I thought Deven was good at playing a variety of sports.

"I played tennis," Rodrigo says.

"You did?" Deven asks. I don't know why Deven seems surprised. Rodrigo may be gay, but he has an athlete's physique and did play in team sports at school.

"Of course, I did. I maintained my figure at a young age," Rodrigo replies causing Rylee to giggle.

Deven keeps the conversation flowing. From what I am observing, she's happily answering his questions and appears to be comfortable speaking to him and Rodrigo.

Aimee excuses herself to prepare lunch. While I want to get to know my sisters, I feel obligated to help my stepmother with lunch. I get up from the couch and offer her my assistance, but she politely refuses my help insisting she has it all under control. I sit back down between Hunter and Harper.

Aimee informs us lunch will be ready in ten minutes. Deven, Rylee, and Rodrigo are engaged in conversation, so I turn to Harper hoping to learn more about her. Max joins us. He's accurate about Harper. She is very sweet. It doesn't take long before Harper becomes comfortable with both Hunter and I.

Aimee announces lunch is ready, and we follow my father to the formal dining room. We all sit down and help ourselves to the assortment of salads and sandwiches.

"Cari, what are your plans for Christmas?" Max asks.

"We're –"

"We are going away." Deven cuts me off with a curt response.

I feel the need to explain. "The office will be closed for the holidays, and we made plans in advance to go to Miami."

"We're going with them," Rodrigo adds.

"I see. Well, it certainly will be warmer there. Do you have property in Miami, Deven?"

"I am looking into an acquisition or two," Deven replies without elaborating.

"What are you looking to acquire?"

"I don't believe I need to disclose that to you," Deven retorts in a rude tone.

There is immediate silence around the table. *What is the matter with him?*

My father's jaw locks. I don't know him well, but I believe he is trying not to make this anymore awkward than it already is.

"I understand. Business dealings sometimes need to be kept confidential until the deal is sealed. I wish you the best in your acquisition conquest."

Deven gives him a nod as a silent gesture to thank him instead of saying the words.

"Mrs. Lew, this salad is *amazing*! I would love to make this. What ingredients did you use?" Rodrigo asks trying to dilute the tension in the room between Deven and Max.

Aimee slowly turns her attention to Rodrigo. "Thank you. I will be delighted to email the recipe to you."

"That will be wonderful. I'll give you my email address before we leave."

She nods and for now we try to finish lunch in peace.

~ * ~

The remainder of the afternoon remained calm between Deven and my father. I had a really nice time getting to know my new family, and it was kind of Aimee and Max to invite us over for lunch. Rylee still did not warm up to me. I'm going to need to make an effort to work on my relationship with her.

We choose to leave before dinner. We thank them and bid them farewell. I promise my father that I will reach out to him during the week despite the annoyed glance coming from Deven. Deven and I say our goodbyes to Rodrigo and Hunter outside of the house before getting in our cars.

Once we are on the road, I bring up Deven's attitude towards my father.

I look over at him. "What is your problem?"

"What problem?"

"You were extremely rude to my father."

"I wasn't being rude, Cari."

"Really? He asked you about your possible acquisitions, and you seemed bothered and uptight that he even asked the question. It's not like he was trying to compete with you on acquiring the potential properties. He isn't even in the same trade as you. He was just trying to make conversation."

"It's really none of his concern what my business plans are."

"He was merely asking a question. He wants to get to know you. After all, you will be his son-in-law."

He scoffs.

"What is that supposed to mean?"

He doesn't respond and focuses on the road ahead. I turn in my seat and lean back staring at the scenery outside my window.

The drive back home was a quiet one. We walk into the building together, but he continues to remain silent. He's never been this way with me, and I have no idea what he's feeling nor do I know what to expect. He goes straight to his home office and shuts the door as soon as we're inside the penthouse. I feel a lump in my throat as my eyes well up. I want him to talk to me instead of ignoring me. *Was I wrong to have questioned his attitude?*

I go into the kitchen and pour myself a glass of Riesling. I bring the glass with me into the living room and turn on the fireplace. There's a picture of us on the wall unit. I look at it. The picture was taken at my first BG holiday party and it's one of my favorite pictures of us. I sit down on the couch and pick up the remote control hoping there's a show on to distract me. Perhaps I should go apologize to him, but for some reason I can't bring myself to do so. I end up watching whatever baking show is on The Food Network and gradually my eyelids start to drop.

~ * ~

DEVEN

I lean back in the chair with my feet up on the desk. I had no intention of being such a dick to her father. I definitely didn't mean to upset her, but the timing of his reemergence continues to trouble me. It's been exasperating not to be able to find anything else on Max.

From the moment he found out Cari's mother was pregnant, Max made his decision. What kind of man was he to run away from his parental responsibility? *Such a caitiff!* And now he wants to be part of her life. *He and his family.* I really should be supportive, but instead I have been looking at it through different lenses.

The image of Cari's face hasn't left my mind. She is disgusted by my attitude towards him. It doesn't give me any satisfaction to know this. The silence that loomed in the car on the way home did not help the situation, but I did not want to upset her anymore. I need to snap out of this funk and go to her.

I leave my home office and hear sounds coming from the television in the living room. When I reach the living room, I find Cari curled up and asleep on the couch. I sit on the floor and stare at her beautiful face. I push back some of her hair and stroke her cheek with my thumb. Her eyes flutter open.

"Hey," I say softly.

"Hey."

"I'm sorry for the way I acted."

She gives me a nod, and it's her way of accepting my apology. I lean in and gently kiss her luscious lips. She gives me a weak smile when I pull back. *She's such an angel.*

"I owe you an answer to the question you asked in the car. I think he was a coward for running away from his responsibility as a father no matter his age. And I am still suspicious of why he has unexpectedly emerged when we are about to get married."

She sits up and pats the couch. I move to sit beside her, and she covers my hands with hers.

"I don't think you need to be suspicious of him. As you saw for yourself, he has done well on his own. I really don't think he wants anything from me other than to be my father."

I rather not get into a quarrel over this. In a relationship there has to be trust, love, honesty, respect, communication, and sometimes compromise. I will let it be for now, but if his intentions are otherwise, I will take matters into my own hands.

"I will do my best to try to abandon my suspicions."

"Do you promise?"

"Let's start with *trying* first."

It's the best I can do for now.

CHAPTER EIGHT

DEVEN

Christmas will be different this year. A couple of months back, I decided to break from the normal Christmas tradition of celebrating the holidays at home. I thought it would be better if we were to all go somewhere warmer instead. I had various destinations in mind such as Miami, Barbados, and our private island. Miami was the winner partially because of business reasons. I extended the invitation to Ken and Kaitlin, but they had made prior arrangements. Kaitlin had already made plans to go skiing in Park City putting Cari at ease. As for Ken, he wanted to spend it alone with Mandy since it will be her first Christmas without her mother.

We leave for Miami tomorrow morning, but first, we have the company holiday party to get through tonight. Mom and May will be coming. It's been a few years since they have attended the company holiday party, and it'll be nice to have them there.

Cari went home earlier to get ready for the party and will meet me at the venue in about an hour. I cannot wait to see my angel tonight. If I could, I would whisk her away from the party. I rather fuck her all night long instead. That thought alone has my dick wanting to stretch. Now is not a good time to have a hard-on.

Looks like it's time to get changed for the party. I remove my cufflinks first and then unbutton my dress shirt. I take off my shirt and toss it on the couch before moving into the bathroom to wash up quickly. I pull out my tuxedo from the coat closet. The next time I will be donning a tux will be at the wedding which is many months away. Stepping out of my shoes, I unhook my pants and let them drop to the floor. I reach for the crisp bib tux shirt with mother-of-the-pearl buttons and put it on. Once I have finished dressing, I put the finishing touch on which is the bow tie, and I check myself out in the mirror. *I look perfect.* Women shouldn't be surprised. Men do care about their appearance too.

~ * ~

This year's party is going to be much more spectacular. When I arrive at the restaurant, the manager is there to greet me and walk me inside. He's trying to schmooze me when something striking grabs my attention. *Fuck me.* I excuse myself and hurry to my angel.

She looks like a goddess. She's stunning as always, but tonight, she looks incredibly sexy dolled up in a strapless dress that shows more cleavage than any other dress she's ever worn.

"Hey beautiful."

She smiles at me. I can't resist and lean in to kiss her. I don't care who sees us. *She is mine and I am hers.* She hums softly as I savor her lips and her tongue. I will never be tired of kissing her. She pulls away gently and opens her eyes.

"You must be happy to see me." She grins.

"You can say that." I kiss the tip of her nose. "You are breathtaking."

She lowers her head and shakes it.

I lift her chin up and stare into her sparkling jade eyes. "You need to believe me that you are." I give her a kiss on her forehead and hold her hand in mine. "We have a little bit of time before anyone arrives. I'd like to find a private corner or something to -"

"Oh, good! We got here before everyone else did."

I recognize the voice that belongs to May. She walks in with Leigh. *There goes my idea of wanting to have some alone time with my angel.*

"That dress is amazing on you!" May says admiring Cari's dress while I am wishing I could slip my hands underneath her dress.

"Thank you. Your dress is just as amazing," Cari tells May.

My girl is always so thoughtful, but May's dress is much too short. My big brother radar will definitely be on tonight.

"Thanks! I hope Brad thinks so too."

That's enough. I clear my throat before she shares too much information about her and Brad.

"Hi Mom," I say as I move forward to give Leigh a kiss on her cheek.

"Deven, you look dashing." She turns to Cari and gives her a cheek to cheek kiss. "And you look radiant, Cari."

"Thank you, Leigh," Cari replies softly.

May spins around to look at the decorated place. "I love how the place looks."

"Dalton always loved to make the holiday parties spectacular," Leigh says fondly. Dad always did like his holiday parties to be grand and spectacular.

"I had ice sculptures added this year."

"You did? I'd love to see them." Leigh has a fascination with ice sculptures. If Cari and I were getting married in the winter season, she would very much want us to have ice sculptures at the reception site.

I lead the way to show the ladies in my life the ice sculptures. The pieces are truly magnificent. There is a snowman, a sleigh, a Santa Claus, and my favorite, the "BG" logo sculpture.

May admires my favorite sculpture. "Pretty cool."

"The entire place looks marvelous. Dalton would be ever so proud to see what you have done for the company and how much it has grown."

"Thanks, Mom." *I do miss my father a lot.*

As if on cue, Cari gives my hand a squeeze. I look at her. Damn...there are no words to describe how much I love this woman.

My Human Resources team arrives and Blake family time is over. I introduce Leigh and May to the team. With the exception of the HR Director, Jenna, the rest of the team is new and full of energy and positive vibes. Together, they are a team of five talented individuals with over twenty years of combined experience. May instantly hits it off with them. My garrulous baby sister would be a good fit at BG. I really need to convince her to come on board after she graduates.

"Are we ready to make this party better than last year's?" I ask.

"Yes, we are," Jenna says with confidence.

"I am so ready for the party to start!" May does not make any attempt to disguise her party mood.

The general manager approaches me. "Excuse me. Mr. Blake?"

"Yes?"

"The DJ has arrived."

"Great. Thank you for letting me know."

"You're welcome, sir."

"I'll handle the DJ."

"Thanks, Jenna." I check the time on my watch. "Is there anything you need me to do before the party begins?"

"No. My team and I have it all under control."

"Very well. I will let you and your team finish setting up then."

"Thanks."

I suggest the rest of us go over to the bar. Brad arrives as we near the bar. I notice his eyes rake over my baby sister.

"Hey B."

He shifts his eyes to me. "Hey D."

After everyone says hello to each other, he looks around the restaurant. "This place is even better than where we had the party last year."

Of course it is. Jenna had suggested this restaurant for the holiday party. I brought Cari here for dinner one night to get her feedback on the place and the food. Hmm. I think back to that night and how aroused she made me as I watched her eat the oysters.

"Can I have a drink?" May interrupts the memory I was having in my head.

"No," I say.

"Ugh!" May crosses her arms.

I expect her to pout, but she doesn't. *Thank God.*

"I'll join you tonight and not have anything alcoholic," Cari offers May.

"Thanks, Cari," May says happy to know she won't be the only one not consuming alcohol.

What a nice thing for Cari to do when she does not have to. She should be able to enjoy at least one drink. If we were not in these surroundings where

May is visible to my staff, I would bend the rules. I'm sure she's had a few drinks while at school, but she needs to follow the rules tonight. The last thing I need is for the office gossipmongers to make my sister part of their daily coffee talk which she probably will be once they discover she's dating Brad.

"May, whomever you speak with tonight, please do not divulge any secrets or speak out of turn. There will be some gossipmongers amongst us," I warn her.

"Oh my God. Really? You are treating me like I don't know how to behave or know what to say."

"I don't want people to gossip about you. You're my sister."

"And I'm an adult. I know how to handle myself."

Leigh flashes me a look to let it go.

I suck in a deep breath. "I'm sorry, May. You're right. You're an adult."

"She'll be with me most of the night," Brad reassures me.

"And May can stay with me as well," Cari adds.

I smile at May. "Great! You're all set then."

"I don't need babysitters."

She actually does, but I put my hands up in surrender to keep the peace between us.

"Thank you," May says.

"Let's enjoy tonight. Dalton wouldn't have been happy to witness that exchange between the two of you," Leigh says drawing May and I in for a hug.

I couldn't agree with her more.

CHAPTER NINE

CARI

The restaurant is filled with the employees of BG from the New York office. Everyone is in a festive mood, and the music is luring some of them onto the dance floor. People have been constantly approaching Deven since the party officially started so Deven and I agree to separate a bit and mingle with the team. I am pleased when I run into Alana and her husband. It's so good to speak to people I actually know. Alana is glowing as she nears her sixth month of pregnancy. Pregnancy agrees with her. I hope I look half as good as she does when I am pregnant again.

"There you are!"

I whirl around and see Hunter and Rodrigo each with a drink in their hands. "Glad you both made it here."

Hunter points at Rodrigo. "This one had to make sure everything on the checklist was packed for Miami."

"I don't want to spend any time running around buying items that should have been packed. I want to enjoy this vacation. Don't you agree with me, Cari?"

"I am not taking sides, Rodrigo."

Alana eyes Rodrigo's drink. "What kind of martini is that?"

"The dirty kind." Rodrigo wiggles his eyebrows. "Is the baby kicking?"

Alana places a hand on her round belly. "Not at the moment."

"I want to feel the baby kick."

"If it kicks, I'll let you know."

"Good." Rodrigo looks at me. "Where's Deven?"

"Somewhere," I reply.

"Watch out for those piranhas."

I nod my head.

"This place rocks," Hunter says.

"Better than last year's," Rodrigo says helping himself to one of the passed hors d'oeuvres.

"Good evening."

The voice streaming through the speakers is Deven's, and the chattering starts to wind down as everyone turns their attention to the stage. Deven begins by thanking the team for their dedication and diligence into making it a successful year for the company. In appreciation, Deven announces everyone will receive an additional bonus. The room explodes with clapping and cheering. Deven gets the crowd to settle down so he and Jenna can announce the winners of the year for various company distinguished awards.

Dinner is served after all the recipients receive their recognition. It is an extravagant buffet spread with several carving stations. Deven finally comes back to me and along with May and Brad, we wait for the line to thin out before we get food.

"Are you having a good time?" Deven asks May.

"I am! Holiday parties are so much fun!"

"My HR team does a really good job with all of the company events."

"And for each event, I question if it's necessary to spend so much," Brad tosses in.

May cocks her head. "How expensive can it be? They deserve to have a nice party. They work hard."

"I agree they work hard, but nice can be done on a budget."

"Then give them one."

"They have one. They just have a very steep one."

May doesn't seem to understand much about the company's budget. Brad starts to explain the budget to her.

Deven faces me. "What about you, angel? Are you having a good time?"

"Yes. I was in good company."

"Do any dancing?"

"I didn't have a chance to."

"Good because no one should be dancing with you other than me."

Of course, Mr. Caveman.

"Why don't you dance with your Mom before the night is over?"

"I'll do that."

My eyes skim over him. *He looks so hot in his tux.* I move my hand and place it on his thigh. He holds my gaze for a few seconds.

"I want to pull you into a private room right now and make mad love to you."

"We can't do that now."

"Why not?"

"I don't want to be the subject of gossip if I can help it."

"Babe, I'll fire them all if they gossip."

And he will.

"I love this song! Come on!" May reaches for Brad's hand and drags him with her to the dance floor.

The song playing is "Sweet Caroline." It is the perfect song to get everyone in the mood to sing along and dance to. Deven gets up from his seat and escorts his mother out to the dance floor. I move over a few seats next to Rodrigo and we sing along while watching everyone dance.

~ * ~

The company party was a success. The food, the music, the ambiance was better than the previous year's party. It's not just my opinion. I happened to have overheard a lot of the team members agreeing that this year's party topped last year's.

Deven and I stayed with the HR team until midnight making sure everyone was sober enough to go home. If they were not, Deven personally paid to have a car service bring them home. It's what Dalton used to do, and it's what Deven will continue to do.

After Jenna and her team leave, we take a cab over to the hotel. We have reservations at the same hotel where Hunter and Rodrigo, and Deven's family are staying. A limo is scheduled to pick us up at eleven in the morning for our flight to Miami which allows us only a few hours of sleep.

Once we are in the room, I kick off my heels and throw my arms around the neck of my gorgeous man. He holds me close to him making certain I can feel how aroused he is, and then our mouths fiercely meet. His hands slide down my back and his palms land firmly on my derrière.

He disengages himself from the kiss and brushes his thumb across my bottom lip. "Can't wait any longer, angel."

The meaning is clear, and we rush to disrobe. He sits on the edge of the bed and pulls me towards him. I stand naked in front of him and place my hands on his shoulders. He leans forward and kisses my midsection. His fingers find my wet spot, and he easily slips two fingers inside making me toss my head back and whimper.

"I want to plant my seed inside you."

My eyes widen. *Oh. My. God.* I look down at the top of his head.

He leaves a few more kisses near my belly button before peering up at me. "I want to make a baby with you tonight."

His words are like gasoline igniting the passionate flames inside me.

"Angel, let me make love to you now," he implores.

Yes, yes, yes. I push him onto his back sending a look of surprise to his face. He grins as I climb over him and trap him, placing a knee on each side of him. I lower myself down on his engorged shaft and gyrate my hips. His eyes flutter as his breathing starts to become shallow. He places a hand on each of my breasts and massages them as I continue to ride him. Heat courses through my body as I close my eyes and emit a raspy moan.

"On your back," he says and rolls me over gently without breaking our connection.

The sensation of him inside as he flips me onto my back has me seeing fireworks. His eyes lock with mine as he thrusts into me. Each thrust becoming fiercer like waves violently crashing onto the shore during a storm.

"So perfect. Love being inside you." His voice is rough.

The love between us is palpable. I brush back some of his hair dampened by sweat and stare at his handsome face. "I want your baby, Deven."

He brings his lips to mine. Our mouths connect with fervency and urgency. The temperature between us can shatter a thermometer. When he withdraws from the kiss, there's a wild look in his eyes. In one swift motion, he plunges deep into me with such force it sends us soaring until we reach the summit and come together. Echoes of our cries bounce off the walls. *It gets better and better each time we have sex.* He drains every drop inside me and then carefully lays his chest on top of mine as we both struggle to regain our breathing.

Some minutes pass before he lifts himself slightly off of me. He engages my lips in a tender kiss and then rolls onto his back. He takes my hand and holds it in his. His grip is loose indicating his exhaustion and within seconds, he's snoring. I splay my free hand on my lower abdomen and silently pray that a miracle did happen tonight before I succumb to sleep.

CHAPTER TEN

January

CARI

Hiring a professional wedding planner to manage most of the details is extremely helpful, but certain things still require Deven and I to handle on our own. One such thing is choosing our wedding party. Deven has already asked Brad to be his best man, and he wants Mandy to be our flower girl. Hunter happily accepted when I asked him to be one of my men of honor, and May knew she was going to be my bridesmaid from the time she learned of our engagement. The only person left I need to ask is Rodrigo.

Rodrigo and I made plans to have lunch together at the penthouse. Hunter and Deven give us our alone time by going car shopping. *Like Deven really needs another car.* I make lunch for us, and we discuss the wedding. He and Belle are surprisingly getting along thus far, but Rodrigo thinks it's because she knows he wears the crown and has the power of approval. He acknowledges that she does have a lot of connections and has booked one of the best caterers in Rhode Island to cater our extravagant wedding. Deven will be extremely pleased to know this as he wants the food to be from a top notch caterer.

"Do you think I should ask my sisters to be part of the wedding party?"

He mulls over the question. "I don't think so."

"Why not?"

"You just got to know them. When you ask someone to be a part of your wedding party, it should be someone you are close to and have known for a while. You shouldn't have to feel obligated to include them."

I don't know if I completely agree.

"And if you do include them, Deven will have to add two more guys on his side. For some reason, I don't think your man wants to ask anyone else to be in his wedding party."

"He has friends everywhere. I think he doesn't want to show preference."

Rodrigo rolls his eyes. "So what?"

"I leave it to him who he wants in his wedding party." I look down at my empty plate. "I have something I would like to ask you."

"What is it?"

The first time I ever saw Rodrigo was when he sat next to me in social studies back in elementary school. He greeted me and made an attempt to befriend me, but I was shy. Little did I know, he was assigned to every class I was already in. He has always been confident, smart, direct, and proud to be gay. He accepted he was different at an early age and never let anyone bully him nor walk all over him. In due course, he got me to crawl out of my shell of bashfulness, and it was the beginning of a beautiful lifelong friendship.

"I remember the first day you walked into Mrs. Washburn's class. Do you remember?"

Rodrigo snorts. "Do I ever. Everyone stared at me because of the way I was dressed and I didn't give a hoot. I said 'hi' to you and you ignored me."

"I was shy."

"And still are. I knew the moment I sat next to you that we would be friends. I could tell you weren't like those other arrogant fools. It took forever to get you to talk to me."

"It did. Your friendship is one of the best things that ever happened in my life. You're Godsent and have been a pillar to me through good and bad times. You've been with me every step of the way since the day we became friends. Everyone should have a best friend like you in their life like I do."

"You're such a darling."

"I do want to ask you a question."

He places his hand over his heart. "Oh my God! I'd be honored to be your man of honor. I was wondering when you were planning on asking me."

He knew that was coming. "Well, that's part of it."

He's befuddled. "Part of it? What is the other part?"

"Will you walk me down the aisle and give me away?"

Rodrigo's face lights up for a brief moment. "Oh! I'd be honored to, but don't you want your father to walk you down the aisle instead?"

"You've gone through so much with me. So many times you have picked me and my broken heart off the floor and kept me marching onward. I can't imagine asking anyone else other than you. I'd be honored if you say yes to walking me down the aisle and giving me away."

"It means so much that you want me to." His eyes are misty, and he locks me in an embrace. "I would love to be the one to walk you down. I accept. Thank you, Cari."

"There is an extraordinary bond you and I have and will always have."

"We certainly do. It's indestructible."

~ * ~

I had been giving a lot of thought as to whether or not I should have my father walk down the aisle with my stepmother. I ran the idea by Deven and he opposed it right away. It took a whole lot of convincing in bed to get him to change his mind. We ended up compromising. Max will escort Leigh down the aisle, and Aimee will be introduced at the wedding reception.

I'm excited to share this news with my father. We make plans to meet for lunch while Deven is at a business meeting. Max and I catch up on the week's events. He asks me how the wedding plans are coming along, and it's the perfect segue to what I want to bring up.

"Deven and I would like for you to be a part of our wedding."

He looks astonished. "I'm flattered."

"We would like for you to walk down the aisle with Leigh, Deven's mother."

"Ah, I see."

I can hear the slight disappointment in his voice. *Isn't he happy to be part of our special day?*

He leans forward. "I won't be walking you down the aisle?"

Uh-oh. I have to break the news to him, and I hope he understands.

"Rodrigo has always been there for me. We've gone through so much together and I want him to be the one to give me away. He's my family too."

"Of course. I understand, and I'm sorry. It was a selfish comment. You're absolutely right. He should be the one to give you away."

"Thank you for understanding."

"I should be the one thanking you."

"Why?"

"For including me on your special day. Now, since Deven is paying for the wedding and doesn't need any help with it, I would like to offer to pay for your dress and the dresses for your wedding party."

"Oh. I only have one bridesmaid and that is Deven's sister. I am going to have Rodrigo and Hunter by my side as well, and Deven's niece is the flower girl."

"Then let me pay for your wedding dress and their wedding attire."

"Deven is not going to let you pay for his sister's dress nor his niece's dress."

"I accept that. Then I will pay for your dress and the tuxedos. I'd like to do this."

Deven wanted to pay for my dress too, but I refused as I had set aside enough money to purchase my dress. I can easily decline my father's offer, but it seems like he really wants to contribute to the wedding in some way.

"Okay. Thank you."

"No. Thank you, Cari. Don't fret over the price. I want you to have your dream dress."

"I'm not a big spender."

"Learn to be for this occasion. It's your special day."

Spending money is more of Rodrigo's specialty and I am certain he will have no problem with helping me find an expensive designer wedding dress.

CHAPTER ELEVEN

CARI

Rodrigo scheduled an appointment for us to go wedding dress shopping at a renowned bridal boutique in Manhattan. The bridal consultant assigned to help me with my quest to find my dream dress is running behind schedule. We wait in the busy store and are offered complimentary coffee while we wait. We politely decline and browse through the racks of silk, tulle, and lace dresses instead.

"Rodrigo, why did you choose this place? These dresses are very expensive."

"This is the crème de la crème of bridal shops. You're marrying a multibillionaire, and you need to be adorned in an exquisite gown. Do you know how many people will be taking pictures of you?"

I do not want to walk down the aisle in a fancy designer gown that will cost more than a thousand dollars even if I'm not paying for it. A simple and pretty white gown will do. The dress will only be worn once; therefore, I don't see the point in spending that much money.

"If Grams was here she would agree with me. It's your wedding day. Why care how much the dress costs?"

I close my eyes and draw a deep breath in wishing Grams was here as well. I visualize Grams looking through the racks of dresses. She would have already selected a few dresses for me.

"Yeah, she would have agreed with you," I admit and pull out a dress. My eyes enlarge when I notice the numbers on the tag forcing me to hang the dress back on the rack. "But I don't care to spend a lot of money on my dress."

"And that's why I am here. I am here to persuade you to spend, and I will help you spend a lot of money on the dress."

I roll my eyes and then watch as some of the other brides-to-be comb through the dresses trying to find their dream dress. My eyes come upon a dress I find somewhat fitting for my Gilded Age fusion wedding. I pull it off the rack to get a better look at it. It has a lace overlay with a high ruffled collar and long sleeves.

"*What is that?!* It's ghastly!" Rodrigo looks horrified.

"It seems to be suitable for the wedding."

Rodrigo shakes his head. "No, no, no. It's hideous. That's more appropriate for…what was the name of that show Grams and my mother loved? The one with the country family living in the pioneer days?"

"*Little House on the Prairie?*"

"Yes, that show. The dress is more befitting for a country wedding. You are not having a country wedding. We need to find you a Gilded Age inspired dress. Something with much prettier lace and is also sexy on you."

"Sexy? I am not going for sexy."

"You have a body others envy. Why not show it off on a day when thousands of pictures will be taken of you? *You're doing sexy.*"

I sigh and put the dress back. I continue to browse through the racks but cannot find anything that suits my taste and is affordable.

The consultant assigned to me finally comes over to us. She introduces herself in a perfunctory way and asks me what kind of dress I am looking for. I tell her and she shows me several dresses that she thinks will be perfect. Sadly, not one of the dresses really appeals to me.

"Cari, there must be one dress you like."

"I cannot seem to find one I like."

"There is no other bridal boutique better than this one. This is the only place that has the largest selection of designer dresses."

"But there's not one dress that has grabbed my attention. Even the dress I just showed you cost five thousand dollars."

Rodrigo turns to the consultant. "Do you have any other dresses or suggestions?"

She looks at us as she gives our question some thought. She snaps her fingers and a huge smile appears. "I think I may have something. I'll be right back."

"God, I hope she finds something for you."

"I hope so too."

The consultant returns with a couple of dresses. She hangs them on a hook and I see that they are Cinderella style dresses which are not my style. Rodrigo is shaking his head.

"These dresses are classic princess style dresses and perfect for any wedding," the consultant says as she fluffs out the tulle on one of the dresses.

Rodrigo faces me and rolls his eyes.

"Thank you, but it's not what I had in mind," I tell her kindly.

"Are you sure? I think you should try it on first and then make your decision."

"Unfortunately, she doesn't have time to try them on. We have another appointment, but we'll think about the dresses. Thank you for your time," Rodrigo says.

"Let me give you my card. Just call and make an appointment when you are ready to try on the dresses." She reaches into her jacket pocket and hands me her business card.

"Come on, Cari. Let's go."

"Thank you," I say to her before leaving. I toss her card into my purse knowing I will not be returning.

~ * ~

I come back to an empty home after dinner with Rodrigo and Hunter. Deven must still be at his mother's with Brad. They had been summoned to clean out the garage where Dalton's belongings had been stored after his passing. I check my phone to see if Deven sent me a text message, but there's a text from my father instead. I give him a call.

"Hi sweetheart."

"Hi."

"How did the dress shopping go?"

"Dress shopping was unsuccessful."

"Well, that's surprising to hear. I thought every bride who goes there walks out with a dress."

I let out a sigh before responding. "Every bride but me. The dresses are costly."

"They are known to carry the finest dresses."

"They have a vast selection, but I couldn't find one that I liked."

"Aimee has a good friend who owns a small bridal boutique in Tribeca. I can have Aimee arrange an appointment for you if you'd like."

"I would like that very much. Thank you."

"You're welcome and we're glad to help any way we can."

There is another matter that I need to speak to my father about. I think now is a good time to bring it up.

"On another note, Deven and I had discussed setting up a date so our families can meet."

"Of course. Let's plan for it. Which date are you looking at?"

"We're thinking of a date within the next couple of weeks."

"Next couple of weeks?" He is quiet for a few seconds. "Hmm. Let me check with Aimee first and get back to you."

"Okay."

"It will be good to meet Deven's family before the wedding."

"You and Aimee will like them."

"I hope they like us."

"They will. Leigh is lovely. She's so kind and is a fantastic chef. And May is very amiable. I would also like for you to meet Rodrigo's family. They are my family too and have taken such good care of me."

"I would very much like to meet all of them and thank them."

Since our first lunch meeting, Max and I have grown closer. He has proven his intention is to be my father contrary to Deven's theory. Even though I have yet to close the gap with Aimee and my sisters, I am confident that our families will forge a wonderful friendship and relationship.

CHAPTER TWELVE

CARI

Aimee's friend, Holly, was very accommodating when I called for an appointment. Saturdays are her busiest days, but she was able to fit May and I in first thing this morning. May came up for the weekend and spent last night at Brad's place. Deven made plans to spend the morning with Brad after he was disappointed to learn he could not go into the bridal boutique with me. He insisted on driving into the City to pick up May and Rodrigo, and then dropping the three of us off at the bridal boutique. Rodrigo rings the bell and announces our arrival. We're immediately buzzed in.

An elegant Asian lady with a folder in her hand approaches us. "Hi. Are you Cari?"

"Yes."

"Nice to meet you. I'm Holly," she says offering a handshake.

I shake her hand. "It's so very nice to meet you, Holly. Um, this is my best friend and man of honor, Rodrigo."

"Hi Rodrigo. Nice to meet you too."

"Pleasure is mine," Rodrigo replies as they shake hands.

"And this is May, my soon-to-be sister-in-law."

"Hello May. Pleased to meet you." Holly extends her hand.

"Likewise," May says reciprocating with a handshake.

"Can I get you some coffee, tea, or a Bellini?"

"I'd love a Bellini," I say.

"Same for me," May says quickly.

I glare at May but she avoids looking at me. Deven is not going to be pleased to learn she had some alcohol.

"I'll have one as well. Thank you," Rodrigo says graciously.

"You're welcome. Brenda?"

An older lady emerges from behind a curtained entryway. "Yes, Holly?"

"Please bring three Bellinis for our guests."

"Yes, ma'am."

Holly opens up her folder and asks me what type of dress I am looking for. Rodrigo steps in and answers the question for me. *He knows best.* After a few more questions, she takes us to the back of the store where there are a lot more wedding dresses. This store by far is not as small as I had thought it to be. She shows us the section that has a collection of dresses inspired by the Gilded Age era and invites me to take a look at the dresses. While Rodrigo helps me look for a dress, she shows May where the bridesmaid dresses are so she can also search for her dress.

I shuffle through the line of dresses and find three that I like. Holly carries the dresses for me into the fitting room and hangs them on three separate hooks. The first dress I put on is made of lace and silk with a sweetheart neckline and a flowing bottom. It also has cap sleeves made up of tiny delicate pearl strands. I model the dress for May and Rodrigo and receive favorable responses. I set it aside as a possibility.

The second dress I try on is ivory with a demure neckline and an open V-back. It is sleeveless and also made of silk with a delicate lace overlay. It's fitted and flares out at the bottom. This dress did not garner the same reaction from them.

I slip into the third dress and instantly fall in love with it. It's sleeveless as well as backless. The dress is comprised of silk and delicate lace. It has two lace embroidered panels in the front which form a very low cut neckline that nearly reaches my navel. *Hmm…definitely eye-raising.* The dress is cinched at the waist by a thin ribbon of lace which is embellished with tiny pearls. The thing that I absolutely love the most about this dress is the lace cape that detaches at the shoulders.

Rodrigo whistles when he sees me in the dress. "Damn. You look hot in that dress. That's the kind of dress I picture you in." He really does know what looks best on me.

"Is it too revealing?"

May has her hands over her cheeks. "No! It's so sexy and pretty and perfect!"

"That *is* the dress. It's like the dress was made for you. It is the perfect combination of sexy yet delicate just like you." Rodrigo draws the letter "V" on his chest with his finger. "Holly, does the dress come with double-sided tape?"

"The panels will stay in place, but we can supply double-sided tape," Holly answers.

"I unhooked the cape to put the dress on."

"No problem. I'll attach it back on for you." Holly goes into the fitting room to get the cape.

I turn around to take another look at myself in the mirror. I agree with Rodrigo and May…this is the perfect dress for me.

"You make a beautiful bride," Holly comments as she attaches the cape back onto the dress. After attaching it, she bends down to smooth out the folds on the short train of the cape. "The front of the dress has a more modern look to it, but the cape in the back gives it the look from that era. It's a good combination."

"It is. A vintage and sexy style," May adds.

Rodrigo agrees nodding his head. "Definitely sexy."

I cannot come up with one reason why I should not purchase the dress. Even the price is reasonable. "This is the dress I want."

"The dress is yours. I will take your measurements and put your order in. Normally, this dress takes about six months to produce, but I will speak to the designer and let her know she needs to make this dress a priority."

I thank Holly and head back into the fitting room where she pulls out a measuring tape from her pocket. She takes my measurements, writes it down in the folder, and then helps me out of the dress.

"What do you think of this dress?" May asks when I step out of the fitting room after changing back into my clothes.

She holds up a champagne color dress that is reminiscent of the Gilded Age. It has a sweetheart neckline with lace cap sleeves and a thick sash in the midsection with a huge rhinestone applique. The bottom of the dress has a sheer overlay with lace trimmings towards the hem. She flips the dress around to show the back side which is open but not entirely. The sash can be tied into two pretty bows and there is a slight train. *What a beautiful dress.*

"That dress definitely is it," I respond.

"Without a doubt it is," Rodrigo agrees.

"Go try it on," I encourage her.

"Okay."

As she changes into the dress, I consume the rest of my Bellini.

"Would you like another?" Holly asks.

I wouldn't mind having another one but hold off. "No, thank you."

"Are you ready?" May asks.

"Yes." Rodrigo and I practically sing the response in harmony.

May steps out and twirls around. "What do you think?"

"You look very pretty in it," I say to her.

"I like the dress, but the decision is yours."

"This dress is a winner."

Rodrigo gives the nod of approval. "I totally agree with Cari. Definitely a winner."

"We'll take this dress as well," I tell Holly.

"Two stunning dresses. Let me measure you, dear," Holly says to May.

Holly confirms everything with me after taking May's measurements. Right before we leave, I ask Holly how I should proceed with payment. She informs me that my father has already arranged to pay for the dresses. I thank her again. I can cross dress shopping off the list. I am content and relieved to have found my dress, and it's all thanks to Aimee and Max.

"I have to text Max and thank him and Aimee," I say when we are outside on the sidewalk. I reach into my bag and pull out my phone.

"Please let him know that I thank him as well for purchasing my dress."

"I will. Don't make mention of it to your brother that Max paid for your dress. He won't be pleased."

May winks her eye. "Got it."

"Why don't we have them meet us for brunch?" Rodrigo suggests.

"Good idea," I say as I start typing the text to my father.

"Rodrigo, you text Hunter, and I'll text the other two," May dictates.

The three of us send our text messages and head off to brunch.

CHAPTER THIRTEEN

February

DEVEN

I promised May some time ago that Cari and I would make a trip with Brad to visit her at Princeton. And this weekend, we are going to do just that. I will never hear the end of it from my sister if we don't go visit her.

There are very limited days in the office when I'm not motivated to work and today happens to be one of those days. I'm grateful for the short day we have. Running an empire is not easy.

It's been dull staring at the stack of files and paperwork on my desk, so I turn my attention to Cari instead. It's hard to resist looking at her. She is quite distracting in the low cut blouse she has on. I sit back in my chair and watch as she does work on her laptop. The explosive sex last night is still fresh in my mind and I wouldn't mind having a repeat of it now. *Hmm…office sex with Cari sounds fucking fantastic.* She senses my eyes on her and breaks away from her computer.

"You're ogling me."

"I'm the boss, and I can do what I want."

She smiles and shakes her head.

"You should take a break," I tell her.

"I don't need one. I actually have work to finish before we leave in a couple of hours."

Her response makes me raise an eyebrow. My girl is being sassy.

"As do I, but work can wait. You need to take a break."

"Why do I need to take a break?"

I'm starving and need some pussy now. "Because I'm hungry."

"You're hungry?"

"Mmm-hmm."

"Let me finish this first, and then I will take a break."

That's not the response I am seeking. I get up from my chair and make my way over to her desk. She continues to type as I stand behind her. I lean down over her, brush her hair to the side, and kiss the back of her neck. She lets out a soft moan. My hands cover her breasts and I give them a light squeeze making her moan a little louder. *Oh yeah, baby.* My cock is ready to spring into action just from the sound of her moans.

"Take a break now," I whisper and nibble on her ear.

"Hmm…" Her hands reach behind and muss up my hair which only makes my cock harder. *Damn, what my angel does to me.*

She tilts her head back and her lips meet mine. With our lips still connected, I move in front of her and pull her up onto her feet. She throws her arms around me as my hands glide along her perfect curves. Waiting no longer, I push her skirt up above her hips, get on my knees, and pull down her lace panties. I admire her exposed pussy. *So sexy and luring.*

My nose grazes up her leg and stops at her tattoo. I trace the butterfly tattoo with my tongue as she runs her fingers through my hair. My nose maneuvers its way to her succulent pussy, and I take a lick of it. *Mmm.* Gripping the edge of the desk, she parts her legs wider for me. *Fucking perfect.* My hands clutch each buttock while I fondle her clit with my tongue. She gasps. Her legs are trembling as she leans against the desk for support. *Yes, baby. Let me fuck you.*

I drag myself away from her delectable pussy and take another look at my beautiful angel half naked before me. The sight of her is making it unbearable on my dick, and I shed my pants and boxers. *I need to be inside her.* She bites on her bottom lip as her eyes take in the length of my cock…evidence of my lust.

I close her laptop and push it to the side. She lies on top of the desk and I position myself in front of her. Her slick pussy makes it very easy for my hard cock to enter. I can feel her pussy stretching to accommodate my huge cock.

Fuck. It feels so damn good every time I am inside her. She winds her legs around me and pushes me closer to her. I'm trying to maintain control of my need otherwise this will be over real soon. She has no idea what she does to me.

I slide in and out of her multiple times before pumping her hard. I no longer have any restraint on my self-control. *I'm so very close to exploding.* I bang her with force and my body stiffens. Seconds later, I empty myself entirely inside her. My dick softens and shrinks, and I can barely stand. I slowly try to steady myself on my feet so I can go get a towel and wipe us clean.

She's insatiable. There is nothing like having sex with Cari. Sex with her is fucking amazing, but office sex with her is even more fucking amazing. I need to clear out my calendar and make time for it to happen each day we are in the office together. No ifs, ands, or buts to it.

~ * ~

At about half past two, the three of us finally leave the office. I gave Jordan the weekend off and do the driving to Princeton. Traffic is light and we arrive earlier than anticipated.

May is still in class, so we check into the luxury hotel first. The hotel is small and inviting. It's also close to town and the campus. For months, I have been entertaining the idea of expanding my company into the hotel industry. *Where would I want to build a hotel? And how big of a hotel do I want?* A smaller hotel will be much easier to handle than a larger one. It is an interest I will definitely need to conduct more research on before committing to such a project.

The suite we are in is modern and well-appointed. I sit on the bed and check the time on my watch. We have about forty-five minutes until we need to leave. I pat the bed. My angel comes over and sits next to me. *I want to make love to her now.* A yawn escapes her lips and it's probably because she's tired from our office activity earlier. I ask if she wants to nap before we meet up with May and she nods leaving me and my dick disappointed.

I watch some TV and answer text messages and emails while Cari is

74

snoozing. I wake her up fifteen minutes prior to leaving to give her time to get ready. As we wait for Brad, I wander through the lobby taking in the surroundings and décor. The manager sees me and engages me in conversation until Brad finally comes downstairs.

The drive to the campus is relatively short. The visitor parking lot is practically empty when we arrive.

I'm concerned about May's safety. "Is this lot always so empty?"

"Not really."

"Good because I wouldn't want May to park here and walk back to her dorm alone."

I lock the Porsche and put my arm around Cari's shoulder. We follow Brad to May's residence hall.

"I hope her roomie is not there."

Brad laughs. "You're going to be disappointed. She usually is when I visit."

I have a sudden urge to go into town and wait for May and Brad at the restaurant instead.

"You saw for yourself how she tends to cling to May, but you don't have to worry. I already told May that Crystal is not invited to dinner tonight."

Bravo. "Did she give you a hard time?"

"No, she didn't. I think it's also because she's being selfish and wants it to be just the four of us tonight."

"What about the remainder of the weekend? I hope she does not have any plans for the five of us."

Brad shrugs his shoulders. "You'll have to ask your sister about that."

It wouldn't come as a surprise to me if my kind sister did ask Crystal to join us. I make a mental note to speak to May about *not* inviting her roommate to the wedding.

I recognize the building May resides in. Brad leads the way to the lobby and signs us in as visitors while I text May letting her know we're here. Brad and I agree that May should bring Cari back to her room and show her the living quarters she shares with Crystal. I want to avoid Crystal if at all possible.

"Hi!"

The three of us spin around. May is smiling from ear to ear. I love seeing my baby sister happy. I stretch my neck to look behind May to make sure her irritating roommate is not around. It pleases me she's not. We catch up briefly before she takes Cari back to her room.

"May is ecstatic to have you and Cari come visit this weekend."

"Yeah, I see that. If it wasn't because she loves Cari, she would never let me live it down that I don't make time to come and visit." I scratch the back of my head.

Brad chuckles as he knows it's the truth. "Sometimes she thinks you kick your feet up and do nothing."

I laugh at the absurd thought.

"She's quite popular here. A lot of them here seem to know who she's related to."

"Good. Then they know not to fuck with her."

"May is tough."

"I know that. Remember who her big brother is."

"How can I forget? I'm glad to be on your good side."

"Keep it that way."

A group of female students pass through the lobby fixing their eyes on Brad and I. They take their time walking out of the building and giggle as they do. Having a handsome face can be so annoying at times.

Brad crosses his arms. "I have an idea and want to run it by you."

"Sure. What is it?"

"I think we should go to Vegas for your bachelor party."

"Bachelor party?"

"Yeah. Why do you sound surprised?"

Because my bachelor party is more for him than it is for me. "I wasn't expecting a bachelor party."

Brad spreads his arms. "Come on. I'm your best man. Do you really think I wouldn't plan one for you?"

"Is this bachelor party more for you?"

"Absolutely not. It's a tradition."

"Tradition or not, my schedule is pretty much tight until the wedding."

"You can always rearrange your schedule. You've done so before."

He desperately wants me to agree to this. I think I'll have some fun and continue to let this ex-manwhore grovel.

"You need some male bonding time."

"Do I need male bonding time or is this just an excuse for you to go see strippers?"

"Why would I need an excuse to go see strippers?"

"Why do you need to go see strippers anyway? Did you forget you're dating my sister?"

"Of course not."

"You are really trying hard to sell this bachelor party trip to me."

"It's one last hurrah for us guys before you get hitched."

Cari will feel insecure if she finds out about the strip club. I will not allow her to feel that way. I am committed to her and have no interest in going to a strip club where those women are constantly lap dancing with other men.

"We can consider Los Angeles or even Miami if Vegas isn't where you want to go."

"Whoa! Did I even say I want to go?"

"It's your bachelor party."

"I told you I don't have time for a bachelor party."

"It's tradition to have one whether you have time or not. It's only one weekend. We can leave early Friday morning which will give us Friday night and all day Saturday."

"I don't want to leave Cari alone."

"You've got to be kidding me."

"Why would I be?"

"She has security detail. She'll be fine."

"What is she supposed to do while I'm in Vegas having some male bonding time?"

"May can stay with her that weekend, or she can spend time with Rodrigo and Hunter. Her father and her sisters are also around, and she can go visit them."

"I prefer she does not spend time with her father while I'm away."

"Does that mean you agree to Vegas then?"

"Just because I say I don't want her to spend time with her father doesn't mean I agree to the trip."

"Then I'll speak to Cari."

He is unrelenting. I let out an exasperated sigh signaling defeat. "Very well, then. I agree."

"Yes! This is fucking great!"

"Don't say a word about it to Cari. I'll inform her of your plans."

"She'll be fine with it. She's so easygoing."

She'll pretend to be fine with it, but deep down inside she won't be. I'm going to have to think of something to keep her mind off this trip that Brad is planning. I hope I don't regret agreeing to this.

May and Cari finally return to the lobby after what seems like hours. And right behind them is none other than Crystal. *There goes avoiding Crystal.*

She greets me and I reluctantly return her greeting. I narrow my eyes at May, and she begins to explain that the food in the dining hall doesn't seem appealing tonight. Cari stops her from saying anything further and admits it wasn't May who invited Crystal to have dinner with us. It was my angel who did. She gives me a kiss on the cheek erasing the scowl on my face. Crystal offers to pay for her portion of dinner, but I refuse. She doesn't realize it's not a matter of paying. I guess this weekend will be a party of five after all. *How fucking wonderful.*

CHAPTER FOURTEEN

CARI

Leigh is hosting brunch today. I'm extremely happy our families are going to meet but also apprehensive of Deven's attitude towards my father.

Rodrigo and his family are the first to arrive. We gather in the gourmet kitchen chatting while sampling the appetizers Leigh made. Mrs. Sanchez requests to speak to me alone. Deven hears this and offers us Dalton's former home office. She has a small bag in her hand which she must want to give to me. We go over to the office. I have her take a seat on the couch and close the door.

"What did you want to speak to me about?" I ask as I sit down next to her.

"Your grandmother loved you so much. Before she died, she gave me something to hold onto. She wanted you to have this on your wedding day." She hands the bag to me.

I reach in and pull out a small box. I open it to find a pair of gorgeous pearl and diamond earrings inside.

"She wore them on her wedding day, and she had hoped you would do the same and wear them on your wedding day."

My eyes are brimming with tears. "They're beautiful, and I will definitely wear them on my wedding day. Thank you for holding onto this. I will cherish these forever."

We hug and rejoin everyone in the kitchen. I put the earrings away safely before helping Deven and May set up the table. Rodrigo's mom keeps Leigh company as she finishes preparing the dishes. The rest of the family has moved into the family room to play with Rockie. As we're setting up, the bell chimes signaling someone is at the entrance gate.

"They're here!" Mayleen announces.

"Why is she so excited?" Deven is perplexed by her enthusiasm.

I shrug. He shakes his head as May checks the camera to make sure it is my family before granting access. She finishes setting up and leaves the dining room to welcome them.

"Maybe she finds it fascinating that I finally have my father in my life, or maybe..."

"Maybe what?"

"Maybe she wonders about her own parents. Has she ever expressed wanting to know who her biological parents are?"

"At some point when she was much younger she did, but I think it's natural for anyone who is adopted or orphaned to be curious. I'm sure you understand the feeling of being curious about your biological parents."

I nod my head as I can relate to Mayleen's curiosity. "Does she know anything about her biological parents?"

"She knows as much as Dad knew."

"Do you think she will ever want to meet them?"

"I'm not sure, but there may be a possibility. Come on. Let's go welcome your family."

"Before we do, please don't make it uncomfortable today for my father."

"I will try not to."

"Thank you."

He opens his mouth to say something but closes it right away. On our way to the front entrance, we stop by the family room to announce their arrival. Deven and I wait in the foyer. My father smiles when he sees me. I close the gap between us and we embrace each other.

"It's so good to see you, Cari."

"Good to see you too."

Embrace released, he extends his hand to Deven.

"Hello Deven."

"Max," Deven says stoically as he accepts the handshake. He does not fully trust Max yet, but at least he will try to make an effort to maintain the peace with him for my sake.

Deven greets and welcomes Aimee while I greet my sisters. Then Deven goes to give each of my sisters a hug. *What a cheeky thing to do when he knows I did not hug them.*

"Hi Aimee," I say as I go to hug her. She doesn't quite return my hug, and I surmise it's because she's still having difficulty accepting me as Max's daughter. Perhaps in time she will accept the fact that I am. "I'm glad you're here."

"We brought a cake." Max points to the Lady M bag May is holding.

"That's kind of you. Thank you," Deven says and shoots May a look.

May goes to bring the cake into the kitchen.

"Let me take your coats," Deven offers.

Deven and I hang their coats in the closet.

"I'll introduce you to my mother first, and then we'll introduce you to Rodrigo's family."

Deven takes them into the kitchen. The aroma in the kitchen is making my mouth water as Leigh puts a casserole dish into the oven.

"Mom, our guests have arrived." Leigh turns around and Deven introduces them.

"Hello everyone and welcome!" Leigh goes around and hugs each of them. "It's such a pleasure to meet Cari's family."

"And it's a pleasure to meet you," Max tells her.

"It smells so good in here," Rylee comments.

Aimee takes in the enormous kitchen. "Yes, it does. And thank you for inviting us to your home."

"Come to the family room so we can introduce you to the Sanchez family," I say.

Max nods his head. "Sure. I'd love to finally meet the wonderful people who have been so good to you, Cari."

We go on over to the family room and I make the introductions. Rockie starts to bark. He's excited to have so many people around him. The girls immediately take to Rockie and pet him.

"Cari has spoken so lovingly of all of you. I cannot thank you enough for all you have done for her. You've been there for her, and she's very fortunate to have you as her family."

"Cari is a blessing. We are the fortunate ones to have her in our lives," Mr. Sanchez tells Max.

My eyes well up and Deven puts his arm around me.

"And I also am fortunate and will be forever," Deven adds before placing a kiss on the top of my head.

"Hey, why don't I give you a tour of our house before we eat?" May suggests.

"That will be awesome!" Harper responds.

"Come with me," May says volunteering to be the tour guide.

~ * ~

Leigh is a consummate hostess and chef. Not only did she make a most delicious brunch but she made our families feel as if we have been gathering like this for years. There was never any awkward silence especially when we all sat down to eat.

We're all sitting around the table again enjoying the desserts including the cake that Aimee and Max brought over.

"Lady M makes the best cakes," May says sharing her opinion. "I should bring one back to campus."

"They have many different flavors, but the green tea one is the best," Esmeralda tells us.

"How are those wedding plans coming along?" Max asks changing the subject.

"Good," I answer him.

"They will have the samples of the invitations next week," Rodrigo chimes in. He helped Belle with narrowing down the samples for Deven and I to choose from.

Rodrigo informs our parents they have to submit to him a list of guests they would like to invite to our wedding. Aimee and Max both look shocked. I suppose they didn't think they would be able to invite the extended family.

"Where are you both going for your honeymoon?" Mr. Sanchez poses the question to Deven and I.

"We're going to be spending it on our private island," Deven tells him.

A hush falls over the room as I take another bite of the delicious cake. I look up from my plate to find all eyes are on Deven. Leigh, May, Hunter and Rodrigo are the only ones who know about the private island.

"You have a private island?" Harper asks in a disbelieving manner.

"*We* sure do," Deven corrects her.

"So cool!"

Max clears his throat and finds his voice. "Wow. That's really something to own an island."

"Well, I can afford the island," Deven snaps back.

My jaw drops open. *Why does he have to rub it in like that?* My father is quite aware Deven can afford it.

"Where is this private island located?" Max asks in an even tone.

"It's in the Caribbean." Deven chooses to be vague about the exact location.

"That is like total awesomeness! I want to go there." Thank goodness for Harper breaking up what could have been another uncomfortable situation between Deven and Max.

Aimee gives Harper a stern look and says, "You need to be invited to go there."

"You're all welcome to come to the island. Just let me know when and I can arrange for the jet to take you there."

"You have a private plane too?" Harper's reaction is priceless and reminds me of my own reaction when I discovered he had his own plane.

"I do."

"Cool! Is there any shopping there?" Harper is by far the more curious and inquisitive sister.

"Harper, dear, it's a private island. There are no shops there," Max informs her.

"Oh. So what do you do there?"

Rylee rolls her eyes. It seems to me shopping is not her thing. My sisters are more different than I realize. I do need to spend much more time with them so I can get to know them better.

"There is a pool and the beach. You can walk to the beach from the house," I tell Harper.

May puts down her fork. "Doesn't sound like I would have a good time there. I need an activity like shopping."

"The island was acquired for the purpose of rest and relaxation," Deven throws back at her.

"Maybe Brad would enjoy that rest and relaxation thing."

"Who's Brad?" Harper asks.

"He's my boyfriend."

"And my best friend," Deven mentions.

"*What?!* You're dating your brother's best friend?" The shock is clear on Rylee's face.

"She is," Deven answers for May.

I don't consider this to be an appropriate subject we should be discussing at the table. My sisters are still young and do not need to know about May and Brad's history at this time. It's not a topic to discuss with our families here. This conversation needs to shift back to the wedding.

I look at Max. "Have you made reservations for the weekend of the wedding?"

"I'm glad you brought it up. I looked at a couple of hotels online. We wanted to stay where you're staying, but the hotel is already sold out. So, we chose another hotel that's not too far away," my father apprises us.

I am gobsmacked to learn the hotel has no availability. "The hotel is sold out?"

"Newport gets really busy beginning in May and it's not unusual for some hotels to be sold out already," Deven explains.

I'm disheartened to learn my family won't be staying with me. "I thought Belle was going to block some rooms for our guests at the hotel where I'll be."

"Don't worry. I have it all under control. I'll speak to Belle," Rodrigo reassures me.

"I've never been to Newport," Harper confesses.

"Never? There's a lot of history to Newport. You will like it," Leigh tells Harper before putting another forkful of cake in her mouth.

"This wedding is going to be like none other," Rodrigo informs everyone.

I wish Deven and I could just elope and forget about this lavish wedding more fit for a prince and a princess than for me.

"You're so famous, Deven. Are there going to be any super famous people there?" Harper wants to know.

"There may be, but I can't mention who will be invited," Rodrigo replies for us.

"Guess you'll just have to wait until the wedding," Rylee tells Harper.

"Well, I can't wait!" May says.

Deven reaches for my hand under the table and looks at me. "Neither can I."

"Will you continue to live in White Plains after you're married?" Max inquires.

"That's the plan for now," I reply.

"We are looking to eventually build a house," Deven reveals.

"In White Plains?"

"Not in White Plains. We're thinking of moving here to Greenwich."

"This is a good place to raise kids."

"I know it is. I grew up here." Deven's tone carries a hint of sarcasm.

"It makes sense to move here. The schools are excellent and we'll be close to Leigh," I contribute hoping to prevent any more sarcastic replies from Deven.

"Westchester also has excellent places to raise a family," counters Max.

"It does, but we like Greenwich."

"Greenwich is a lovely place to live in. I will be delighted to show you around Greenwich. When it's warmer, we'll take you to the downtown district. There are great shops and restaurants there," Leigh offers.

Harper's face lights up. "Shopping?"

"They have the cutest boutiques in town," May happily adds knowing she has found a shopping partner with one of my sisters.

After a couple of more hours, the brunch party comes to an end. Thankfully, Deven displayed a much better attitude towards Max. Overall, it was a wonderful afternoon as our families became united.

CHAPTER FIFTEEN

Mid-March

CARI

Holly was true to her word and had the designer prioritize the production of my dress. My wedding dress has arrived, and today is my first fitting. May, Rodrigo, and a very pregnant Alana are accompanying me. We're greeted by Holly upon arrival, and she shows me the fitting room where the dress hangs. I stare at my wedding dress. *My wedding dress.* It's more beautiful than I remember it to be. Holly tells me she will be right outside if I need any assistance getting the dress on. I thank her and she draws the curtain closed behind me.

The dress is quite delicate and I carefully put it on. It's slightly loose on me and probably will not require significant alterations. I spin around glancing into the mirror admiring my dress before stepping down from the riser and pulling open the curtain.

"The dress is stunning on you, and it just about fits you. I don't think too much will need to be altered. The cape won't need any adjustment," Holly says as she clamps the extra fabric on the sides of the dress for the proper fit. "There."

"What do you think?" I ask.

Rodrigo gives me a thumbs up. "Only you can wear the dress so well."

"What a dress! Very sexy," Alana says giving me two thumbs up.

"My opinion hasn't changed since you first tried the dress on," May expresses. "Deven is going to die when he sees you in it."

"The dress is befitting and such a perfect blend of then and now." Alana appears to be uncomfortable on the bench as she shifts into different positions.

"There's a cape that attaches to the dress, but I don't want it on now," I tell Alana.

Rodrigo holds up his phone. "I want to take a picture of you in the dress so we can decide on how to style your hair." He takes a few pictures.

"Uh-oh."

We all turn our attention to Alana.

"I think my water just broke," Alana says looking at the water trickling down her leg.

May's eyes are wide like saucers. *"What?!"*

This is not the right time for May to start panicking.

"I'll go get some tissues," Holly says.

Rodrigo is nearly hyperventilating as he paces back and forth. "Oh my God! Hold that baby in until we get you to the hospital."

"I can't hold this baby in! I have to get to the hospital now. Please go get a cab, Rodrigo," Alana beseeches him.

"Got it. I'll go get a cab. And don't panic," he says running out.

"Hurry!" May screams after him.

Alana and I look at each other. May and Rodrigo are in panic mode, and we burst out laughing.

May turns to us. "This is so not funny."

"I'm sorry, May. I find it funny that you and Rodrigo are more nervous than I am," Alana tells her.

Holly returns with a wad of paper towels. "Are you experiencing any pain?" Holly kindly asks Alana.

Alana shakes her head as she takes some of the paper towels to wipe her leg. "Not yet."

"Let me quickly take off this dress so we can rush over to the hospital as soon as Rodrigo hails a cab."

"Allow me to remove the clips first," Holly tells me.

She removes the clips, and I go back into the fitting room to change out of the dress. I return to Alana's side afterwards. Alana continues to wipe her leg, but the water keeps streaming down.

"I sent a text to my doctor and Vinny to meet me at the hospital." Alana's gaze remains on her leg. "I don't think wiping is of any help. It's not stopping."

I look at Holly. "Thank you, Holly. Will you call me when I should come in for my next fitting?"

"I will." Holly turns back to Alana. "Good luck to you."

"Thank you, and I'm sorry about this."

"Don't be. I gave birth to two kids of my own."

Rodrigo comes back in to announce the cab is outside waiting for us.

"We need to get you to the hospital," I say taking a paper towel and placing it on the floor to wipe up a small puddle of water.

I help Alana to her feet and together, we make our way outside. Rodrigo helps Alana into the cab while May and I get in from the other side. Rodrigo shuts her door and hops in the front.

The cab driver steps on the gas pedal giving all of us whiplash. Alana is doing some sort of breathing thing with her hands resting on her baby bump. She moans from what I presume to be contractions.

"Can you not go any faster?" Rodrigo asks the driver.

"Sir, there is traffic in front of my cab. I cannot move around the cars."

"Well then, you better know what to do if she has the baby in your cab."

"I have four kids. She will get to the hospital on time."

"*On time?* Do you happen to know what time the baby is due?"

Alana, May, and I look at each other suppressing the urge to laugh as we watch Rodrigo and the cab driver exchange words.

"Oh!"

My full attention is on Alana. "What is it?"

"I can't be sure, but the contractions seem stronger. I think the baby wants to push its way out very soon."

"You need to hold the baby in until we get to the hospital," Rodrigo warns Alana again.

"She can't do that," I speak for Alana.

"You have to, Alana. It's more sanitary to give birth in a hospital. Why would you want to have the baby in a dirty taxi?"

"Excuse you, sir, but my cab is *not* dirty," the cab driver informs Rodrigo.

Rodrigo has an incredulous look on his face. I must agree with Rodrigo that giving birth in the hospital will be better.

"It sure is filthy. You pick up many passengers. How often do you sterilize the back seat?" Rodrigo questions him.

"You listen to me. My cab is not dirty." The cab driver seems irritated by Rodrigo's comment.

I notice Alana closes her eyes as she continues to inhale and exhale short breaths. "Just get us to the hospital," I interject.

The driver looks at his mirrors and squeezes the cab in between two cars in the right lane.

~ * ~

We arrive at the hospital safely and Rodrigo rushes in. I offer my assistance to Alana as she gets out of the cab. May goes to pay the driver. As we start to make our way into the waiting area for the ER, Rodrigo returns with a wheelchair. Alana sits down in it, and Rodrigo pushes her down a different corridor. May and I follow them. Alana starts to moan again as we wait for the elevator.

"The baby has to wait until we get up there," Rodrigo says in a panicky tone.

"I don't think the baby is going to be born in the next few minutes," Alana tries to assure him.

"I should hope not."

"Vinny is upstairs waiting for us, so don't worry. I think he will be quite disappointed if this baby didn't wait."

The elevator doors open up and we wait for everyone to step out before getting on. May pushes the button for the fifth floor.

"I am looking forward to meeting either baby Alberto or baby Lola," I say.

"I am looking forward to babysitting, and I'm so glad I am gay. There is no chance that I could possibly be calm with a pregnant wife in labor if I was straight."

The doors open and Vinny is pacing back and forth like an expectant father.

"Thank God!" Vinny says rushing to Alana. He kisses her forehead. "You ready, babe?"

"I am." She looks at us. "Thank you for getting me here."

"Yeah, thanks everyone. It's time to have our baby," Vinny says anxiously.

"Good luck. We'll be in the waiting room," I say as the doors to the maternity unit opens and they go on their way to have their baby.

Alana smiles and waves to us as Vinny pushes her to the nurse's station. They will be parents the next time we see them.

"Oh!"

"What's wrong, Cari?" Rodrigo asks.

"I forgot to call Deven to let him know we were on the way to the hospital."

"You better call my brother before he calls the police and have them put a missing alert on you."

"And he will since your bodyguard isn't with us today."

"Yeah. Let me call him." I call Deven.

His phone doesn't even ring when he answers.

"Cari?"

"Hi."

"All's well?"

"Yes. Alana's water broke and we're in the waiting room at the hospital."

"I'll meet you there. I need to take care of a few things with Leigh first."

"Yes, of course. You don't need to rush. Rodrigo and May are here with me."

"I want to be there with you as well."

"I'll see you soon then."

"Yes. Hey, I love you."

"I love you too."

The call disconnects. He will do anything to be with me and for me. Sometimes I wonder how I can be so lucky. He's such an incredible guy, and I am so in love with him. I can't wait to marry him and have a family with him.

~ * ~

We have been at the hospital for nearly six hours now and have yet to receive any news. Both sets of expectant grandparents arrive and wait with us in the waiting room.

"There's no telling when the baby will come. Why don't all of you go home? We'll have Vinny text you when the baby arrives," Doris (Alana's mother) suggests.

"Please have him text me," I tell her.

We put our coats on and swap goodbyes. Deven recommends dinner in the City before heading home since May, Rodrigo, and I skipped lunch. May and Rodrigo call their respective partners to have them meet us in Little Italy. The intimate restaurant we chose is known for their huge portions. Best of all, it's inexpensive. My best friends and I use to frequent the place when we first moved to Manhattan.

"Ooh! Everything looks so good on this menu. I am most definitely starting with the arancini," May says.

"Good choice," Hunter agrees.

"We have to watch our waistline for the wedding," Rodrigo reminds him. He is cautious of what they eat as Hunter doesn't always pay attention to what he consumes yet he still maintains his great shape.

"Let him eat what he wants. The wedding is over two months away." Brad sides with Hunter.

"We can always wear a cummerbund," Hunter says.

Rodrigo scowls at Hunter. "Really?"

I hope they're not about to have a spat now over curve lines. Lately, Rodrigo has been on Hunter about his eating habits.

"I think we should decide what we want so we can satisfy our hunger," Deven says preventing them from having a tiff.

Whew!

May nods her head. "I agree. I'm famished."

When the server comes to our table with bread, Deven orders five appetizers to start.

"Five appetizers?" asks Rodrigo disapprovingly.

"Yes, five," Deven answers in a tone that dares Rodrigo to make any further comment about it.

I put my menu down. "I wonder how Alana is doing."

"I can't wait to hold the baby!" May's voice is full of excitement.

Brad rolls his eyes.

"Me too. You seemed to be in panic mode when Alana's water broke," I say to May.

"It's the first time I have ever witnessed anyone go into labor. Now that I have seen it, I know what to expect and will be calm and prepared. If Deven isn't around when you go into labor, then I will be."

Brad breaks off a piece of bread. "It's too soon to talk about them having babies."

"I don't think so. I'm excited to be an aunt."

"That's good to know. Then you should plan on doing a lot of babysitting in the foreseeable future." Deven reaches for the bread.

"I can only babysit when I am not in school."

"We'll babysit as well, but Deven, you will have to be there in the delivery room. I don't think I can handle the labor and delivery stuff." Rodrigo shakes his head.

"I wouldn't be able to handle it either," Brad reveals.

May's eyes widen. "Why?"

"I've heard stories about how women can get when they are about to give birth."

"Not all women are the same, Brad." May cannot hide her annoyance.

"Well, I am not at that point in my life; therefore, I refuse to say anything further."

"Anyway, did you lovebirds pick your wedding song yet?" Rodrigo inquires moving to another topic.

I turn to Deven as he takes a sip of his wine before answering. "Yes, we did."

"Which song did you pick?" May is now eager to know.

"Let me guess," Rodrigo offers.

"Go ahead," Deven says challenging him.

"Is it 'All Of Me'?"

"No."

"I know which song," May says confidently.

"Do you now?" Deven sounds skeptical.

"Yes. I bet it's 'A Thousand Years'."

"It's not."

"How did you not pick that song? It's perfect for the both of you."

"Because we found a song that really is perfect for us."

"So what's the song then?"

"You'll find out at the wedding."

"Why can't you let us know which song it is?"

"It's a surprise."

May is miffed by Deven's response. "We won't share it with anyone."

"I know that, May."

My phone is buzzing and I grab it out of my bag. It's a message from Vinny. I unlock it to retrieve the text message.

"It's a girl." I hold my phone up so they can see the picture.

Everyone is gushing over the picture of the baby.

Hunter leans back in his chair and crosses his arms. "That seemed to be pretty fast. Some women are in labor for many hours if not days."

"That's a scary thought."

Deven turns to May. "What exactly is scary, May?"

"Being in labor for days."

"Every pregnancy is different."

"I hope mine is quick. The less pain, the better."

"Well, that won't be happening for some time."

"Here are your appetizers," the server announces placing the plates in the center of the table.

The timing is perfect. There is no better way to end that conversation than to start stuffing our mouths with food. We all help ourselves by reaching for what we want. For now, we'll enjoy our dinner.

CHAPTER SIXTEEN

CARI

The following morning, we meet at the hospital to visit Alana and her baby. The hospital has a limit on the number of visitors allowed into her room even though she has a private suite. Hunter and Brad volunteer to stay behind while the rest of us go to see her first.

The maternity unit is large and inviting. It's carpeted, and the walls are painted in a soothing warm beige tone with pictures of babies hanging in the corridor. We pass by the nursery on the way to Alana's room, and I stop to look at the babies.

May puts her face close to the window. "Aren't they cute things?"

"Babies are human beings," Deven corrects May.

Rodrigo has a hand on his chest. "Look at that one yawning! Oh! Their cuteness kills me. They're so precious."

Babies are cute, precious, and small miracles. They bring happiness, love, and lots of smiles. There are moments when my heart is still heavy over the loss of my baby, and sometimes I wonder if it will ever subside.

"Hey."

I peer up at Deven. He knows what is going through my heart and mind. Without saying another word, he takes my hand and holds it tightly in his.

"Rodrigo, are you and Hunter going to adopt any kids?"

"We want to, but we're looking to move out of Manhattan first," he answers May.

"Move to Greenwich. Greenwich has great schools."

"So does my hometown. Cari was the valedictorian."

"But you'll be closer to us if you move to Connecticut. Westport has good schools too, but Greenwich is better."

"Good point about being close, but my parents will also want us close to them. I'll speak to Hunter about it. Let's go see Alana and Lola."

A nurse is inside when we reach Alana's room.

Alana's face brightens as soon as she sees us. "Hi! Come on in."

The nurse finishes up and leaves. We congratulate her as we step inside her huge room. *Wow!* The suite resembles more of a hotel room than it does a recovery room. There is a couch and a chair in the room, two televisions, and even a desk.

"How are you feeling?" I ask Alana.

"I feel so much lighter now that the baby is out of me," Alana tells us.

Rodrigo looks around the room. "Where's Lola?"

"Vinny went to get her from the nursery."

"We just passed by the nursery and didn't see him there."

"He probably had to wash his hands and put a gown on first. They won't let him in unless he follows procedures."

"This is for you." Deven holds up a large blue bag containing a few baby gifts from Tiffany.

"You shouldn't have. You've already given her so much from the registry. Thank you."

"I'll put it down on the table." Deven walks over to the table in front of the couch and places the bag next to the flowers.

"What was it like delivering the baby?" I want to know what to anticipate.

"It's a lot of work to push. The contractions became more intense the closer it got to birthing. I thought I would be pushing for hours, but the doctor said it was one of the fastest deliveries he ever had."

"You *were* there for hours," Rodrigo reminds her.

"Some women are in labor for a very long time, but because my water broke, it sped things up."

"Did you feel uncomfortable spreading your legs and exposing your vajayjay for them to see?" Rodrigo asks.

Our mouths drop open.

"What?" Rodrigo asks looking at us.

"This conversation is over," Deven tells him.

The door opens and Vinny comes in with the bassinet. Lola is bundled up in a blanket with her eyes closed and her lips puckered. We are all in awe over baby Lola.

"She's so small!" May says not taking her eyes off of the baby.

Vinny lifts the baby out of the bassinet. "You guys are just in time for her feeding."

"I want to feed her," May volunteers.

"Me too," Rodrigo says.

It's a battle to feed the baby, but I know exactly who should get the honors of doing so. "I think Deven should feed the baby."

"Me?" Deven asks surprised by my suggestion.

~ * ~

DEVEN

I sanitize my hands with the foam that is in the dispenser on the wall, and then sit in the chair ready for my feeding duty. Vinny comes over with the baby and puts her in my arms. She's so light. He shows me how he stimulates her with the bottle to get her to open her tiny mouth, and it takes a few tries before she latches onto the bottle.

I haven't held a baby in my arms since May first came home. I look at the baby as she slowly drinks the formula in the bottle. When she stops sucking, I move the bottle to stimulate her. It's amazing to watch as she sucks on the bottle with her eyes closed.

"You look good with a baby in your arms," Alana implies.

"This is good practice," I tell her.

Cari sits down beside me. Someday soon there will be a moment like this when Cari and I will be holding our baby.

"Ready for fatherhood?"

I glance at her twinkling eyes. "I am."

"I wanted you to have the chance to hold the baby first since you never got to hold ours."

Sometimes it's hard not to think of the baby we lost, and that I wasn't there for my Cari during such a dark moment. But we're here now, and I love the feeling of a little one in my arms.

"Deven, you have to burp her," Alana tells me.

Right. *How the fuck do I do that?* Cari realizes I need assistance. She tells me to pull the bottle out of the baby's mouth. When I do, some of the milk oozes out of her mouth and drips down her neck. Cari takes the bottle and gets up. She comes back with a piece of cloth and some tissues. With care, she gently wipes around the baby's mouth and neck.

"You're supposed to have this on your shoulder, then hold her up, and pat her back until she burps." She lays the piece of cloth on my shoulder.

I follow her instructions. The baby's head is bobbling. Cari comes around me and carefully lays the baby's head to rest on top of the cloth sitting on my shoulder. "I'm glad you know what to do."

"I kind of do. You look hot holding her."

My eyes comb over her sexy body. "Let's raise the temperature together later."

She gives me that seductive smile of hers, and I can feel my cock getting stiff. *Fuck me.* Just then the baby lets out a burp, and my cock softens.

"She burped," I announce.

"Good. You can change her diaper now," Alana says.

"No, thank you. May, you can have the honors and change her diaper."

"No way! You fed her so you should be the one changing her," May responds.

"It's a piece of cake. I'll walk you through it," Vinny offers.

"May, you and I can change the baby together." Rodrigo walks over to the bassinet and pulls out a diaper from the shelf underneath.

I hand the baby back to Vinny, and he lays her down in the bassinet. May and Rodrigo stand alongside the bassinet as Vinny guides them through the process. The baby cries as soon as her bottom half is exposed to the cold air.

May looks like she is about to throw up. "Yuck! Is that her poop?"

"Yes," Vinny responds.

My sister grabs a wipe and carefully holds the baby's ankles up to clean the baby's ass and her genital area. I am trying to keep from laughing. This is a task I rather not take on even with my own kid, but I know I won't be able to get out of it.

Once she finishes wiping the baby clean, Rodrigo tries his hand at putting the diaper on the baby. He doesn't succeed on his first try so he tries again and again and again. After several attempts, he finally secures the diaper on her. Vinny wraps the baby back up like a burrito. Then Cari, May, and Rodrigo all take turns holding the little bundle of joy as she sleeps.

CHAPTER SEVENTEEN

April

DEVEN

A couple of weeks back, Ken dropped the news that he has to leave the west coast and build a new beginning with Mandy elsewhere. He felt ashamed to admit he could no longer afford to live in California. His current teacher's salary isn't enough for him to make ends meet as he has a child to raise, and Kait doesn't earn a steady income. I expressed to him my concern about Mandy's well-being and her future. Once again, I offered him an executive position in my Los Angeles office and doubled his salary, but he declined the offer. He made it clear to me that teaching is his passion.

There is one big obstacle with relocating. Other than Kait, there is no one whom he could entrust the care of Mandy to while he works. God forbid his mother flies halfway around the world to help babysit her own granddaughter. From what Ken told me, she was not accepting of the fact he had a child out of wedlock and with someone she did not approve of. *It's so fucking typical of her.* Everyone is beneath her standards.

Kait does not want to leave Los Angeles. I don't know where she will end up living, but my hunch is she'll probably move in with Rochelle. Ken couldn't do this himself, and I gave him a suggestion. I ran the idea of him and Mandy moving to this side of the country. It took some persuasion, but he finally agreed to it.

Ken loves the beach and wants to live as close as possible to one, but the location must have good schools. He did the research and narrowed the possibilities to Long Island and the Jersey Shore. *Why in God's name does he want to live so far away from us?* I want him to be closer to Cari and I so our children can be close. With the semester nearly over, he is unable to take any time off from work and graduate school; therefore, I volunteer to help with scouting the towns he is interested in moving to.

There is one particular small seaside town with a highly rated school system along the Jersey Shore that is on the top of his list. The town is very different from Los Angeles, but he wants Mandy to grow up in a small community rather than a large and dense city. My brother put a plan in place, and one of the immediate things he did was apply for a teaching position at the nearby high school there. He won himself an interview right away.

Time is really of the essence. I meet with a local realtor this weekend and will see what he has to show me. Most of the houses are more than what Ken will be able to afford unless I can find them a rental. With the beach season just around the corner, there are no available rentals until the season is over. If he gets the teaching job, the two of them will need a temporary home before school begins in the fall. But there may be one possible solution.

~ * ~

CARI

I contain my excitement when Jordan announces we are finally in Stone Harbor. The humdrum trip has been a long one. Deven kept himself busy with work while I alternated between napping and looking out the window. Jordan finds a parking spot and pulls into it. He remains in the car while Deven and I walk into the real estate office together.

The receptionist can barely take her eyes off of my fiancé. I quickly flash the rock on my left hand hoping she can see he's taken and then push back the hair away from my face. Deven does not wait for her to speak and lets her know we have an appointment with Jim. A gentleman sitting behind a desk towards the back of the office rises from his chair and comes up front. He introduces himself as Jim and takes us back to his desk. He hands us a list of the houses he has lined up for us to look at and quickly goes over the features of each house before we go to see each one.

All the houses on the list are beachfront homes. The location of each house couldn't be more ideal with close proximity to the beach. The last two houses are the largest ones we've been shown and practically identical in terms of number of rooms. Each of these two luxurious houses has five bedrooms, four bathrooms, two half bathrooms, and a pool. Both oceanfront homes are situated at the end of a short street with direct access to the beach.

Deven thanks Jim for showing the houses to us, and we leave for our weekend retreat in Cape May. The drive is rather quick. It's impossible not to notice the historic homes as we drive by. I am enthralled by the charismatic Victorian homes in this seashore town. I have never seen anything like it. Deven suggests we return during the holiday season as the town is decked out in lights and there are walking tours. I love the idea and look forward to coming back during the holidays.

~ * ~

"You always manage to book the best room." I sit down on the couch in our suite.

Deven crosses his arms and looks out the window. "Certainly. Why not stay in the best room the hotel has to offer?"

"We're only here for the weekend."

"Money is not an issue."

Money is never an issue with Deven Blake. I would have been content staying in one of the cheaper rooms, but he is accustomed to staying in the best room the hotel has to offer.

He turns around and faces me. "Which house did you like the best?"

"It's a toss-up between the last two houses we saw."

"I concur. The last two were the best. Those houses are newer."

"But isn't a house of that size going to be too big for Ken?"

"Ken will eventually need more space if he marries and his family expands. It's best to invest in something larger now." Deven thinks of everything.

"He chose a very nice location to live in. I like it there."

"Do you?"

"I do. It's very charming and tranquil and less populated than Los Angeles.

It will be nice to visit on the weekends."

"Tell me which one of those houses is your pick for them."

I think it over. "The first one is the better choice for Ken and Mandy."

He tilts his head. "Why is it?"

"That house has the one bedroom with built-in shelves which will be ideal for Mandy's room. The shelves can be decorated with beautiful books or whatever she wants to display. And the master room is not far from her room whereas in the other house they're on different floors."

"Good observation. Then it's settled. The first house will be theirs, and the other house across the street will be ours."

I'm not sure I heard him correctly. "Ours?"

"We'll take the other house."

"You can't be serious."

"I am."

Of course he is.

"You don't seem excited."

"I'm still trying to acclimate myself to your world of wealth. We went there to look at houses for your brother. I wasn't expecting you to buy a house for us as well."

He sits beside me and places a hand on my thigh. "It will be our weekend house, and we can invite guests to come and stay with us. Ken will love the company and the help with Mandy."

Ken is a single parent and will welcome the help.

"I can't dispute that he will need the help."

"Perfect. We have ourselves a weekend home. I'll email Jim and get the contracts for both houses." *Spoken like a businessman.*

I put my head on his shoulder. "You are full of surprises."

He gently leans his head on mine. "I don't think I'm full of surprises. I'd like to think I'm full of money."

"That you are full of."

He lets out a soft laugh. "I love you very much."

"And I love you more than that."

"I will always love you more than you love me. I think we should go take a walk into town and have an early dinner. Then I'd like to come back and spend most of the night showing you how deep my love for you is."

When he puts it that way, how can I say no?

We meet Jordan at the main entrance, and the three of us stroll into town. There's a light cool breeze and I'm glad I have on a warmer coat. When the sun goes down in a couple of hours, the chilly night air will return.

The town isn't as crowded as I thought it might be. There is a plethora of shops and food establishments in the area. I cannot resist stopping into some of the local boutiques to make a few purchases. Deven waits for me outside while I look around in the stores. Thankfully, our bodyguard stays with him.

When I exit the soap shop, I come to a halt. The sight of Deven standing on the sidewalk speaking on his phone leaves me breathless. I've seen him on the phone many times, but there's something striking about him right this moment. He looks like he's posing for a fashion photo shoot in his quilted Burberry barn jacket, fitting jeans, and driving loafers. He catches me staring at him when he turns. He ends his call and comes over to me.

He looks down at the large bags in my hands. "Did you purchase everything in the store?"

My cheeks heat up. "Um, just about."

"Ms. Snow, I'll be happy to carry your bags," Jordan offers.

I am capable of carrying my own bags. Jordan is only trying to be helpful so I hand my bags over to him. Deven threads his hand with mine and we continue to explore the town.

The afternoon seems to be ending as twilight is now upon us. Soon the night sky will settle in. Deven proposes we go have dinner. I want to do a little more shopping, but he is hungry and tells me we will come back into town tomorrow. Shopping will have to wait then.

CHAPTER EIGHTEEN

CARI

Lately, Deven has been spending a lot of hours in the office securing new development projects, conducting performance reviews, and preparing to move ahead with an aggressive expansion plan for his company. His days are filled with meetings, video conferencing calls, visits to job sites, interviews, and annual reviews. His day crosses into his night and it seems like the day never ends for him. There have been nights when he's had Jordan drive me back to the penthouse first while he stayed behind at the office working until well after midnight.

Tonight is another one of those nights when I come back home alone and dine alone. I take a shower after my workout and then lay down in bed. I attempt to force myself to sleep but can't and reach for my phone. It's nearly midnight and he isn't home yet. I call him.

"Hi. Still at it?"

"Yeah. There's much happening in L.A. and Hong Kong that requires my attention, and I still have the Miami contracts to review."

"It's very late. Can't you leave it for tomorrow?"

"I prefer if I don't have to. I need to try to get as much done as possible."

"It's lonely in this bed without you."

"Angel, I promise I will be home soon."

"How much longer do you think you will be?"

"Probably another hour max."

I try to keep the disappointment out of my voice. "Okay."

"Get some rest. I love you."

"Love you."

I contemplate going back to the office. After a few seconds, I send a text to Jordan letting him know that I want to go into the City and to be ready in five minutes. He swiftly replies that he will meet me in the foyer.

I run into the bathroom, pull my hair back into a neat ponytail, and don't bother with putting any makeup on. Moving to the spacious walk-in closet, I search for a pair of heels. I grab my favorite pair of nude Jimmy Choo pumps and slip them on my feet. Hurrying to the coat closet near the entrance, I pull out the Burberry raincoat Deven insisted on buying for me to match his. I'm tightening the belt on the coat as I walk to the door when I realize I don't have my phone. I rush back to the bedroom and take my phone with me.

When I open the door, Jordan is in the foyer ready and waiting. The car is out front when we get to the lobby, and the valet opens the back passenger door for me. I climb in, and Jordan shuts my door before getting into the driver's seat.

Entering the building, I greet the overnight security officer who is apparently surprised to see me at this hour. Jordan escorts me up to the thirty-fifth floor. He waits by the elevator bank as I head inside the north wing.

The door to our office is open. Deven is looking down at some papers as he holds a pen in his hand. *I can do this.* I stand under the doorframe with one arm propped against it and one hand on my hip trying to look as seductive as possible.

I clear my throat. "Hello."

He looks up, and I have to catch my breath. *Hello, hotness.* His hair is disheveled, his tie is gone, several buttons on his shirt are undone, and his sleeves are rolled up. Making him look even sexier are the glasses he has on. *He's pulled a sixteen hour day…how can he possibly still look so hot at this hour? Is it possible to have a sexgasm just from looking at him?*

"What are you doing here?" He takes off his glasses and places the spectacles on top of the papers he was just looking over.

I strut over to his desk and stop in front of it. Running a finger from my neck down to my cleavage, I tell him, "I was lonely." My hands move swiftly to untie the belt on my coat. Then I begin to unbutton it observing Deven shift in his chair as I do.

His eyes enlarge when the coat opens up. "You came here with just the coat on?"

I nod a couple of times. "There wasn't much time to decide on an outfit."

He comes around his desk. "This is a much better look," he says as he cups my breasts and then licks my neck.

I roll my head back as my body burns from his sultry touch. He removes one of his hands from my breasts and uses it to part my thighs. His fingers glide back and forth down there relishing the dampness. Easily, he slips his fingers inside me making me yelp.

"First time I ever heard you yelp."

"Your fingers took me by surprise."

"Like you took me by surprise coming here with only that coat on."

"Come home." I pout and fidget with the buttons on his shirt.

"Hmm. You're a siren."

I didn't plan on having sex in the office. I want to go home and have it in our bed instead. The expression on his face clearly depicts hunger for me. I cup my hand on his arousal. "Come home with me then."

~ * ~

DEVEN

Cari's hand on my cock is fucking hot, but her beseeching eyes are what convince me that my work will just have to wait until the morning. I button up her coat and pack up the files to take home with me. I plan to spend tonight and part of tomorrow in bed.

When we arrive back home, I tell her to wait for me in the bedroom while I drop the files off in my home office. My knees nearly buckle when I enter the bedroom. Her back is towards me and she's standing there naked in heels. *Fuck me.* My cock is instantly rock hard.

"What took you so long?" she asks tossing her hair back.

Oh, so sassy. I stand behind her and rub my swollen cock up against her luscious ass. *I am so damn horny.* I quickly undo the buttons on my shirt, remove it, and fling it onto the carpet.

"Don't move," I order her as I take off my pants and drop to my knees to kiss her perfectly smooth round ass. My fingers caress her moist pussy before sliding them in and out of her. From the corner of my eye, I notice her coat on the bed. With my free hand, I reach for the belt and tug it off the coat.

I use the belt to tie her wrists together. Then I direct her to stand with her back against the wall. She complies and spreads her lovely legs apart. *Good girl.* I get back down on my knees in front of her and part her legs just a little wider inhaling her scent as I do. My nose skims her inner thigh as my tongue concurrently licks her silky flesh. Having made my way to her pussy, I consume it voraciously. *Cunnilingus is hot and fucking amazing. I give it five stars and highly recommend it.*

Every inch of my cock needs to be buried deep inside her. I pull away from her bare pussy and get up off my knees. She squeals when I lift her and throw her over my shoulder. I carry her to our bed and lay her down. She throws her tied hands above her head and arches her back. *Fuck.* I climb over her in bed, hold down her tied wrists with one hand, and lock eyes with her.

"I need to be inside you now," I say stroking the tip of my cock against her wet folds.

"What are you waiting for?" She licks her upper lip.

She doesn't have to ask me twice. I slam my cock into her with force. *Lord Almighty.* What an amazing feeling every time her tight pussy hugs my cock. I thrust fast and hard watching her voluptuous tits jiggle. She can't do much with her hands tied, but she sure as hell can match my tempo with her body. *Oh, yeah. That's it, angel. Move with me.* I am about to unravel at the seams. My breathing is becoming more labored, my heart is racing, and my pace accelerates. I can feel her contracting around my dick as I struggle to say her name. Then my body hardens and the dam bursts inside her releasing the rapid currents. *Holy fuck.*

"Hmm," she croons.

I try not to hurt my delicate angel with my entire weight as I gently fall on top of her. She's fuckalicious and I am not quite done with her yet. Our bodies are sticky with sweat, but I don't care. I untie her hands. She rubs her wrists and then places her hands in my hair. I love when she runs her fingers through it. Starting at her neck, I kiss my way down to her divine tits. I feed greedily on her big tits and suck on each stiff nipple until I have satisfied my appetite.

"You have the sexiest breasts," I murmur laying my cheek on her bosom. *Hmm.* A wave of exhaustion overpowers me and my eyes close as I begin to fall into the world of sleep.

CHAPTER NINETEEN

CARI

The honor of your presence is requested at the marriage of
Carilyn Jade Snow
to
Deven Aidan Blake

Saturday, the eleventh of June
At two o'clock in the afternoon
The Breakers
Newport, Rhode Island

☙❧

Cocktail Reception at The Marble House

Followed by Dinner Reception at The Elms

Transportation will be provided to each venue

Delicate gold lace damask encrusted with small faux pearls and tiny rhinestones frame the words on the heavy flat white invitation. It's a beautiful invitation and fitting if not ornate. With about two months to go, everything is gradually coming together.

I had seen the guest list Aimee and Max submitted to Rodrigo. It isn't a long list, but it did leave me curious as to what the relationship is that these guests have with them. I didn't hesitate to ask my father. He clarified the relations and told me he wants to have me meet the extended family prior to the wedding. Max considered having a get-together at his house, but Deven and I are booked every weekend right up to the wedding. It took some coordinating but after checking everyone's availability, it was determined that dinner on a Friday night would work for all of us.

And tonight is *that* Friday night. Max chose to have the dinner at his parents' favorite restaurant in Flushing, Queens. I've only been to Flushing a few times, but the heart of Flushing is similar to Manhattan's Chinatown. The streets and stores are usually bustling, there are plenty of good restaurants to choose from, and mass transit is convenient.

I'm about to freshen up for dinner when my phone chimes. It's a text from Deven. His meeting is running late, and he promises to be at the restaurant as soon as the meeting is over. *Why does this have to happen tonight?* There are times when I wish he could just cut the meeting short, and this is one of those times. Deven excels at breaking the ice whereas I am shy and more reserved. I reply to his text asking if there's a possibility he can end the meeting early. I lean back in my chair and close my eyes.

"Is everything okay?"

I open my eyes to see Brad at the door.

"I just received a text from Deven letting me know the meeting is running late."

Brad comes over and takes a seat in one of the chairs facing my desk. "He can't help it. It's business. This is going to happen from time to time."

"I wish it didn't have to happen tonight."

"He'll try to accelerate the pace of the meeting. Would you like for me to accompany you until he gets there?"

"That's so considerate. Thank you, but I should probably go alone."

"How are things going with your father?"

"It's going very well."

"That's really great, Cari. I'm happy for you. I wish I knew my father."

A look of surprise registers on my face. *What does he mean?*

"I guess Deven never told you about my father?"

"The only thing I know about him is that he and your mother live in Boston."

"My father is not my biological father. It's why I have two last names. Wong is my biological father's name, and Wu was added once my father legally adopted me."

Oh. "I see."

"Deven probably didn't feel like it was his place to share that information."

"May I ask what happened to him?"

"He was murdered."

My mouth is agape as questions flood my head. Brad must know I have questions and shares the details of what went down the night his biological father was taken from him. Brad was so young when the tragedy struck that he barely has any memory of his father. We're both connected by tragedy that occurred in our young lives. No child should ever have to experience a loss of a parent or both parents at such a young age.

"I'm so sorry."

"It happened so many years ago."

"You didn't get to really know your biological father, but the man who adopted you became your father. You have a father and a mother, and that is a blessing. The three of you became a family. You're very lucky."

"I can say the same about you. You're lucky too. You had your grandparents."

"I did. And they loved me very much."

Brad looks at his watch. "Hey, I better not take up any more of your time. I know you have to leave soon. If you change your mind about me accompanying you, let me know."

"Thank you, Brad."

After freshening up, I check my phone again before I leave. There are no messages from Deven. I put on my spring coat and shut the office door behind me. I bid Catrina a good night and a good weekend. When I reach the lobby, I see Jordan outside ready to drive me over to the restaurant.

On the way there, I review the notes I had taken. Max had gone over with me how to address each family member in Chinese. He said it shows respect. I have practiced the pronunciations many times and hope to nail it tonight. I want to make a good impression.

Jordan drops me off at the restaurant and then heads back to Manhattan to wait until Deven is done with his meeting. I enter the restaurant. The place is huge and outfitted with gaudy tiered chandeliers. The tables are draped with white tablecloths, and a glass Lazy Susan turntable is set in the middle of each table. I see Max waving to me from the back of the dining room. It does not appear that anyone has arrived yet except for the two people at the same table with Max.

Max gets up from his seat as I come near the table. "Cari. Good to see you as always." He envelopes me in a hug.

"Hi."

Hug dispensed with, he looks over to the couple sitting at the table.

"Mom. Dad. I'd like to introduce you both to Cari."

Max shared with me what transpired when he told his parents about what he did in high school. At first, his parents were dismayed that he impregnated my mother. Then they became angry with his decision to run away from his responsibility of being a parent. The anger and shock eventually faded and they wanted to meet me. Knowing they acknowledge me as their granddaughter is deeply satisfying.

His parents rise from their seats. They are both shorter than I am. His father looks to be in his late fifties or maybe early sixties with a slim built. He has thinning gray hair and sports a pair of metal rim eyeglasses. His mother seems to be in her mid-fifties. She's a bit plump with a short layered hairstyle and has a very sweet smile.

His father offers a smile and extends his hand to me. "It's nice to meet you, Cari."

"It's very nice to meet you, *Ah Yeh,*" I return addressing him as my paternal grandfather while shaking his hand.

"Very good," he responds seemingly impressed.

Yes!

Max's mother tilts her head and stares at my face. Then she takes my hand and sandwiches it between hers. "*Ah Cari.* Nice to meet you too," she says in a voice laced with a slight Chinese accent.

"The honor is mine, *Ah Ma.*" I address her as my paternal grandmother like Max had instructed me to do.

She smiles and turns to Max uttering something in Chinese.

"Welcome to our family," my grandfather says.

"Thank you."

"Please sit," my grandmother says gesturing to the chair with her hand. "Where is your boyfriend?"

"He has a late running meeting. He will be here as soon as it's over." I'm hoping the meeting *is* over with.

"We can't wait to meet him."

"He's excited to meet you and the rest of the family."

"Max told us your grandparents raised you."

"Yes, they did."

"Max said they did a good job."

I turn to Max and smile. "Thank you."

"You live in Westchester?"

"Yes, I do."

"Uh, where in Westchester?" Max's father inquires.

"White Plains."

"It's almost like living in New York City." He chuckles.

"Dad, they plan to move to Connecticut," Max informs.

"Ah. Connecticut is very nice," Max's mother comments. "Rich people like Connecticut."

"Mom, her fiancé grew up there."

"That's why I said rich people like it there. *He's rich.*"

Max says something to her in Chinese.

"Max. Mom. Dad."

Along with my father and grandparents, we turn our heads towards the voice. There stands a lady with hazelnut color hair dressed in a lavender business suit toting a large Chanel bag. She is surrounded by a man also wearing business attire and two young girls probably around Harper's age.

Max stands up and greets them. "Hello."

She goes over to greet the parents next. The man and the girls follow suit. She must be one of Max's sisters. Max directs her back to me.

"Elisabet, this is Cari."

"What a pleasure to meet you," she says offering a handshake and a friendly smile.

"Likewise," I respond accepting her handshake. "Should I address you as *Goo Ma* or *Goo Jeh*?"

"Heavens no. Please call me Aunt Lisa."

"This is my older sister, Elisabet. She prefers to be called Lisa as she just mentioned. And this is her husband, Luke."

"You can call me Uncle Luke," he says and shakes my hand.

"And their children, Bailey and Katerina."

They wave and I wave back. Max has Elisabet and Luke sit down at the table with us and the kids at the table behind ours. Aimee and my sisters arrive shortly after, and we all go through the formalities again. My sisters sit at the other table with the cousins while Aimee sits beside Max's father.

Everyone else except for Deven begins to arrive. Max introduces me to Remi, his youngest sister. Like her older sister, she also exudes sophistication wearing a pretty pale green silk blouse with perfectly pressed dress pants carrying a Louis Vuitton tote. She's married to a nerdy looking guy who likes to be called by his first name, Owen. Together, they also have two children of their own. The oldest is their daughter, Peyton. And the youngest is their son, Jerry. Both are in elementary school.

Max's aunts, uncles, and cousins all seem to be friendly and warm towards me making me feel comfortable. These are the people my father wants to invite to the wedding, and I'm so happy to meet all of them. I check my phone once again to see if Deven has left a message, but there's no message from him.

"Cari, do you have any aunts and uncles on your mother's side?" Remi asks.

"Remi, that is not an appropriate question," Max says with a hint of anger in his voice.

"I don't mind answering her question. My mother was an only child."

"Well, you have all of us now," Aunt Lisa tells me. "Aunts, uncles, great aunts, great uncles…we're all family."

"What line of occupation are you in, Cari?" Owen inquires.

"I own a web site development company."

"How impressive!" Aunt Lisa says.

"It is, isn't it? I'm extremely proud of her." Max is grinning.

"And your boyfriend –"

"Fiancé," Aunt Lisa says cutting Owen off to correct him.

"I beg your pardon. Your fiancé is a huge real estate developer. Everyone knows of him. Do you see yourself changing careers and going into real estate later on?"

"I am learning more about the trade, but that will be determined at a later time."

"Focus on what you're doing now. There's plenty of time to decide if you want to veer onto a different career path," Aunt Lisa advises.

"Cari, I couldn't help admiring your ring," Aunt Remi expresses not being subtle at all. "It's enormous and lovely."

"I did not see your ring," my grandmother says.

How could she have missed it? I lift my hand and show it to her.

"Wah!" She says and murmurs something else in Chinese.

"She said it's really stunning," Max translates.

"Let me see that rock."

I turn my hand so Aunt Lisa can look at it.

"That is some ring," Uncle Luke says.

"It's a gorgeous ring," Aunt Lisa comments.

Aimee agrees with her. It's the first time I have heard Aimee compliment the ring.

"She's worth it and more," Max adds.

My aunts want to know how Deven popped the question so I tell them even though Max has heard it before.

"Look there. Is that him?" Aunt Lisa asks motioning with her chin to turn around and look behind me.

I rotate slightly in my chair and see Deven walking towards us. *Thank goodness he is finally here.*

"Hello everyone. My apologies for showing up so late."

Max stands up and introduces Deven to everyone at our table first. Then my father takes him to each table to meet the rest of the family. Once that is over with, Deven sits down to my left and my father returns to his seat.

My grandfather stands up and lifts the teapot. He pours some tea into Deven's cup. Deven thanks him and takes a sip of his tea.

"Ah, you like tea," my grandmother says.

"Yes, I do," Deven replies.

He does? I've never seen him drink tea.

"We're glad you could come," my grandmother tells him.

"As am I," Deven responds ever so politely.

"Sometimes you can't predict how long the meetings will last. Isn't that right?" Owen asks.

"That's correct," Deven concurs.

"You two like Chinese food?" my grandmother asks.

Deven smiles at her. "We love it. In fact, we sometimes go to Chinatown for dim sum." *Oh, he's turning up the charm.*

My grandparents are impressed.

"I love dim sum. Hong Kong has the best dim sum."

"You've been to Hong Kong then?" my grandfather asks Deven.

"I have an office in Hong Kong."

"Oh. Do you speak Chinese?"

"I've learned a little bit."

He has? How is it I am not aware of this?

My grandmother says something to him in Chinese and he responds with a short answer in Chinese.

"Very good!"

And just like that, he's won her over.

"My sister is Chinese."

Confusion crosses her face. "Huh? Your sister is Chinese?"

"Yes. My father adopted her from China when she was a baby."

"Does she speak Chinese?"

"Not really, but she's learning the language in order to converse with her boyfriend's family."

"Her boyfriend is Chinese?"

"Yes. He is also my best friend."

"Your sister is dating your best friend?" Aunt Remi asks in an astonished tone.

"That's correct."

"And it doesn't bother you?"

"Remi, please," Max says sternly.

"It's fine. To answer your question, no, it does not bother me. These things happen."

The waiter comes to our table and places a large platter of food on the glass turntable. None of the items on the platter are recognizable to me except some meat that resembles ham. Max serves his parents first and then everyone else afterwards. I stare at the items on the plate he's handed me.

Owen notices my hesitation. "Don't be afraid. It's all good stuff."

"I don't know what it is I'm about to consume."

My father shows me what each item is. There is jellyfish, beef, ham, pork, bean curd, and century old egg. It does not look appetizing to me, but I don't want to offend my family so I pick up my chopsticks and force myself to try the sliced beef first.

"Do you like it?" Deven asks in a low voice.

"I only tried the beef." It didn't taste bad. It was just cold.

"You'll enjoy all of it. Try the jellyfish."

I push the slimy translucent stringy food back and forth with my chopsticks. It looks unappealing to me. I pick it up and put the slippery thing in my mouth. It's crunchy, but it doesn't taste bad.

"At Chinese banquets, this is a traditional dish that is served." Max educates Deven and I.

"Will you both be incorporating the Chinese customs into your wedding?" Aunt Remi inquires.

Deven and I look at each other. We are both clueless as to what those customs are.

"We're not familiar with any of the customs," I confess.

Aunt Remi turns to Aimee and Max. "You didn't go over the wedding customs with them?"

Max shrugs his shoulders. "There will be a lot of guests there and it seems inconsequential."

"*What?!*" Both Aunt Lisa and Aunt Remi react at the same time.

I want to know about the customs and ask. Between my aunts, Aimee, and my grandmother, they tell us.

Deven speaks first. "Quite a list."

"Maybe we can speak to the wedding planner about integrating a few of the customs," I offer.

"But the wedding is in Rhode Island," says Max.

"So? Why does location matter?" Aunt Remi interrupts and questions him.

"Their wedding is not the type of wedding where the traditions will blend in."

"Rubbish! Many Chinese weddings blend eastern and western customs. There are many traditions we follow and occasions we celebrate. Did you even mention any of that to them?"

"*Ai-yah!* Enough you two."

Everyone's heads turn to the matriarch of the family.

"*Ah Cari. Ah Deven.* You go talk to your wedding planner first."

"We certainly will. Thank you," Deven says kindly.

Aunt Lisa sets her chopsticks down on her plate. "Are you getting married in the same church that Jackie and John Kennedy got married in?"

"We're not getting married in a church," Deven states matter-of-factly.

"Oh. No church wedding?"

Deven shakes his head. "No."

"Then where will the ceremony be?"

"On the grounds of one of the mansions in Newport."

Except for Aimee and Max, everyone around the table appear to be surprised. *Sheesh. Didn't Aimee and Max mention anything about the wedding to them?*

"Well, that's going to be one hell of a wedding," Owen lets out.

"You just wait and see," Max tells him.

"We're invited?"

"Of course," Deven answers.

The faces of my aunts, uncles, and grandparents light up in unison like Christmas lights being plugged in. *They're family.* We may have just met, but it is the beginning of a beautiful union for all of us. I can't imagine excluding them from the joyous occasion. I'm perplexed as to why they would think they wouldn't be invited to the wedding. Perhaps Aimee and Max wanted to wait until after tonight to tell them.

"What an honor to be invited! Thank you." Aunt Lisa is overjoyed.

"Not necessary to thank us. We are family now," Deven says.

"That we are," my grandfather agrees.

The evening comes to an end too soon. We learned a lot about each other as we ate and talked for several hours. Deven and I bid farewell to everyone before getting into our car to head home.

My mother and my grandparents are long gone and along with it our family ties. When they departed the world of the living, there were no surviving Snow relatives. In a sense, I was alone. And now, I feel as if I have found my pot of gold at the end of the rainbow. I have new family ties with Max and the entire Lew clan. And soon, I will marry my love and we'll have a family of our own. My life has never been better.

CHAPTER TWENTY

May

CARI

Spring decided it will hide this weekend while we're in Newport. The bitter cold wind makes it feel as if winter has made a temporary return.

Hunter and Rodrigo are with us again on this trip and took up Deven's offer to stay at the house this time around. We get up early to meet with Belle as we are her first appointment of the day. This appointment should be taking place in a couple of weeks, but it happens to be the only weekend Deven is available to make the trip here. With not much time for a sit down breakfast in a restaurant, we opt for Starbucks instead to grab something quick. The guys are chatting as I fight to stay awake.

"Cari?"

"Hmm?"

"Are you feeling alright? You seem sluggish."

"I feel quite tired."

Deven puts his arm around me and I lean into him. "Would you rather go back home and we'll handle this with Belle?"

The offer to go home sounds ideal right this minute, but I should be at the appointment too.

"No, I'll be fine. The caffeine will kick in soon, and I'll be okay."

"We should go then," Rodrigo tells us.

We get up and dispose our trash before leaving the popular coffee shop. It's a very short drive to her office. As we wait for Belle, Hunter walks over to the credenza and helps himself to the tiered tray filled with mini breakfast pastries.

Rodrigo puts his hands on his hips. "Really? We just ate."

"I'm still hungry, so why not? Besides, they have great pastries," Hunter says and shoves a mini breakfast quiche into his mouth.

"Darling, we have to be mindful of our figures." Rodrigo is constantly reminding him of this.

"Hello!" Belle cheerfully says as she saunters in.

My eyes open wide. She is wearing a clingy dress with a low cut neckline that shows off her cleavage making me look underdressed in a long sleeve T-shirt, jeans, a puffy vest, and UGG boots.

"We'll go into the conference room. Follow me." She turns around and sashays down the hall like a fashion model does on the runway.

We are led into a conference room with a large cherry wood table and leather rolling chairs. She starts by going over what's on the agenda and then hands out samples of the wedding program to each of us. The beautiful six-tiered wedding program has a translucent vellum overlay with a pretty gold organza ribbon at the top. The first tier has our names, the date, and the location of the ceremony printed in gold ink. The second tier is the order of events during the ceremony. It is quite detailed as this is the most important event of the day. The rest of the sections in the program include the names of our wedding party, the cocktail and dinner receptions, and a thank you message from us.

After Belle finishes going through the wedding program and has our approval, she shuttles us over to the mansions for a final walk through. On the way, she delivers the good news that we have approval to use the Chinese Tea House for the traditional tea ceremony. My relatives will be very pleased to know that this custom will be accommodated.

~ * ~

The past couple of hours spent at the mansions have worn me out. Belle went into great detail on how everything will be set. The biggest lawn transformation will be at The Elms where the dinner reception is to take place. A structured tent will be erected on the spacious grounds. She also ordered restroom trailers that have individual stalls with flushable toilets and working sinks as per Deven's request. He wants to have these trailers instead of a bunch of porta potties lined up for the guests. *There is nothing money cannot buy for this wedding.*

I can barely hide my excitement when we arrive at the restaurant for the tasting as it's the last item on the agenda. The owners and the chef profusely thank Deven and I for the business. They are very pleasant and quite generous with the portions of food we are about to sample. My mouth is watering from the array of food set out on the table. Deven wants at least three choices of meat, chicken, and seafood on the menu. He is still considering adding lamb chops, and possibly a surf and turf. *He can be so over the top.*

Rodrigo looks at the food displayed before us. "Everything looks scrumptious."

"I thought you were watching your figure," Hunter tells him.

"This is an exception. We have to help decide on the food."

"And we do need your feedback," Deven adds.

"We will give you our honest opinion."

The chef encourages us to try the food. All that mansion hopping has made us quite hungry. I pierce the Dover Sole Francese and taste the fish. *Mmm.* This is definitely a keeper on the menu. Deven is trying the prime rib. There is no expression on his gorgeous face as he chews the piece of meat, but I do notice Hunter's facial expression as he tries the filet mignon. He loves it.

"What do you think?" the chef asks after we practically finish everything presented to us.

"Anything you didn't like?" Deven asks me.

"No, not at all. Everything was very good."

Deven looks over to Rodrigo and Hunter. "Guys?"

"Everything deserves a place on the menu," Hunter says.

Rodrigo looks at the chef. "I found the chicken to be just a tad bit too salty."

"You have sensitive taste buds," Hunter tells him.

Rodrigo dabs at his mouth with his napkin. "I certainly do not."

Deven turns to the chef and the owners. "We will keep everything as is on the menu then. Check the amount of salt used on the chicken. The execution must be flawless. There will be nearly five hundred guests attending, including some high profile ones."

"Mr. Blake, I can assure you everything will run smoothly and be nothing less than perfect," Chad promises. He is one of the owners.

"I have been to many events, and I cannot express the number of times I have been disappointed with the execution and sometimes the quality of the food. I have had cold steaks served to me. None of our guests shall have their entrées or any hot items served cold unless it is prepared that way. I am spending an obscene amount of money on catering."

"You have our promise. We will not disappoint."

"We appreciate you giving us this opportunity to serve your event," the chef tells us.

"Very well."

The owners offer us coffee and dessert. We decline the dessert but accept the coffee. They insist we take dessert back home with us. We remain at the table enjoying our coffee and learning about the experiences of the chef and the owners until Belle announces she has to be back for her next appointment.

Once we are back at Belle's office, we thank her outside and walk to Deven's car. Hunter and Rodrigo want to go to Providence. I'm enervated and prefer to go home instead. Deven has them drop us off at the house first before taking the car.

"Brrrr!" I say as I enter the family room shivering. The cold air suddenly wakes me up.

"I'll turn up the heat. Why don't you go upstairs and warm up?"

I admire his backside as he walks to the thermostat and turns up the temperature. *He has such a nice behind.* I move into the kitchen and put the bag of desserts in the refrigerator. Now I need something to keep me warm. Wine will assist with the warm up process. I grab two wine glasses from the cabinet and search the wine cooler for a bottle of port. My eyes locate the Taylor Fladgate bottle.

"I'm going to go lay down in bed." I bring the wine, the glasses, and the wine opener with me.

"Okay. I'll be up shortly."

I place the items on the nightstand and then go to turn on the gas fireplace. I remove my coat and hang it in the closet. The warmth coming from the fireplace is comforting. I slip underneath the cold bed cover and can't seem to keep my eyes open.

A ringing sound brings me out of my sleep, and I hear Deven's voice.

"What's up, Kait?"

I open my eyes pondering the reason for her call this time. She has been calling Deven more than usual over the past couple of months. She has been having difficulty making a decision on whether or not she should give up her acting career and go back to school. Deven has been encouraging her to go back to school and pursue a degree. It befuddles me why this is such a difficult decision for her to make.

"The house is my gift to him. Who lives under his roof is up to him."

Hmm. She must be having a change of heart about staying in California. I turn on the television and lower the volume. I flip through the channels, but nothing seems to hold my attention.

"Bye, Kait." Deven hangs up and puts his phone down on top of the dresser. He climbs into bed and I move to be closer to him. He draws me into his arms and I lay my head on his strong chest. "Sorry about that."

"Is everything all right?"

He rubs his hand up and down my arm. "I think so. Her new plan is to move to New Jersey with Ken."

I pull away to look at him. "Why?"

"She wants a fresh start too." He purses his lips.

"You don't approve?"

"I approve. I don't want her to stay in L.A. and go back to that asshole, Cal. A fresh start is what she really needs. It will also be nice to have her close by, but I'm not sure how Ken feels about it. I think he wants it to be just him and Mandy…their new beginning. And he also wants you and I to be a big part of Mandy's life. He didn't factor Kait into this move."

"Does she still want to get a degree?"

"The topic wasn't approached this time. Kaitlin will have to figure that out herself, but there was something else she brought up to me."

"What's that?"

"Her mother wants to know if she will be invited to our wedding."

Oh, no. She can't be serious. After the incident at the restaurant following Dalton's funeral, I never want to see that woman again. But I can't really tell Deven that right now. Nothing will change the fact that she is his biological mother even if he cut her out of his life. If he wants her there, I will do my best to avoid her. *How hard can that be amongst five hundred guests?*

"You're quiet."

"What is there to say?"

"Are you worried she will be there?"

I am reluctant to respond and press my head to his chest. I will just silently pray she is not invited.

"Cari?"

"Yes?"

He squeezes me. "I have no intention of inviting her to our wedding."

His statement gives me relief, and I nod my head before returning his squeeze. I shift my thoughts on the new beginning for Ken and his daughter, and the new beginning for Deven and I as husband and wife.

"We're going to have a beautiful life together."

I pull back again and stare into his adoring blue eyes. "I want us to have a family more than anything."

He leans forward and drops a kiss on my nose. "And you will have that. *We* will have that."

I can't control my yawn.

"I think you need more sleep."

"Hmm." I snuggle up to him. "When are those two planning to return?"

"I don't really know, but it won't be at least for a few hours."

"Oh. That should be enough time to delight in each other."

His hands skim my waistline. "I concur, angel." He smiles and cups my butt as he draws me in for a deep kiss.

CHAPTER TWENTY-ONE

CARI

After returning from our weekend in Newport, Deven and I will be spending the week apart. He is on his way to the other side of the country with Los Angeles being his first stop. Ken will be receiving his master's degree and Deven wants to be there to celebrate his brother's accomplishment. While he's there, he also plans to check on things at the office. He will then travel to Seattle midweek and stay a couple of days to ascertain all is in order before heading off to Las Vegas for his weekend bachelor party.

Leaving me alone in the house did not bode well with Deven. My overprotective fiancé not only kept Jordan in New York to guard me, but he also requested Rodrigo and Hunter stay in the penthouse with me. I am happy the three of us will have this time together, but how many bodyguards do I possibly need?

The weekend has left me quite drained. I have my final dress fitting today and make a last minute decision to take the day off even though I had planned to work a half day. My bodyguard, Rodrigo, requested the day off from work to go with me. When we get there, we are informed that Holly is finishing up with another client and will be with us shortly. Brenda offers us a drink and we both ask for a bottle of water.

"Have you decided which hairstyle you're going with?"

"Not yet, but I am leaning more towards having it in a twisted bun."

"A classic choice and very suitable. Can't go wrong with that style."

"A simple and pretty style is what I want."

"I can't believe that in a few weeks, you will be having the wedding of a lifetime and become Mrs. Deven Blake."

"*Deven* will be having the wedding of a lifetime. This wedding is going to be an insanely lavish event because that's what he wants."

"It should be a lavish event. After all, you are marrying one of the richest not to mention one of the hottest guys in the world. Did you expect anything less?"

"Less people maybe."

"Not possible. I'm surprised he didn't invite the President and the First Lady to the wedding."

"He doesn't know them."

"But if he did, they would have been on the guest list too. You're going to have to get used to his lifestyle."

Deven and I come from different lifestyles. He grew up in a mansion in an affluent town, went on extravagant family vacations, and never had to worry if he could afford to purchase something or not. I grew up in a small Cape Cod style house in a suburban town northwest of New York City. My vacation with my grandparents was to the Jersey Shore each summer where we stayed in a rented house for a week. Gramps had worked hard to put aside money so we could have those vacations. And there were times we had to watch what we spent.

Brenda returns with a bottle of water for each of us. We thank her.

"It is not easy to adjust to Deven's world."

"You'll get the hang of his world soon."

"Hello to you both!" Holly warmly greets us. "How are you?"

"We're great," I answer Holly.

"How is your friend? Did she have a boy or a girl?"

"She's good. She had a girl."

"Oh, how nice. Are you ready for your final fitting?"

"I am."

"You can go on into the dressing room and just call my name when you have the dress on."

I follow her instructions and go into the changing room. I put the dress on and it's a bit snug. *Oh no!* I probably put on some pounds after the tasting and need to shed those pounds before the wedding. I call Holly in.

"I'm having some trouble buttoning up the dress. I'm afraid I splurged at the tasting this past weekend."

"How can you pass up anything at a tasting? It's important to try everything. Okay, you need to hold in your tummy just a bit."

I do as she requests, and she manages to button up the dress. I step out of the dressing room to show Rodrigo.

Rodrigo puts his hand on his cheek and shakes his head. "The dress is amazing on you. I can't get over how perfect that dress is. You're going to be such a beautiful bride!"

"I couldn't agree more," Holly says.

My face turns crimson from their compliments. "Thank you." I exhale.

"What's the matter?" Rodrigo asks.

"I had too much to sample this weekend so the dress is snug on me right now."

"I'm putting you on my diet."

"This can be an easy fix. The tailor can add a button extender or two. I've had button extenders added on dresses for brides who gain a few pounds or are pregnant."

The latter part of what she just said sounds the alarm in my head. I have been feeling very tired recently and the last pregnancy made me feel the same way. Rodrigo's eyes widen immediately and we look at each other. I can't let her know there is a possibility that I may be pregnant.

"What if I lose the weight? Wouldn't the dress then be too loose on me?"

"You will still have the original buttons you can use. Let me just mark off where she needs to make the adjustment." Holly grabs a pin to mark the area. "All done."

"Will I need to try it on again?"

"I don't think you need to."

"Okay. Thank you."

Holly helps me unbutton my dress and then leaves the room pulling the curtain shut behind her. I step out of my dress and turn to the side to take a better look at myself. I place my hand over my slightly protruding belly which I did not even really notice because I haven't been paying attention to my body. It's not obvious to the naked eye unless I point it out. *Can it be that I am finally pregnant again after months of trying?* I have to know, and I know what I need to do after we leave here.

I confirm a date to pick up my dress and May's dress. I thank Holly again and leave with Rodrigo.

"You know what I'm about to ask you?"

I do know. "And the answer I'm going to give you is that there is a possibility."

Rodrigo smacks his forehead. "Have I taught you nothing about using protection?"

I have a sheepish grin on my face. My sexual activity with Deven is not something I want to discuss with my best friend on the sidewalk in New York City.

"Why don't we stop at the pharmacy and get one of those home pregnancy tests to confirm if you are?"

It's exactly what I was thinking and we do just that. We stop into the pharmacy a couple of blocks away from the bridal boutique. *Goodness.* There is quite a selection of home pregnancy tests to choose from.

"I don't know which brand to get," I tell Rodrigo.

"Don't look at me. I know nothing about home pregnancy tests. I only know about condoms."

I pick up a box and read the instructions on it.

"I'm going to ask her," Rodrigo says spotting an employee. "Excuse me."

The employee stops and ogles my best friend.

"Yes?"

"I want to know which home pregnancy test is the best one to purchase."

She sees me and probably assumes he and I are a couple. She looks at the shelf and shows us which test is the popular choice.

"Thank you."

"Sure. Good luck to you both."

I stifle a laugh. *If she only knew Rodrigo's preference.*

"Okay, daddy. We should definitely get this brand then."

"Okay, honey. I do hope you have a little junior in there."

I end up purchasing two tests to ensure I don't get a false result. I don't want to allow myself to be ecstatic about this in case both results indicate I am not pregnant. I call Jordan to have him pick us up from the pharmacy making sure to shove the purchase to the bottom of my handbag so he can't see what I bought.

I am anxious to find out the results. As soon as we get home, I open my bag and pull out the tests. Rodrigo seems to be anxious to know as well and urges me to hurry and take the tests. I bring the boxes with me into the bathroom. I read the instructions and pee on the stick. The positive sign immediately appears in the window on the first test. I gasp and quickly tear open the next test and repeat the process. The same result appears. I put the toilet lid down and sit there fixated on the results.

"Are you okay in there?" Rodrigo asks knocking on the door stirring me out of my reverie.

"Yes."

"Can I come in?"

"Yes."

He opens the door and steps in. "Well?"

I point to the tests sitting on the vanity.

He looks at the results. "How accurate are these?"

"Very. Both tests display the same results, but Deven cannot know yet."

I catch the look of disapproval on his face.

"Why not, Cari?"

"He'll fly back immediately and miss out on his bachelor party."

"He's not going to care if he misses out on his bachelor party. It will be the least of his concerns."

"Ken's graduating tomorrow. It's a big moment. Deven also needs to take care of some stuff at the offices over there."

"Ken will understand. As for the offices, he can always go back later."

"He just got there. I can't ask him to turn around and come back. And given what happened with the last pregnancy, I want to see the doctor first to confirm this."

"Fine."

"Thank you."

"Do you have a doctor?"

"Not yet, but I will ask Alana for her doctor's information."

"You may have to tell her why you're asking."

"I can tell her I want to see the doctor for a routine examination."

"Oh. Good plan. I'll go with you to the doctor's."

"Okay. And please don't let Hunter in on this just yet."

"I won't say anything to him. Only the three of us know about this."

"The three of us?"

"You, me, and the baby."

I grin and splay my hand over my belly. "Yes, just the three of us for now."

CHAPTER TWENTY-TWO

A FEW DAYS LATER

CARI

I sit on the exam table flipping through a parenting magazine while I wait to be seen by the doctor. There are many things Deven and I will need to learn as first time parents and many things we will have to purchase if the doctor confirms the pregnancy. The knock on the door pulls my attention away from the magazine.

"Come in," I say.

"Hi Ms. Snow. It's nice to meet you. I'm Dr. Tober," she says as she goes over to the sink to wash her hands. She looks to be in her late thirties and has a very soothing voice.

"Nice to meet you as well, and please call me Cari."

She nods and sits down in the chair. She reads the information displayed on the computer screen in front of her.

"I see here you had a previous miscarriage."

"I did."

"I'm sorry to learn of it." She continues to look at the information on the screen. "The pregnancy test results show that you are pregnant again, but..."

My heart sinks. *Please don't let it be bad news.* I don't know if I can handle it if she tells me that I cannot carry this baby to term.

"You will be monitored more closely to make sure everything is progressing as it should be and that there are no other issues with your health."

"Are you saying there is a chance I may not be able to carry this baby to full term?"

"There is a slim chance, but the probability is very low. It's nothing to be concerned about right now. The worst thing you can do is worry and stress yourself and the baby." She puts on latex gloves. "Lean back. I am going to perform an internal examination."

I have a million questions floating in my head, and I ask the doctor as many as I can while she does the examination. She patiently answers all of my questions. After the doctor finishes the exam, she gives me a bottle of prenatal pills and tells me to make an appointment for an ultrasound in a couple of weeks. She will have a better idea on the due date when the ultrasound is performed. *Is it possible to be both happy and fearful at the same time?*

I make an appointment for the ultrasound prior to leaving the office. Rodrigo gets up from his seat when I return to the waiting area. We make our way out of the office and to the elevator in silence.

"You're killing me. What did the doctor say? Are you pregnant?"

I can't hold back my smile any longer. "Yes!"

He hugs me and lifts me off the ground. "Congratulations!"

A couple exits the office and waits for the elevator with us. Rodrigo puts me back down on my feet. I see them smile, and they probably assume Rodrigo is my husband.

"Did you tell the doctor about the last pregnancy?"

"I did, and she said I will be monitored closely."

"That's good."

The elevator arrives and we get on.

"I'm so very happy yet I'm petrified I could suffer the same misfortune."

"Stop with the nonsense. It's understandable you feel trepidation, but don't let it overshadow this happy moment to start a family with Deven again. Everything is perfect and exactly the way it should be." Rodrigo always knows how to make me feel better. "It's a good thing the bachelorette party is a non-alcoholic event. No one will notice if you don't have a drink."

I forgot the bachelorette party is tomorrow night. "It didn't even cross my mind."

"When do you plan on telling the baby daddy?"

"It needs to be a special moment when I share the news with him."

"What are you thinking? Telling him over a romantic candlelight filet mignon and lobster dinner?"

"No. I intend on telling him when we're away in a couple of weeks."

"Why wait until then? What if he finds your prenatal pills?"

"I'll put the pills in a clear plastic bag and keep it at the bottom of my purse. Deven never looks through my bag."

"But why wait until the trip to tell him?"

"Because that's where I want to create the special moment. It's the ideal place to do so."

Ever since I got the results from the home pregnancy tests, I have been devising various ways to tell Deven. I want it to be memorable like it was when he proposed to me.

"Do you plan on telling anyone else before the wedding?"

"It's something I will discuss with Deven. Perhaps it may be best to wait until after the first trimester."

"I strongly agree. I think it's best to wait."

"I only hope I don't show too much on the wedding day. There will be so many people taking pictures and looking at me."

"The wedding is less than a month away. You cannot possibly show that much. Besides, people will be too busy socializing and talking about your ostentatious wedding to even spot your tiny belly."

"You're right. The mansions alone will be distracting."

"And if it is noticeable, you can always wear a tummy control that day."

What a good idea, but will it hurt the baby?

"Don't you worry your pretty self about any of it. Promise me."

"I promise."

Deven and I have been given another chance at having a family. It doesn't matter to me that this happened before we're married. All that matters is that our baby survives.

"Now, let's focus on this weekend's bachelorette party," Rodrigo says.

CHAPTER TWENTY-THREE

DEVEN

The enormous lobby of the hotel is very busy. Las Vegas is like New York City. It never sleeps.

Where the fuck is Brad? He told me he would meet me right in front of Starbucks.

"Dude!"

I recognize the voice and turn around. We greet each other with a bro hug.

"You're ten minutes late."

"I was on the way here when this cute lady stopped me to ask for directions to the pool."

My eyes narrow at him. Does he remember who he is dating?

"You noticed she was cute, huh?"

"Come on, Deven."

"Did the Vegas air already make you forget about my sister?"

"Of course not. I didn't make a play on the lady."

"Say no more. You better not act like a manwhore in my presence."

"I swear I won't. Scout's honor."

"You were never a boy scout, so it doesn't mean anything. Let's go up to the room. I want to get rid of this suitcase."

We head towards the elevators. Brad and I are staying in a two bedroom suite. I wanted my own suite, but Brad thought it would be more fun to share a suite. I acquiesced but on the condition we have separate bedrooms.

"What do you have planned for us this weekend?"

Brad wags his finger. "Good try. You'll see when we get there."

"Listen, whatever it is you have planned better not cause any trouble between Cari and I. The last thing I want is to have her hurt."

"I would never want to hurt her. Look man, this weekend is about being with the boys and having fun. What is it they say about Vegas? Oh, yeah. 'What happens in Vegas stays in Vegas.' Don't sweat it. Besides, Cari is going to be enjoying her bachelorette party."

There is not an iota of reassurance from what he just told me.

"The difference between her weekend and my weekend is that she knows what is planned; therefore, I don't have to worry."

"Loosen up. Just enjoy what's in store this weekend."

"Well, don't you forget that you are seeing my sister."

"I will not forget your sister, but let's remember why we're here. We're here to celebrate your last days as a bachelor. This isn't an everyday occurrence. Why not just live a little and have some fun?"

"Spoken like a manwhore."

"Correction. *Ex-manwhore*." He says it with pride.

I shake my head. "Keep your dick in your pants while we're here."

"I have given up my manwhore crown."

I playfully clutch my heart. "I feel so much better now knowing that."

"Good."

"My siblings and niece will arrive early afternoon. When are the guys getting here?"

"Everyone should be here later this afternoon."

Brad kept the list short. He invited our college pals from Boston, Brayden (my VP of Development and Construction), Adam (my Project Development Manager), and Ken. It thrills me that he didn't feel compelled to invite anyone else from the company. Kait is tagging along only because Ken needs her to babysit Mandy while he is out with us guys.

"Hey, I want to get Cari something before we leave."

"You should."

"Are you planning to get something for May?"

"Of course."

Right.

"I'm starving. After we drop my suitcase off, let's go get something to eat."

"What are you in the mood to eat?"

"Something light like a sandwich or a salad."

"That sounds good. Eat light now and save your appetite for later."

And so our Vegas weekend begins.

CHAPTER TWENTY-FOUR

CARI

It's going to be a delightful weekend with my best friends, my sisters, and my soon-to-be sister-in-law. This is far from the typical bachelorette party mainly because my sisters and May are all under the legal drinking age. With Brad in Vegas, Mauricio was given the task by Deven to pick May up from Princeton and then my sisters on the way to the penthouse.

Deven and I have been communicating daily. He called me this morning when I was in the office knowing we wouldn't have a chance to speak later. He was at the airport waiting to board his early flight to Vegas. There was concern in his voice when I mistakenly told him that I am still feeling weary. I quickly blamed it on the workload I had. He can't know the real reason yet.

May calls from the lobby to announce their arrival. Their timing is perfect as I am ready to have dinner. After the round of greetings, I show my sisters to the other spare bedroom first before giving them a quick tour of the penthouse. My sisters love the place and the views it offers. Then we all gather in the living room and talk about our day.

My hunger pains are intensifying. "I think it's about time we go to dinner."

"Oh, yay! I'm so hungry," Harper admits.

"Where are we going for dinner?" Rylee asks.

Rodrigo stands up. "We have reservations at this really good Thai restaurant."

May claps her hands together. "Good! I've been craving pad thai for a while now."

"Let's go eat then." Hunter is never shy about eating. He is always ready and willing to eat.

May goes to the door. "Which car are we taking?"

"We're not taking any car. The restaurant is within walking distance," Rodrigo says.

I call Jordan to let him know we're ready to go, and he agrees to meet us in the lobby. My sisters are excited to walk there and check out the area I live in. Jordan is in the lobby ready to accompany us on our walk to the restaurant. My sisters are in disbelief that I have security detail. I'll have to eventually explain to them why I do. May stays by my side as we head there, and my sisters keep pace with my best friends.

"Does Jordan go with you everywhere?"

"Most of the time."

"My brother tends to go overboard sometimes."

"It's surprising that Deven doesn't have him follow me into the ladies restroom."

May giggles. "There's always a first time. I wonder what the boys are up to tonight."

"Didn't Brad share the plans with you?"

"He sure didn't."

"Oh."

"Did Deven share it with you?"

"Deven wasn't told anything except to show up at the hotel."

She giggles again. "That's the best part of it. Everything is going to be a surprise."

My instincts tell me that one of the surprises will include a stripper which doesn't sit well with me, but I don't want to think about it especially now in my condition.

"Are you worried that Deven will do something you don't like?"

"It's hard to answer that when I don't know what the plans are." I have never met the guys from Boston. "Have you met the friends from Boston who are invited to Vegas?"

"I have. They're typical guys. They're nice to look at. They flirt a lot. They're not committed. But you have nothing to worry about. Deven is nothing like them. I know my brother, and he is so in love with you. He wouldn't do anything stupid. They're going to enjoy themselves, so we girls should enjoy ourselves this entire weekend too. Forget the boys for now."

As we walk down the street, a couple of guys whistle at us oblivious that we are surrounded by Rodrigo, Hunter, and Jordan.

Rodrigo spins around. "Are you guys flirting with us?" he asks batting his eyes at them.

They appear embarrassed and quickly walk away in the opposite direction making us all laugh.

Rodrigo tosses his head back. "See how easy it is to get rid of those perverts?"

Jordan doesn't want to stay for dinner and goes back home until we're done. It's Friday night and the restaurant is busy. Every table is taken in this popular establishment.

"Order whatever you want. It's on Deven." Rodrigo is never shy accepting Deven's offer to pay.

"We've never had Thai food before," Harper discloses.

"What? Never? You both have been deprived. You must hang out with us more often. Cari loves Thai food," Rodrigo tells my sisters.

"You'll love the food. Why don't we start with some appetizers?" I offer and then suggest a few dishes to my sisters.

Once the ordering is done, Rodrigo raises his glass. "A toast to our beautiful Cari. Here's farewell to the single life and hello to a happy ever after."

Everyone raises their glass.

"Thank you. I'm very happy to be spending this weekend with all of you."

"We wouldn't want to be anywhere else this weekend. We love you. Cheers," Hunter says.

We clink our glasses and take a sip of our drink. Rodrigo and Hunter declare tomorrow to be Divas Pampering Day. We will be going a private spa nestled in the hills of Connecticut. We are booked for spa treatments and will also be spending the night at the hotel there. It's going to be a serene and relaxing weekend and exactly what the baby and I need. I won't think about what Deven is up to in Vegas. Nope. Not at all.

CHAPTER TWENTY-FIVE

DEVEN

Brad invited the guys up to our suite an hour prior to leaving for dinner. We're laughing and talking when Brad excuses himself to get something from his room.

"You guys met in college, huh?" Adam inquires.

"We did, and the five of us also belong to the same fraternity," says Dylan who is an HR manager for a pharmaceutical company.

"We had a fucking wild time in college." That's Franco. He owns a small restaurant in downtown Boston.

Brad comes back with a bunch of bags.

"What do you have there, Brad?" asks Nolan. He works for a public relations firm and enjoys being a manwhore too. He has no desire to commit.

"We're all going to wear this shirt tonight." Brad pulls out a shirt and holds it up. It's a raglan T-shirt with the words "Groom Squad" printed on the front and our initials on the back. My T-shirt identifies me as the groom.

"Where are we going tonight that we need to wear these?" I probe.

"Wouldn't you like to know?" Brad replies as he hands out the bags.

"Any of you guys going to tell me?" I look at each of them and they all shake their heads. "Ken, you're not going to tell me either?"

"I've been sworn to secrecy."

Damn.

Brad looks down at his Apple Watch. "We need to wrap up. Go back to your rooms and put that shirt on. Meet us at the main entrance in about half an hour."

"You got it, Brad," Nolan says.

We all split up to get ready. I wonder if Brad thought of the matching T-shirts on his own or if my sister fed the idea to him. I step out of my room and find Brad in the living room all set to go.

"Ready to get this night started?" The excitement is hard to miss in Brad's voice. He's been looking forward to this weekend for months.

I'll admit I'm looking forward to hanging with the guys. "Hell, yeah."

"Let's do this then."

The guys are at the main entrance donning their shirts. We look like the fucking *Brady Bunch* with our matching shirts on, and people can't help themselves from staring at us. Brayden wants a group shot and asks the bellman to take a picture of us while a group of ladies salivate as they walk by us.

"What a bunch of hot ass guys," one of them says.

"Did you hear them call us 'hot ass guys'?" Dylan has drool dripping from the side of his mouth.

"Yeah. I always knew I had a hot ass," says Nolan.

Franco stands behind Nolan and points to his ass. "Really?"

"I've been told it."

I look over to my left and catch Brad smiling flirtatiously at a few ladies.

I disrupt his attempt to flirt. "Where are we going, Brad?"

He turns away from the ladies to answer my question. "Follow me." He looks back at the ladies and waves to them.

"I'm going to get wasted tonight," Franco informs us.

"Well, that's good to know. Thought we were over those days from college," I say.

"This is a special occasion," Brayden says in Franco's defense. He's probably going to get hammered as well.

"Why not get drunk? We don't have anything planned in the morning," Brad encourages.

"I don't want to have to drag you back to the room if you're inebriated," I warn him in case he is considering the same thing.

"Hopefully, you won't have to."

Great.

Brad brings us to a burger bar where he has secured a table for us. The hostess, decked out in a very low cut tank top and hot shorts, has a wide grin when she sees us. As she takes us to our table, I hear the guys comment on her ass making me peek at it. *Hmm*. Not bad, but Cari's ass is so much sexier.

"Which one of you is the groom?"

"He is." Brad points to me.

Her eyes focus on my face then slide downwards to my shirt.

"You look familiar."

Brad chuckles. "He gets that a lot."

"He's hot, rich, and taken. But I'm not," Dylan quickly informs her.

I attempt to refrain from rolling my eyes at his feeble effort to pick her up.

"Enjoy your dinner boys," the hostess says and winks at us before walking away.

"I just got a hard-on from her wink," Dylan announces.

"Such a juicy piece of ass," Nolan shares.

"Oh, yeah," Dylan agrees looking like he's lost in love.

The waitress shows up to our table. Her huge tits command our attention. The guys are slobbering. Brad somehow finds his voice and orders a round of beer for us while never taking his eyes off her chest.

"Fuck me, fuck me, fuck me," Dylan chants.

"I have never seen tits so big," Brayden says in a mesmerized state.

As the guys continue to compare notes on the best tits they've seen, I glance around the restaurant. All of the female staff here are busty, but the award for outstanding tits goes to my Cari. The waitress comes back to the table with our beers.

Brad raises his bottle. "D, this PAT party would not have been possible if you did not get engaged. To you," Brad says.

"PAT?" Ken asks.

We all stare at him dumbfounded. Nolan explains what it stands for…pussy, ass, and tits. A look of comprehension appears on Ken's face.

"To D," the guys say together raising their bottles to me.

I clink my bottle with theirs and we all take a swig of our beer. Let the festivities begin.

CHAPTER TWENTY-SIX

CARI

Rodrigo booked three rooms at the hotel. I am sharing one suite with my sisters, and May is sharing the other suite with Rodrigo and Hunter. Jordan has a suite to himself right next to my room. I want my relationship with my sisters to flourish as we've hardly had any bonding time together since learning of our connection to each other, and I am counting on this weekend for it to happen.

Rylee plops down on the couch. "Is there nothing to do around here?"

"Rodrigo mentioned dinner at Mohegan Sun," I tell her.

"Where is that?"

"Not far from here."

"But it's dinner. There's nothing to do except to eat."

"It's a casino with shops and restaurants."

"We're not old enough for the casinos."

"I don't need to go to the casino. We can walk around and do some shopping either before or after dinner," I suggest.

"What kind of stores are there?" Harper asks with interest.

"It's not the mall, but there are a variety of shops. Why don't you check the website and see if there are any stores you like?"

"Okay." She takes my suggestion and pulls out her phone to search for the list of stores.

"Is there anything else to do other than shopping?" Rylee clearly does not like to shop as much as Harper.

"Um, I'm not quite sure. Harper, would you also check to see what else there is to do other than shopping?" I'm not sure what will interest Rylee, but

I hope there is something for her so she can enjoy the evening.

"Okay."

"Cari?"

"Yes, Rylee?"

"Do you have a picture of your wedding dress?"

"Yes."

"Are we allowed to see it?"

"Definitely can." I go into the bedroom to get my phone and scroll through the pictures to find the ones from my final dress fitting.

"Here are some pictures," I say handing over my phone.

"It's so pretty." Rylee surprises me with her compliment. She's reserved with her compliments just like her mother.

Harper goes over to Rylee to look at the pictures. "I think you look very pretty in it."

"Thank you."

"We have our dresses for your wedding," Harper shares with me.

"Any pictures by chance?"

"We didn't take any."

"Well, I'm sure the dresses are beautiful. I can't wait to see you both wearing your chosen dress."

"They cost a lot of money."

Rylee hands the phone back to me. "Father didn't complain about the price. How shocking."

I am interested in knowing what Max is like with them. "Does he normally not allow you to spend a lot on clothes?"

"He tells us that clothes are the biggest waste of money because styles are always changing."

My two sisters share some stories of our father and how tight he can be with money. It's another thing I learn about him even though he was generous with offering to pay for my dress and my wedding party's attire.

"Can we go to the pool now?" Harper pleads obviously bored with the conversation of Max.

She likes swimming and couldn't wait to get here. The outdoor pool is not yet open, but the indoor pool is. I don't see why we can't go now since our spa appointment is not for another couple of hours.

"All right. Go get changed and we'll head on over to the pool." I call Rodrigo to apprise him of our plan. He and May will go with us while Hunter takes his beauty nap. I send Jordan a text to meet us in the hall in ten minutes.

The pool is larger than most indoor pools I have seen and even has a small waterfall in one corner. Chaise lounges and large potted plants border the edge of the pool while the wraparound balcony allows visitors a view of the pool from the second level. Natural sunlight flows in from the surrounding windows.

"You two look like you've never seen an indoor pool before," Rodrigo tells my sisters.

"Not one like this. This is way nicer than any indoor pool we have been to," Rylee admits snapping a couple of photos with her phone.

"We're at a very chic spa. Their facilities have to be updated and well-maintained otherwise they would not be able to attract the clientele that they do," explains May.

"I'm going in," Harper announces and removes her flip flops leaving them next to one of the chaise lounges.

Rylee places her phone on the lounge chair adjacent to Harper's and follows her sister. The rest of us sit down. I try to hold back my yawn but I can't.

"You seem to be very tired."

I glance at May. Does she suspect my condition?

"Cari has been working way too much trying to get as much done before the wedding. She needs to relax, so I think we should all get in the pool and do some relaxing." Rodrigo saves the day. *Thank you, Rodrigo.*

"You need to hire an assistant to help you. Why don't you speak to my brother about it?"

"Because it's my company. I don't have the budget to hire someone right now."

"Deven can give you the money."

"Your brother can't just give money to her like that. This is business," Rodrigo interjects.

"Oh. I get it now. Okay. Well, let's go in the pool so you can relax," May says.

Rodrigo stands at the edge of the pool. "Girls, is that pool water cold?"

"No, it's warm," Rylee replies.

May looks over at Jordan. "Do you want to go in the pool too?"

"Thank you for offering, but I'm fine here," Jordan answers her.

Jordan probably has directions from Deven to be on guard protecting us at all times.

Harper is floating on her back. "Come in the pool, Cari."

"You don't have to worry about what Deven will say if you want to go for a swim. I will explain it to him," I tell Jordan.

"I don't doubt you will, Ms. Snow, but I also did not come prepared to go swimming." He tugs on his shorts.

"Ah, I see. Well then, I better get in that pool before Harper pulls me in."

He gives me a nod. "You enjoy your swim."

"I will. Thank you." I go to join the rest of the crew in the pool.

CHAPTER TWENTY-SEVEN

DEVEN

The buzzing coming from my cell phone wakes me from my slumber. *Ugh!* My head is throbbing as I try to open my heavy eyelids. *Shit.* I haven't felt this way since college. Managing to unlock the phone, I see it's a text from my angel. I open it to find a picture of her and the gang at dinner last night. She tells me how her evening was and informs me they are on their way to the spa. Her last text asks me about my night. *My night...*

Brad and I didn't get back to our room until a few hours ago. After dinner and prior to casino hopping, Brad took us to a beer garden for more drinking. I don't remember much of what happened at the casinos except for Nolan getting really wasted. Too tired to fight staying awake, my eyes shut and I surrender to much needed sleep.

I finally wake up at half past noon. On the night table is a white box with my picture and the word "Hangover" printed above my head in the picture. *Wait a minute.* I don't recall the box being on the table last night. Brad must have snuck it in here while I was passed out. I sit up and open the box to see what contents are in this hangover survival kit. I pull out one packet of aspirin and a bottle of water. *Just what I need.* I swallow the pills immediately.

There's a light knock on my door.

"Are you up?"

"Yeah. Come on in."

Brad opens the door and comes in with a cup of coffee.

"Thanks man."

"Sure. How are you feeling?"

"I have a headache, but I should be fine for tonight. Don't worry. I'll make it."

I have not consumed that much alcohol in quite some time. My partner in crime here has always been able to consume more liquor than I ever could. I need to scale back on my intake of liquor tonight.

"Hey, I know that. I just wanted to check on you. It's been a while since you've had so much to drink."

"Yeah. I appreciate the hangover kit."

"All the guys got one."

"Good planning on your part."

"Do you want to order room service?"

"Yeah. Let's do that. I don't know what you have planned for tonight, but I think it's going to be another late night with heavy drinking."

He shrugs. "Possibly. Just dress up for dinner. We're going to a steakhouse tonight."

"And then what are we doing after dinner?"

He grins. "It's a surprise. You'll find out later."

Yep. I can tell by that grin of his what he has planned.

"Your sister called."

"Which sister?"

"Kaitlin."

"What'd she want?"

"She said Ken is still sleeping and she's taking Mandy to the pool."

"Good. Mandy loves pool time."

"And she will soon have a home with a pool."

The closing on the houses is in the next couple of weeks when Ken comes to the east coast.

"I was thinking I should make an investment and buy a house close to you and Ken down by the shore."

"That'll be great man. It'll be a good investment. You can set up an appointment with my realtor if you want to have a look at some of the homes."

"I'll do so. My parents can live there and go between the Jersey shore and Boston."

"Wouldn't you prefer your parents to be in the City instead?"

"They already live in the City. The shore will be a nice change. Fresh air and less pollution will be better for them."

"It will be a huge change for them. Do you think they're prepared to deal with summer crowds and a quiet off season?"

"Maybe I need to make a trip there with them to get their thoughts. They can always spend the summer in Boston and winters in Jersey."

"You can rent out the house in the summer if they rather be in Boston."

"I don't think my mom will like having strangers stay in the house if I decide to rent it out. There's time to think about all of that later. Right now, let's order some food."

CHAPTER TWENTY-EIGHT

CARI

"Why are there always so many good choices on the menu? It makes it difficult to decide," May says keeping her eyes on the menu in front of her.

"Someone should order that super expensive seafood thing," Harper says aloud.

"Why don't you order it, Harper?" Hunter suggests.

"No way. Father would tell me it's too expensive."

"*Father?* That sounds so old-fashioned," May comments.

Hunter looks up at Harper. "Your father is not here so order whatever you'd like no matter what the price is."

Harper still seems unsure. "Really?"

"Absolutely," I reassure her.

"Okay." Harper smiles widely.

After placing our orders, Harper turns to Jordan. "What is your favorite thing to eat?"

He lays his chin between his forefinger and thumb and thinks about it. "I like so many different foods."

"There must be one thing that you really like the most."

"I would have to say that sour cream and onion chips are my favorite."

Harper makes a face. "Seriously?"

"Yes."

"I thought you were going to say lobster."

"Lobster is good too. Tell me what your favorite thing to eat is."

"That's easy. I love chocolate ice cream."

"I like ice cream too."

"But it's not your favorite."

"No, but it's delicious and cools me down in the summer."

"Yeah, it does. Do you have kids?" Harper changes the subject as quickly as one snaps their fingers.

"Harper, you're not supposed to ask that," Rylee tells her.

"It's no problem to ask. To answer your question, Harper, I don't have any kids."

I have to put an end to Harper's brief inquisition on his personal life. "Jordan, we are very happy to have your company for dinner."

"And don't you worry about being in any trouble with my brother. We invited you," May adds.

"Thank you very much for inviting me. Mr. Blake is aware that I'm dining with you all tonight."

Of course, Mr. Blake would know. He always wants to know everything. He probably even wants a status report on us every hour. *I wish I could get a status report on him tonight.*

"Rodrigo, does it feel weird to be gay?" Harper questions him out of the blue.

Her inquiry generates the same shocked reaction from all of us except Rodrigo.

"Not at all. It's who I am, and I am proud of who I am. It is imperative to not be ashamed of who you are. You have to be comfortable in your own skin."

"Cool. I like you."

Rodrigo puts a hand over his heart. "I like you too, Harper."

Harper smiles and turns to me. "Cari, if you and Deven have a baby then I will be a very young aunt."

That's another shift in conversation. Hmm. Harper is right. Both of my sisters will be young aunts.

"Does being a young aunt bother you?"

"Nope. I like it and I think it will be fun. None of my friends are aunts."

"Then you can do the diaper duty. That's loads of fun." Rylee happily passes that responsibility to Harper.

"You're going to be an aunt too so you get to share it with me." Harper can really stick it back to Rylee.

"You can do diapers and I'll feed the baby." Rylee sticks her tongue out at Harper.

I can't wait to see how they will react when I reveal to them that I am pregnant.

"I've changed a baby's diaper before. There's nothing to it," May says earning glares from Rodrigo and I. "But let's talk about the wedding instead."

"Are there going to be any cute guys my age at the wedding?" Rylee asks.

Hunter crosses his arms. "Guy shopping, Rylee?"

"Father is going to be mad if he sees you talk to boys."

I turn to Rylee. "You're not allowed to talk to boys?"

"It's more like I can talk to them as long as I don't date them," Rylee clears up.

Rodrigo leans on his elbows at the table. "I don't know if there will be any guys your age, but there will definitely be plenty of hot guys."

"My brother's friends are all hot."

"And his friends are older than she is," I point out.

"Does age really matter if the attraction is there?" Hunter asks waving his hand back and forth in the air.

"Exactly. Brad is older than I am."

"I don't want to disrespect Max's rule."

"Cari, he can't stop me from dating when I go to college."

I cannot disagree with Rylee as she has a valid point. She is free to date then, but she's not attending college yet.

May puts her hands up. "Enough about guys. We got off the subject of the wedding."

Rodrigo cocks his head. "I don't think we ever really got on the subject."

"That's because we got into the talk about hot guys."

"Okay. No more hot guys then. Girls, be prepared as this wedding is going to be epic."

"Give us the details," begs Rylee. She may be tough, but she has a sweet spot for weddings and all things romantic.

Rodrigo shares some details about the wedding. My sisters are excited and happy when I let them know they will be included in the grand entrance at the reception.

"That's so awesome! I can't wait to tell everyone at school and church!"

Rylee rolls her eyes at Harper's statement. "Thank you so much, Cari."

Overall, it's been a perfect day with my family. We stroll through the shopping concourse after dinner. Harper and May do the most shopping. Riley is either not much of a shopper or she doesn't want to spend my money as I offered to pay for my sisters' purchases.

We're back in our room and Harper drops her shopping bags next to the couch. Rylee picks up the remote and turns the television on. I sit on the oversized chair and join them in watching whatever it is Rylee chooses.

"Have you been enjoying your time away from home?"

"Yeah, I've been enjoying it," Rylee admits.

"Me too," Harper agrees.

"I'm glad we were able to spend some time together. I know it couldn't have been easy for either of you to accept the news that I am your sister."

Harper speaks first. "We thought it was a joke when Father told us."

"Why did you think that?"

"Because it sounded ridiculous," Rylee explains.

Harper crosses her legs under her. "He told us what he did."

"We were mad at him, but Mother talked to us. She told us we shouldn't be mad at him because it happened before they met in college."

"Yeah. She said we have to accept that you're our sister."

"And she said you set a good example for us because you're very smart and successful and polite."

"And you're marrying a rich guy."

"It's like she wants us to be like you."

Listening to my sisters reveal what Aimee said about me comes as a shock. She's more accepting of me than she lets on.

"How did you get to be so smart?"

I look at Harper and Rylee. "I studied a lot and gave school my one hundred percent."

"Are we allowed to ask you any personal questions?"

I'm puzzled as to why Rylee has to ask for my permission. "Of course. You don't have to ask if you're allowed. You can always ask anything of me."

It troubles me why my sisters have to seek permission from me, and I question them on it. Max does not permit them to ask certain questions due to their age. That is Max's rule but not mine. I won't impose any restrictions on my sisters. I don't want there to be any walls between us. My sisters want to know more about me, and they have many questions they want to ask. They also want to know about Deven and our history. My wish is for us to learn about each other and grow closer, and tonight marks a wonderful start to our sisterhood.

CHAPTER TWENTY-NINE

DEVEN

Brad made reservations for an early dinner. No better way to start the evening than to meet at the bar first for a few drinks. Tonight, dinner jackets are required at the swanky steakhouse located in the hotel. *I'm very much relieved we don't have to dress alike.*

When it's time, we're shown to a private room reserved for VIPs. In the room, there is a rectangular table with tufted leather chairs surrounded by floor to ceiling walls of wine behind locked glass doors. A bottle of specially selected Duckhorn Howell Mountain Cabernet Sauvignon sits on the table waiting to be poured into each glass. Being successful and very rich does have its privileges.

"Do you guys eat like this often?" Adam asks focusing on the menu prices instead of the quality of the food this restaurant offers and serves.

Brad laughs. "No. This is a special occasion. I usually eat quality food that's cheap."

"Cheap? *Really?*"

"He does," I respond for Brad. Brad doesn't normally eat at four or five star establishments. He's all about quality cheap eats.

"Make sure you eat well tonight. I'm picking up the tab," Brad informs.

Nolan puts down his menu. "Lobster it is for me."

The ribeye steak is my choice tonight. *It's tender and juicy like Cari.* The thought of eating her sexy snatch starts to arouse my lonely cock. I don't know how I have survived this long without being inside her.

"Good evening, gentlemen. May I start you off with some wine?" the server asks.

"Please," Brad responds.

The server opens the bottle of wine and pours some into my glass. I lift the glass and give the wine in it a swirl. Then I inhale its aromatic scent before tasting it. It's smooth and perfect. I give the server a nod and he proceeds to go around the table pouring wine into each glass.

Dylan tastes the wine. "This wine is excellent."

Franco agrees. "A superb choice."

"Of course. Only the finest for tonight," Brad says.

We enjoy some of the best food and wine Vegas has to offer. At the end of our meal, the chef stops in to introduce himself to us. He's young with a great sense of humor. We thank him for the delicious meal prepared. After Brad signs the check, he informs us there is a Hummer limo ready to take us to our next destination.

The shiny black Hummer limo is parked outside of the hotel's main entrance. The chauffeur opens the door for us and we pile in. Inside are two bottles of Dom Perignon champagne, a bottle of cognac, and a bottle of Scotch. I open the first bottle of Dom Perignon and fill the glasses as we continue our carousing until we get to wherever it is we're going to.

CHAPTER THIRTY

DEVEN

The limo comes to a stop and the chauffeur announces we have arrived. He opens the doors for us and we get out. The area appears to be desolate except for the gas station down the road and the abandoned looking structure in front of us. Ken's mouth is agape as he points to something. I look to see what it is he is pointing at. It's a flashing neon sign featuring a silhouette of a naked female body with her back arched and tits pushed forward. Here we are at T*tty T*tty Bam Bam in the middle of nowhere. I knew Brad would not pass up the opportunity to visit a titties joint.

Brad spreads his arms wide open. "At last, we're here boys. Titty Titty Bam Bam is the best strip club in Vegas. It's a PAT lover's dream."

"Why are we all still standing out here then? Let's go in," Nolan impatiently says.

"I want some *bam bam* tonight." Dylan releases a hearty laugh.

Horny bastard.

We are met at the entrance by a lady clad in a catwoman suit. *Do they all dress in Halloween costumes at this place? What kind of strip club are we at?* The guys are salivating over her assets defined by the suit. She asks for a name and Brad gives her one. Apparently, reservations are required. She looks at each of us and then instructs us to wait for the hostess inside.

The foyer is spacious. There are several couches, chairs, and tables around the perimeter of the area. A dimly lit chandelier hangs over the center, and pictures of women's torsos in various poses hugging the dance pole flank the walls. One of the wall panels slide open and out steps a lady dressed in a barely there harness leather bodysuit with nipple covers and platform stiletto heels.

158

"Oh my God," Adam and Ken say together.

Nolan and Dylan have their fists in their mouths trying hard not to drool like fools. Brad smiles appreciatively at her admiring her from head to toe. She introduces herself as Priscilla. Priscilla asks which one of us is the groom, and I raise my hand like a shy schoolboy.

"Aren't you a hottie?" She doesn't take her eyes off of me as she slowly licks her lips with her pierced tongue. Her action does not stimulate anything in my body, but from the corner of my eye, I notice Nolan licking his lips. "We have reserved a private room for you and your friends. This way, gentlemen," she says and turns around giving us a full view of her exposed ass. Her ass doesn't compare to Cari's ass which is way hotter.

The guys are immediately right behind the hostess except for Ken. He is having some trouble walking at a normal pace, and I attempt to suppress my amusement. *He's got a boner.*

"Why are you walking so slowly?"

"Kind of difficult to walk," he whispers.

I slap him on the back and walk alongside of him down a darkish hall with lights emitting a dim golden glow. We reach the end of the corridor where music is blaring behind the door and walls. Priscilla opens the door. There's hollering and whistling from the men as the stripper swings around the pole in the center of the stage. The Deven Blake groom squad has come to a stop entranced by the pole dancer. Even Ken seems struck by her.

"Your type?"

Ken shakes his head in slow motion. "Not really."

"You're looking at her like you want to fuck her."

"No. I've just never been to a gentleman's club."

"Are you shitting me?"

"Nope."

"How the fuck have you never gone to a strip club?"

He shrugs. "Just never have. I'm more of an introvert. These places are not my thing."

If my brother didn't have a daughter, I would think he's a virgin.

"When I was your age, I frequented strip clubs and was surrounded by girls all the time."

"I'm not you. You're confident in a way I am not."

"I disagree. You are much more confident than I am. Look at you. You graduated with a master's degree."

"You could have as well if you chose to pursue one."

Touché. I didn't further my education with a master's degree because I wanted to work for my father right after college. Our conversation comes to an end when Priscilla reminds us we have to follow her. We're brought into a spacious room with several booths and tables. Towards one side of the room is a much smaller stage with a dancing pole and chairs arranged in front of it.

Priscilla leans in. "Stop by and see me before you leave," she whispers to me and walks away.

Nope. No fucking way.

"What did she say to you?" Nolan is dying to know.

"She wants me to see her before leaving," I reply.

"We won't tell Cari," Franco says.

"You won't need to. It's not happening," I tell the guys.

"Don't worry. I'll go in your place," Nolan volunteers.

"Please do."

"You're like a magnet with women," Ken says to me.

"We all are."

"Not me. I don't attract them like you do, and I'm also shy not to mention awkward."

I seem to be discovering stuff about my brother. I thought I had him figured out. I have always considered him to be someone who is self-confident with great social skills, but he is just the opposite.

"You underestimate yourself."

"I don't."

"When was the last time you've been with someone?"

"Not since before I got custody of Mandy."

Oh fuck. My poor brother hasn't fucked in nearly a year.

Brad comes up to us. "Guys, show is going to start soon."

"Maybe the stripper will make you feel differently," I tell Ken.

"Chastity belts are not allowed here," Brad mentions to Ken. He throws his arm around Ken's shoulders. "Come on, bro. Sit with me and let me show you how to have a good time tonight."

Our scantily clad waitress comes into the room and presents herself as Venus.

"Now, that's hot," Brad points out to Ken.

Venus bends over to allow us a closer view of her tits which are barely contained in the halter top she has on. Her tits sway from side to side and her nipples are a telltale sign she is not wearing a bra underneath but it's obvious anyway. She has a velvety smooth voice and practically purrs each word that comes out of her mouth. She winks at Ken and asks him what drink she can get for him, but he seems to be grappling with words so I order a Scotch for him.

"She winked at you, bro," Brad teases him.

"She's very good looking," Ken finally says.

"Good looking? Man, she's *hot*. She should be the stripper. Don't you think, D?"

"No one is hotter than Cari."

"You are so fucking whipped."

I laugh. Maybe I am, but that may be a good thing. "SPF."

"SPF?" Ken questions.

How does my brother have a child but fucking lacks knowledge in women and social skills?

Brad and I look at each other and then turn to him. "Same pussy forever," we tell him.

This earns a shake of the head and a chuckle from Ken.

"Dude, what shell have you been hiding under?" Brad asks him.

Ken shrugs. "I am surrounded by guys who are more into their education, video games, and chess."

"Chess? People still are into that?"

"Yes. Lots of people still play it."

"You really have been hiding under a shell. When you move to Jersey, we will take you out."

"Nah, man. I can't."

"Why not?"

"I have my daughter."

He's already finding excuses not to have a social life.

"So what if you do? Are you planning to be celibate forever?"

Ken rubs the back of his neck seemingly uncomfortable with the questioning from Brad. "Not forever."

"Then you can hang out with us. Cari and May can babysit your daughter."

"I don't have the house yet, so why don't we revisit this once I have settled into my new home?"

"Fair, but I'm holding you to it."

Venus is back with our drinks. She winks at Ken again and asks where we are staying. Brad tells her and starts small talk with her. The pro is giving my brother a lesson on how to engage a woman in conversation.

Venus goes over to Ken and slips him a piece of paper. *Did she just give him her number?* Brad beats me to it and asks him first. He doesn't deny it, but he tells us he has no interest in hooking up with her after she gets off using his daughter as justification. Brad asks for the number making me turn and narrow my eyes at him. Ken refuses to give Brad the number and rips up the paper instead.

The dim lights go off darkening the room and signaling the start of the show. The three of us move over to the available chairs set up in front of the stage. I end up in the middle between the ex-manwhore and the semi-virgin. The other guys are already drunk and shouting and clapping loudly.

The music is pumping and the stage is shrouded with a plume of fog. As the fog dissipates, the entire backside of the stripper comes into view. With one hand on her hip and the other hand on her dance cane, she spins around. She's in a sequined bodysuit where the front dips low and her tits are hardly concealed. A glittery top hat sits on her head, and shiny thigh high boots dress up her legs.

All the guys are hooting at the stripper except for Ken who is still in shock from seeing some PAT. Once again, Ken's mouth is agape. The stripper struts around the small stage and stops in front of me. She squats down and parts her legs. *Whoa. What's my cock doing? I think it wants to betray me. WTF?* The stripper takes her finger, licks it, and touches her pussy. *Oh fuck.*

She stands up and shakes her ass in my face before strutting back to the middle of the stage. I let out a breath I didn't even know I had been holding in. I'm glad the room is dark and none of the guys could tell I was nearly aroused. *What was I thinking?* She's not even attractive. I'm going to blame this on the lack of sex with Cari. First thing I do when I return home is fuck my angel to the moon and back. After all, from the moment I first claimed possession of her pussy, I knew I wanted to be in her pussy forever. *SPF.* No one and nothing will ever change that.

CHAPTER THIRTY-ONE

DEVEN

I wake up with a throbbing headache again. There's nothing but darkness as I struggle to open my eyes. All of last night is a blur to me. *Fuck. Whose room am I in?* I feel for the light switch and flip it on. The brightness from the light is blinding and forces me to shut my eyes instantly. *Oh, that was painful.* I take my time opening my eyes again. I let out a huff of air. *Whew! I'm in my room.* I wouldn't have wanted to think of the consequences had I ended up in someone else's room. *But what the fuck happened the rest of last night?*

I try to recall details from last night. I remember being at the strip club, having a lot to drink, and the stripper entertaining us with her grinding and spreading. I just have no recollection how I ended up back here.

I need to know if Brad is awake. He'll remember the details from last night. I try to gather some energy to get out of bed and go to his room but fail. I reach for my phone and call him instead.

"Hmm?" he answers.

"Were you still sleeping?"

"Yep."

"Hungover?"

"Mmm-hmm."

He may not remember then. "What the fuck happened last night?"

"We had a good time."

"I don't remember coming back here."

"Hmm."

"You need to wake up."

"I need to have black coffee injected in me."

What an excellent idea. Why didn't I think of it?

"We need to pull ourselves together. We have to meet the gang for lunch before heading to the airport."

"Hmm."

He is incapable of saying anything coherent at this time, so I let him go back to sleep for another hour. I haven't received a text from Cari, but I did get a message from Jordan updating me that all went well last night and they're about to go back home. That was a couple of hours ago. They should be almost home by now. I take the second packet of aspirin from the hangover kit and return to sleep.

~ * ~

Brad and I manage to get up, pack, and make it to the café for lunch before we leave Vegas. All of us have sunglasses on except of course, Ken.

"Some night that was," Dylan starts.

Nolan rubs his temples. "I feel like I've been hit with a sledgehammer."

I have to know what happened as my memory fails to remember. "What the fuck happened last night?"

Ken looks around the table. "Each of you had way more than enough to drink."

"I remember the stripper inserting that cane of hers into her –"

I cut Brad off and ask Ken, "Did I behave in a manner that I shouldn't have?"

Ken stares at me without saying a word.

Oh, fuck. What did I do?

"Your conduct was mild compared to everyone else's."

"Mild? How exactly did I behave?"

"You want me to say it in front of everyone?"

"Why not? Guys don't kiss and tell."

He appears to be nervous. He and I have to spend more time together because I have never seen this side of my brother. I'm thrilled he will be moving to New Jersey which will give us that opportunity.

"Go ahead."

"You were intoxicated and the stripper knew it too. After her performance on the stage, she came off the stage. She circled around you like you were her prey and then sat down on your lap. She whispered something in your ear that made you laugh. Then she took your hand and moved it to her...you know...her private area."

Oh, shit.

Ken continues, "You pulled your hand back, but she took your hand again and held it to her breast. Then she leaned forward to try to kiss you."

"*What?!*" How could I have allowed myself to drink so much knowing it would affect my behavior?

"Strippers are not supposed to be doing that," Nolan says.

Ken looks at me. "Her face was really close to yours, but I cannot say with certainty that she did kiss you."

I shake my head in shame. I shouldn't have let that happen.

"Nothing happened, bro. Even if she did kiss you, she took advantage of the state you were in. She threw herself on you not the other way around," says ex-manwhore Brad reading my thoughts.

He has a point, but it doesn't excuse the fact that I was so intoxicated and let myself loose like that.

Brad looks at the guys around the table. "Cari can never know about what happened. It stays here in Vegas. We don't bring any of this back with us," he warns them. Leave it to Brad to bury this in the sand.

Ken sits back in his chair. "The rest of you were very hands on with the stripper."

"I can't say I remember much of what happened last night either," admits Dylan.

Franco nods. "Me either."

The other guys mumble something similar.

Nolan looks over at Ken. "You were the only one that didn't get drunk?"

"I did drink, but I limited my consumption."

"I don't believe it."

Not one of them understands why Ken had to monitor his consumption of alcohol.

I speak up in Ken's defense. "Believe it. He is the only one at this table with a child."

"Are you gentlemen all set to order?" our server asks us.

We haven't had a chance to look at the menu but order anyway. Once the server leaves, we go back to discussing the events of last night. Listening to the way the other guys had conducted themselves with the stripper makes me look like a saint. Brad's manwhore ways emerged again, but I will spare May's feelings from this.

"Don't be so hard on yourself. You didn't give the stripper an invitation," Ken tells me.

The guys concur with Ken.

"I don't want to keep this from her either."

"How will she know if we don't say anything?" Brad questions me.

"Fuck the guilty conscience. You didn't fuck the stripper, so forget about it," Nolan advises.

Love is a powerful thing once Cupid's arrow strikes. I fell in love with Cari from the moment I first laid eyes on her. As I got to know her better, the love became deeper. But when she gave herself completely to me one word came into mind...*forever*. All I can see is a future with her. *She is the one.* But the last time I kept something from her it tore us apart. *Is this worth keeping from her?*

CHAPTER THIRTY-TWO

DEVEN

It was great spending the weekend with the guys, but I am elated to be home with my angel again. The sun is up, but I am far from tired right now.

"Good morning."

I turn around to see Rodrigo in the hallway.

"Hey. Good morning."

"Welcome back."

"Thanks."

"How was Vegas? Did you have fun?"

"Yeah, it was good being with the guys." *Do I tell him what happened?* "Everything went well this weekend?"

"Yeah, it did."

I look past his shoulder and see that the door to the master suite is closed.

"I need to tell you something."

Rodrigo eyes me suspiciously. "Oh?"

"Something happened in Vegas."

Rodrigo starts to get dramatic on me with the look of shock on his face and a hand over his heart.

"Listen to what I have to say first before you go on with your theatrics." I look down the hall again to ensure the door is still shut. "It's not as bad as you think."

"But it has to be bad if you need to tell me."

I exhale a deep breath and tell him about the incident between the stripper and I. Rodrigo covers his mouth with his hands.

"I think I should let Cari know."

He crosses his arms and gives me a long hard stare. "No."

"No?"

"She doesn't need to know."

His response isn't what I was expecting. "You want me to keep this from her?"

"Yes."

"The last time I kept something from her it damaged our relationship."

"I know that. But stick with the facts for a minute. You were drunk, and your brother witnessed your attempt to withdraw your hand. You didn't approach her. She approached you. And you have no recollection of what happened which proves you were boozed up.

"Look, I made sure Cari had a very relaxing weekend as she's been inundated with work. She's also been extremely tired lately. But I think she suspected Brad planned a trip for you boys to the pussy club. The wedding is next month, and your relationship does not need a stress fracture right now. Just let it go."

It looks like the consensus is to not mention the incident to Cari.

"Okay. Thanks. I noticed as well she seemed drained before I even went away. She needs to go see the doctor."

"She's stressed between the wedding and work. The birthday trip will be good for her."

I nod my head in agreement.

"It's time for me to eat breakfast and then prepare myself for work."

"I thought you have been working from here."

"I have been, but I have a routine. Look, you should go be with Cari right now. She missed you badly."

"I missed her much more."

"Well, just keep the noise level down."

I chuckle. "All right then. See you later."

"Yeah."

I open the bedroom door and quietly remove my clothes before getting in bed. My weight on the bed causes her to stir. I can't take my eyes off of her. She looks so beautiful and peaceful as she sleeps. I push a strand of her hair behind her ear and kiss her forehead. Her eyes open.

"Deven."

"Hi." I pull her into my arms loving the feel of her in them and not wanting to let her go.

"You're back."

"I am."

"I'm happy you're back."

"Me too."

"Did you have a good time in Vegas?"

Inhale. Exhale. "It wasn't the same without you. Did you enjoy your spa weekend?"

"I did. And I think it brought my sisters and I closer."

"I'm ever so glad. The three of you needed that bonding." All of a sudden, I feel exhaustion take over me. I yawn.

She places a hand on my cheek and looks at me affectionately. "You need some sleep."

"Not yet. I need you first." My mouth takes hers as my hand slides down her impeccable body.

It's been a long week without her. Sleep can wait.

CHAPTER THIRTY-THREE

DEVEN

The past few weeks have been consuming with work, events, and finalizing wedding stuff. The timing of this trip to Kiawah Island couldn't be more perfect. I have no intention of doing much of anything outside of our room except to perhaps eat. I do, however, intend on having a fuck-a-thon with Cari. After all, we are here to celebrate her birthday which I am very much looking forward to.

My insatiable angel is asleep in my arms. I inch a little closer and kiss her ear. She stirs but doesn't awaken; however, my dick is very awake. I'm certain she can feel its hardness against her flawless ass. She responds by rubbing her ass against my hardened cock. *Oh, fuck me.* I need to bury myself deep in her sweet pussy.

Wide awake now, she flips onto her back and parts her thighs for me. *Her pretty pink pussy is a lovely sight to behold.* I take my fingers and gently rub it loving how moist she is there. Then I push two fingers in between the lips of her pussy. Her eyelids close as she takes pleasure in my fingers pressing against her interior walls.

"Like that, baby?"

"Uh-huh." Her voice is barely audible.

I remove my fingers out of her. She watches as I suck on them savoring the taste of her. Her eyes grow big. *Yeah, angel. Bet you didn't know how good you taste.* I snake down her body to her pussy and start eating away. *Mmm...pussylicious.* I pull back and blow a puff of air into her making her body clench. Raising myself over her, I tease her folds with the wet tip of my cock first before driving myself into her. I love how her tight pussy swallows my cock completely. I'm immediately drowning in an ocean of incoherency and pleasure. *Damn…*

Let the fuck-a-thon begin.

~ * ~

CARI

I open my eyes to find sunlight peeking through the gap between each panel of drapes. The time on the digital clock indicates it's nearly nine. My hot fiancé is sleeping soundly after our night of nonstop lovemaking. *Hmm…what a sextacular night.* I roll out of bed, put on a robe, and head into the living room to order breakfast from room service. I speak to the manager to reconfirm this morning's special breakfast order I had requested prior to the trip.

I step out onto the balcony after placing the order. I rest my palms on the railing. Looking out towards the beach on this beautiful morning, I silently pray for everything to go as planned. We're here for my birthday, but little does he know we will have something else to celebrate as well. Finding a way to announce the news…well, that was the difficult part.

"Morning, angel," Deven says as his arms circle my waist.

"Good morning."

He kisses my neck. "That was some night."

I smile. "It was. I bet you're extremely hungry."

"I am very hungry."

"Breakfast should be here soon."

"I'm actually hungry for you." He releases an arm from my waist and moves his hand under my robe sliding a finger into me. "I'd love to fuck you out here." He pulls me tighter to him and slips another finger inside. He is really being daring.

"Indecent exposure is not allowed out here."

"Are you sure about that?" he asks continuing to push his fingers in and out of me.

"Hmm. I'm pretty sure. They may not allow us back if we engage in a lewd act out here on the balcony."

He gradually pulls his fingers out of me. I turn around and my eyes land on his bare chest. I trace each ripple on his hard chest with my finger as his breathing starts to become shallow. *He likes when I touch him.* I continue to outline each ripple and then draw an invisible heart in the center of his chest. He lifts my chin up, and I notice his smoldering eyes. He moves to kiss me, but the moment is interrupted by a loud knock on the door.

"Guess our breakfast is here."

"I'll let them in."

"No. Why don't I do that and you go put a shirt on?"

"Why do I need to get a shirt on?"

"I don't want the employee to stare at your nakedness."

He flashes his sexy dimpled smile and looks me up and down. "You're wearing a robe."

"Thanks for pointing it out, but it's tied *tightly*," I emphasize.

"Touché," he says and heads to the bedroom.

I quickly go to the door and let the room service attendant in. She enters and puts the tray down on the dining room table. I sign the tab and thank her. I hear the water running in the bathroom which means Deven must be brushing his teeth. *Perfect.* It gives me a few minutes to set up.

I move everything off the tray and onto the table. I bring the two coffee cups with me into the kitchenette and place them on the counter switching them out with the special coffee cups and saucers I had brought with me on this trip. Just as I finish pouring coffee into each cup, my gorgeous man comes back to me.

"Smells delicious." He pulls out the chair and sits down.

I pick up my fork and knife and cut my stack of pancakes. "Bon appétit," I say and place the pancakes in my mouth.

Deven takes a bite of his lemon blueberry ricotta pancakes. "These pancakes are awesome. They have this on the menu here?"

"No. It was a special order."

"Thank you, angel, for ordering my favorite pancakes."

"Thank you for this trip. The pancakes are really good." I wish I had thought to order more. *This baby has increased my appetite.*

"What's really good is being inside you again. There's nothing like sex with you, a good breakfast, and more sex with you." He wiggles his eyebrows.

"Why don't we finish our breakfast first?"

"That's what I'm doing. I'm not going to waste my favorite pancakes."

We continue to eat, and I patiently wait for him to take a sip of his coffee. It's some time before he reaches for his cup.

"Is everything okay?"

His eyebrows knit together as he stares at the two little footprints on the saucer. "Did you know there are feet on the saucer?"

I lift my cup and gaze down at my saucer pretending to notice for the first time. "Isn't that something? They're footprints."

He shrugs and places his cup back down on the saucer. Then he swallows another forkful of pancakes. The hint of the tiny footprints did not capture his attention like I thought it would have. *Will he even spot the next hint and connect the dots?*

"More coffee?" I ask.

He looks in his cup and finishes the remaining coffee. He puts the cup back on the saucer and misses the second hint. *This is not going the way I had planned.* I quickly come up with another tactic and reach for the coffee carafe. Before pouring more coffee in his cup, I tell him there's something inside it. Deven takes the cup from me and looks in it.

"What the fuck?" He lifts the cup closer to examine it more closely.

I hold my breath as he reads the words on the bottom of the cup.

"We're expecting?"

A smile stretches across my face. "We're expecting."

"Really?"

"Really."

"I'm going to be a dad?"

I laugh and nod. "Yes, you are."

His face is beaming as he takes my hands in his. "We're having a baby! This is the best news ever!"

"This is a blessing."

"It is. When did you know?"

"When you were in California."

The beaming expression on his face suddenly fades. "Why didn't you tell me as soon as you knew?"

"You would have returned home right away."

"You're absolutely right. I would have."

"I wanted you to have a good time away from home. And then this trip made it perfect for me to share the news with you."

His eyes widen as he runs his hand through his tousled hair. "I get it now. How did I not make the connection? The tiny footprints on the saucer are baby footprints."

I nod to confirm.

"When is the baby due?"

"The guesstimate is somewhere around Christmas. We'll have a better idea of the date once the ultrasound is done."

"A Christmas baby! This is absolutely wonderful!" He gets up from his chair, pulls me out of mine, and embraces me tightly. "Is it safe to have sex while you're pregnant?"

"The doctor said it's fine unless there are complications."

"Complications?"

"Nothing that we need to worry about yet."

Concern shows on his face. "Yet?"

"She went over what I need to be cognizant of. Can we not discuss this now? I don't want to ruin the moment."

He brushes a finger along my cheek. "Okay. I think we should celebrate by letting me love you slowly and gently."

"That's a good way to celebrate. Let me just clean up first."

"Leave it." His eyes are blazing with desire.

"I will then," I say shedding my robe and leading him back to the bedroom.

CHAPTER THIRTY-FOUR

June

DEVEN

I am making breakfast for Cari this morning before we head to our first ultrasound appointment together. As I fold her mushroom and spinach omelet, I think back to the time she made a kale and cheese omelet for me. It was the first time any girl ever cooked for me. I push the omelet onto her plate next to the whole wheat toast and bring the tray into the bedroom. She rewards me with the prettiest smile ever.

"Thank you for making breakfast."

I set the tray down on the bed and kiss her forehead.

"You're not eating with me?"

I'm ashamed of myself because I ate my entire omelet while making hers. The incredible night of sex left me ravenous this morning. I rub the back of my neck and look awkwardly at her. "Sex with you is so damn incredible, and I always tend to be starving afterwards." I smile at her. "I noticed your breasts are a little fuller since you've been pregnant and it immediately turned me on this morning."

She stares at me, cheeks flushed and mouth agape.

I place my finger under her chin to close her mouth. "I can't help myself around you. Eat your breakfast before it gets cold."

"Yes, sir."

I love watching her eat. There's something sexy about it. *Damn.* My cock is getting hard again.

"Mmm. This is good. And I think our baby loves the omelet too."

I love whenever she references "our baby." It's surreal that we're going to be parents before the year is over. How amazing it is to have created the beginning of a little one. Life is just perfect.

~ * ~

I have Cari take a seat when we arrive for the appointment and inform the receptionist she is here. The receptionist hands me a clipboard with some forms to complete. I take the clipboard with me and sit beside Cari. She leans into me and tells me she is capable of completing her own forms. *Right.* She sure is, and I hand the clipboard to her.

Once she's done, I bring the forms back to the receptionist and give her the insurance card in order for her to make a copy. When I rejoin Cari, she shows me something she typed on her phone. She wants me to know some of the few moms-to-be are gawking at me. I hate that this bothers her. I put my arm around her and she places her head on my shoulder. *That's my girl.* I get to have my angel closer to me and make her feel secure.

Cari's name is called, and we follow the assistant into a room where she tells Cari to sit on the examination table. She enters some information into the portable computer and then leaves the room after informing us the technician will be in shortly. I look at the equipment next to the examination table.

"I'm interested to see what is used to view the baby."

"That's what is used." She points to a thick wand-like instrument. "Are you anxious?"

"I absolutely am. It's our baby we're going to be seeing."

The technician knocks on the door and enters the room. She sits in the chair next to the table and types in something. Then she pushes up Cari's blouse and squeezes some clear substance onto her abdominal area.

I watch as the technician rolls the wand-like instrument over Cari's abdominal section. The technician directs me to focus my attention towards the monitor hanging on the wall. I gaze at the image and I am in awe. This is the beginning of the life cycle of the child Cari and I made together. The technician shows us where the baby's head is - *of course, I already know that -*

and then explains she is checking for abnormalities at this stage. *Abnormalities?* Cari sucks in her breath while I keep my anxiety at bay and reach for her hand.

After the technician is done, she confirms everything appears to be fine. Cari and I feel a sense of relief. She puts a few of the images in an envelope and hands it to us before exiting the room.

I assist Cari with wiping off the gooey substance on her abdomen and then help her sit up. "How fascinating it is to see our baby in the beginning phase."

"It's hard to make out much of the baby this early in the stage."

"I was able to make out the baby's head before the technician even pointed it out."

She looks at me disbelievingly. "You were able to make it out?"

"That's right." I had done a little homework on Google prior to today's visit, but she doesn't need to know that. I wanted to prepare myself for what I would be seeing. During one of the nights I was working late in the home office, I searched for images. The images of the fetus did raise my eyebrows but after just seeing our child on the monitor, I can say for sure it is the most beautiful image I have ever seen.

My phone rings as we walk out of the office. It's Catrina. I answer the call and hear the exasperation in her voice as she describes the situation at the office. There is a lady in the lobby of the building insisting she is my mother and needs to speak to me. *WTF?* Catrina told her I took the day off; however, Flora is insistent on seeing me and refuses to leave the building unless she has her way. *Fuck.* She always likes creating drama. I have no choice but to go in and get rid of her.

"What's the matter?" Cari asks as I end the call.

She cannot know. It will only induce stress and she doesn't need that now. "Something's come up at the office. I have to go back after I drop you off at home."

"Why drop me off? I'll go with you to the office. I have work I can finish up."

I shake my head. "You should go home and rest. Our baby had too much activity for one day."

She laughs. "The ultrasound was not too much activity."

I laugh with her because it does sound ridiculous, but I need to keep her home. "I don't know how long I will be, and I rather you be comfortable at home than at the office."

She stares at me like she knows I am keeping something from her. "Why don't you take me to Rodrigo's since it's a lot closer?"

Why didn't I think of that? "I'll drop you off there."

I help her into the car. When I get in on my side, she is on the phone with Rodrigo letting him know we're on our way.

She puts away her phone. "Are you hoping for a boy or a girl?"

I haven't given it much thought what I want. It will be great to have a girl, but it will also be great to have a boy. "It doesn't matter to me one way or the other as long as our child is healthy. What are you hoping for?"

"My hope is that this baby will make it to its birthdate."

I stroke her cheek with my finger. "This baby will make it." I'm worried too, but I will not let her see that I am.

I open my hand and she places her hand in mine. I refuse for her to be apprehensive about the baby. This baby needs us as much as we need him or her. I will always love Cari and do everything in my power to make sure she is surrounded by happy and positive things.

CHAPTER THIRTY-FIVE

DEVEN

My delightful day is cut short by the unwanted visitor in the lobby of my office building. I leave my Maserati parked in front of the building and storm inside towards the atrium. I spot her sitting across from the water wall, and I pick up my pace.

"What are you doing here?" I ask vehemently.

She tears her eyes away from her cell phone and looks up at me.

"Is that any way to greet your mother?"

My mother? "I sent you an email clearly letting you know that I no longer wanted anything to do with you."

"You left me with no choice this time. I had to see you. I am appalled that I am not invited to your wedding."

I glance around the atrium to make sure no one else is around us. It is not the place to have this discussion with her, and I certainly do not want to bring her up to the office I share with Cari. The last thing I need is to have her make a scene.

"I will not have this discussion here. We can go to the park and discuss this."

"The park?"

She's never really liked Central Park or any park for that matter. Parks are beneath her.

"Yes, *the park.*"

She looks down at her expensive designer shoes and lets out an annoyed sigh. "We'll go to the park then."

Well, isn't that something? She's actually going to go with me to the park in her designer shoes. I wait for her as she puts away her phone and pulls out a mirror to check her makeup. *For goodness sake, we are going to the park not a dinner party.*

"Shall we?" I ask extending my arm out to let her go first.

We leave the building without saying a word to each other. Walking alongside her, I lead the way into Central Park.

"Are you ever going to answer my question?"

"You didn't ask a question. You stated your feeling about not being invited to the wedding. That's evidently *not* a question."

"I am your mother and I deserve to be at your wedding."

She's infuriating me. "You have a damn nerve to say you deserve to be at my wedding. I made myself clear what you are to me."

"Don't be absurd. Your guests will notice I am not there. Do you really want people to talk and question why I was not invited?"

It's always all about her, and sadly, Kait carries herself in the same manner. *At least, there is hope for Kait.* She lives apart from her mother and is still young enough to change.

"No one is going to notice that you're not there. In fact, I know for certain that some people will be glad you won't be there."

"How can you be so callous?"

I am seething and look at her with incredulity. "*I'm callous?* You embarrassed Cari in front of a crowd after I had just buried my father. How would you describe what you did?"

"I was only defending you."

I stop in my tracks and turn to face her. "*Defend me?* I have never needed anyone to defend me especially not you."

"I did what I had to do for my son."

I strongly disagree with her. "No. You did what you had to do for you. You never even met her yet you not only passed judgment on her but you did so in front of onlookers. She was humiliated and didn't deserve that."

She should apologize for what she did to Cari, but she hasn't nor will she ever. Her pride and her ego will never let her.

"Perhaps she did not deserve that."

I don't believe what I am hearing. *Perhaps?* How can she not even acknowledge what she did to Cari was uncalled for?

"Is that the reason why I am not invited to the wedding?"

I take in a very deep breath to help maintain the little bit of calm I still possess at the moment. "No. That is not the reason."

The ring and vibration from my phone distracts me and I glance at it to see who is trying to reach me. Rodrigo's number pops up. I'm sure it has to do with the wedding which can wait until I am done with Flora. Cari is with him and will be of more help than I can be right now. I put my phone in silent mode.

"Does Leighton not want me there? She never liked me at all. Your father would have done the right thing. He would have wanted you to invite me to the wedding if he was still alive."

Coming to the park with her is a mistake. I should have had my security team escort her out of the building instead.

"Don't throw Leigh into this conversation. She has been there for me more than you ever have been. You should be thankful she took care of your own flesh and blood."

Her jaw tightens.

"Have you ever thought of anyone else's feelings besides your own? Having you at the wedding will stress not only Cari but quite a few other people as well. Your presence will make some people uncomfortable, and God forbid you start a war at my wedding. I want everyone to be happy and celebrate the day with us, and I can't see that happening if you're there."

"But I'm your mother."

Leigh is the one I call my mother. I am done with this drama. She came here with a mission and that was to have me reconsider allowing her to come to the wedding. She wants the world to know she's my biological mother. The biological mother who left my father and I. She's livid, and I think for the first time in her life, she isn't going to get what she wants. Dad would not have been pleased with the way I'm treating her, but he would have understood why I had to be this way. There is no point in continuing on with this conversation.

"Look, I have to head back."

"Does this mean I am still not invited?"

Ugh! "Yes, it still means you are not invited. There will be a heavy security presence at the wedding; therefore, if you show up uninvited, you will be turned away. In addition, you will no longer be permitted to step foot into my office building. My security team will escort you out if you ever do. And if you dare to defy my request, the NYPD will be called to remove you off my property."

"You can't do that!"

"Actually, I can and I will."

It's not my finest moment for sure, but I have no choice. She only wants to be my mother when it's convenient, and it will not shock me if she is the same way as a grandmother to my child. I start making my way back to the office leaving her standing alone in the park. *Goodbye, Flora.*

CHAPTER THIRTY-SIX

DEVEN

I immediately meet with my Director of Security Operations upon my return to the building. We review the surveillance to see the exact moment Flora entered the building. I instruct him that Flora is to never be allowed back in. If he and his team cannot follow these instructions, they will find themselves out of a job with my company.

I decide to go up to the office since I'm here. Fortunately, I am able to ride up solo in the elevator.

Catrina looks at me when I walk in. "I wasn't expecting you to come in."

"I'm not staying. Is Brad in his office?" I ask raking my hand through my hair.

"Yes."

I head to Brad's office. His door is open.

"Hey."

Brad pulls his concentration away from his monitor. A look of surprise reflects on his face.

"Hey. Thought you were taking the day off."

"I was until I got the call that Flora was here."

"What? What was she doing here?"

I sit down in the chair. "She wants to come to the wedding."

"Seriously?"

"I couldn't be more serious. She thinks people will notice if she's not there."

"Who is going to notice?"

"I don't know."

"You didn't agree to her demand, did you?"

"Of course not. I warned her not to show up in Newport. And she is not permitted into this building ever again."

"You think she will dare to challenge you?"

I shrug. "Can never tell with her, but I will have her removed if she does."

"It's not a good idea to have her anywhere near Cari. Does Cari know Flora was here?"

"No." I suddenly remember Rodrigo's attempt to reach me earlier. I take out my phone and see a dozen calls from him. *That's odd.* I call him back.

"Deven?"

"What's going on?"

"Cari is at the hospital."

Panic sets in and my heart rate jumps. "Is she okay?" My anxiety level is off the charts.

"She's fine and the baby is too."

"What happened?"

"We were just sitting there looking at the sonogram pictures and talking when she felt the urge to go to the bathroom. She came back white as a ghost and told me she was bleeding. It was so scary. We both felt like it was happening again, but thank God they're both fine."

I have to get to her and gather the rest of the information from Rodrigo. I inform Brad that Cari is at the hospital and he insists on going with me. We rush out of the office and get into my car. I weave my way through the city traffic to get to the hospital.

My eyes shift between the mirrors as I change lanes. "I have to make you aware of something, but you need to keep it to yourself."

"I will."

"Cari's pregnant."

"That's great. Congratulations. *Oh.*" Brad just put the pieces together. "You think the hemorrhaging is linked to the pregnancy?"

"Cannot help but think it. She lost the baby last time."

"Don't think the worst. Last time is not this time."

"I know, but the pregnancy is in its early stage."

"Everything will be fine. You'll see. I'm the baby's godfather. I know it will be." Brad really has a way to make the situation slightly better.

Once we are inside the hospital, we find our way to the emergency room. The receptionist has us take a seat first as no more than one person is allowed inside with the patient. I plead with her, but she is unyielding explaining the hospital has rules that must be adhered to. I send a text to Rodrigo explaining the hospital policy. After a few minutes, he finds us in the waiting area.

"How is she?" I ask with urgency.

"She's fine. The doctor came by again and confirmed everything is okay. You should go in and be with her. I think they're going to discharge her soon."

The receptionist allows me to go in. As I search for Cari, I hear a patient scream from what I presume to be excruciating pain. *I can't wait to take Cari out of here.* She's asleep on the gurney when I find her.

I lean over her. "Cari?"

She wakes up.

"Hi, angel."

"You're here."

"I am. How are you feeling?"

"Better now. Oh, Deven. I was so afraid when I saw…"

"Shh." I take her hand and kiss the top of it. "I know. All is well now. Rodrigo said you and the baby are fine. That's what matters."

She gives me a weak nod. "The doctor said it's not unusual to experience bleeding in the first trimester. They had to do an ultrasound to confirm the baby is okay."

"Rodrigo mentioned it. I'm going to take you home soon and you are to do nothing but rest."

"Okay."

I hear the scream again. *That's it.* I'm not waiting for the doctor to make his or her way back here in an hour or so. I tell Cari I will be right back and go to the nurse's station requesting to see the doctor so Cari can be discharged. The nurse pages the doctor and I return to Cari's side.

"Is everything okay at the office?"

There is no chance I will share with her the reason why I had to go back to the office after what she's just been through. "Yeah, it is."

"Why did you have to go there?"

"Just a security breach, but it's all taken care of. Nothing to worry about."

"If you say so."

"I do. Now, where is this damn doctor so you can get out of here?"

CHAPTER THIRTY-SEVEN

DEVEN

Some of us know exactly what we want to go to college for. Some of us change our majors halfway through college. And some of us graduate college and go down a completely different career path than originally intended.

From start to finish in college, I knew I wanted to join my father in the world of real estate development. I also knew I would have a place in his company. What I didn't factor into my future were two significant life changing events. One was losing my father so soon. And the other was the four letter word...*love*. Love was the furthest thing from my mind until fate brought Cari and I together. I was a goner immediately. She won me over and will forever have all of me. I have my girl, and we're going to have a baby. Everything is so right in my life.

With the wedding only a couple of days away, Cari and I will be making our way to Newport tonight. But first, we have to get through a long and busy day. We arrive at the office very early as I have a meeting scheduled for eight o'clock.

"Coffee?" Cari asks as I look through the files on my desk. She's been feeling much better since the trip to the hospital, and thankfully, there has been no recurrence.

"Yes, please." It's definitely going to be a long day. There are many projects that are waiting to begin, but nothing can happen until the contracts are signed and the monies are released.

"Okay. Be right back."

I look up briefly and stare at Cari's fine tight ass as she leaves the office. Just a couple of more days and she will officially become my wife. *I can't fucking wait.*

I'm absorbed in reviewing a file on a residential building in Stamford when Cari returns and leaves the cup of coffee on my desk. Under different circumstances, I would break away from my work and have her lean against the edge of my desk so I can have sex with her. My angel is going to become more voluptuous in the upcoming months. Thank God the doctor gave her clearance to resume sexual activity.

The thought of fucking her during this pregnancy is giving me a hard-on. *Not now.* A distraction is welcome right this minute to get my mind off of sex with Cari so I can plow through these contracts and then go to my meeting. I close my eyes and shake off all sexual thoughts. My swollen cock slowly wilts.

"Are you feeling okay?"

I smile at my beautiful soon-to-be-wife. "Yeah."

She returns my smile. The sexual energy will have to be reserved for our wedding night *if* I can hold out that long.

~ * ~

The plan tonight is for Cari to stay with me at the house. She will move to the hotel tomorrow night prior to the rehearsal dinner. My wish is to have her stay with me both nights. It would be great to wake up and make love to her on our wedding day. But she wants to keep the tradition of not being together on the eve of our wedding. *Who came up with such a ridiculous tradition anyway?*

Jordan left for Newport earlier in the day. He is staying at the same hotel where Cari will be staying tomorrow. What she doesn't know yet is that I booked the entire hotel for the weekend so her family can be with her. When I mentioned this to Max, it didn't go over too well with him. He was not pleased that I did not inform him ahead of time as he and his family had already made reservations elsewhere. It took him long enough to calm down and appreciate what I had done. *Of course, I did it for Cari.* Most brides are usually surrounded by her immediate family and bridesmaids on the morning of her wedding day. Cari should be able to have the same experience as well.

The one thing not coming with us tonight is her dress. She didn't want to take a chance of me sneaking a peek at it. *What's the big deal if I see it prior to the wedding? Stupid traditions.* The dress will travel with Rodrigo and Hunter tomorrow. No matter what her dress looks like, my Cari will be the most beautiful bride in the world.

On the way to Newport, we stop at our favorite barbeque restaurant in Stamford for dinner. It is essential that Cari does not miss any meals now that she is eating for two.

"I'm going to ask you again…are you *certain* you want to stay at the hotel instead of with me tomorrow night?"

She ordered a hearty meal of ribs, chicken, and brisket. I watch as she thoroughly enjoys her dinner. She licks her fingers after finishing the ribs. *Damn. I need my cock to stay down and not up.*

"It's bad luck to see each other right before the wedding."

"Says who?"

"Tradition dictates we be apart."

"If we were sticklers to traditions, we wouldn't be having premarital sex nor live together."

She tilts her head and gives me that radiant smile of hers. "We can abide by one tradition, can't we?"

I pout like a little kid because I really do want to wake up inside her on the morning of our big day.

"It's only for a few hours."

"More like half a day."

"I promise you it will be worth it."

"Okay. Well, I have a surprise for you."

"Oh?"

I nod.

"What is it?"

"The hotel you're going to be staying at is sold out."

"I know it is. It's been sold out for some time now."

"The reason why the hotel has been sold out is because I booked the entire hotel so your family can be with you on Saturday morning."

She stares back at me with her hand over her mouth. It takes a little while for the shock to wear off. "I don't know what to say. What an incredible and generous thing to do."

"Because I booked the entire hotel for the weekend?" It's not really a question.

"Yes, but also because you did it for me."

My girl knows me well. "You should be surrounded by your family."

"But everyone made reservations at other hotels."

"They already canceled their reservations about a month ago."

"I suppose you spoke to Max about this?"

"There was no other option. He had to be the one to inform your family."

"And he accepted your generous offer?"

I let out a chuckle. "He had no choice. He did want to pay for your room and for the rest of the family, but I refused. He wouldn't hear of it, so we compromised and he will pay for half of the bill."

"He didn't make mention of it to me about switching hotels."

"I requested he not mention it to you. I wanted to be the one to tell you."

"Wow." She gazes at me. "There's no one luckier in this world than me because I have you. Thank you for doing all of that."

I will do anything for her. It's simple…I love making her happy. She's dealt with more sadness in her life than she should have. Her father may not be on my list of favorite people, but Cari loves him and she's glad to have him in her life now. She deserves much love and joy, and it's my mission in life to make sure that happens.

CHAPTER THIRTY-EIGHT

CARI

Belle reserved the entire third floor at Deven's favorite restaurant in downtown Newport for our rehearsal dinner. Tonight will be a more intimate setting as only our family and a few family friends have been invited. Deven and I were told to arrive a half hour prior to the start time as Belle needs to review some final details with us.

It's a beautiful Friday evening, and Thames Street is crowded with locals and tourists. The hostess recognizes Deven and tells us we can go on upstairs. The first thing that grabs my attention when we reach the third floor is a large sign sitting on a wrought iron scrollwork easel welcoming everyone to our rehearsal dinner.

The rustic dining room has four long tables set up along one side of the room. Each table is outfitted with cream tablecloths and gold runners. Small hurricane lamps surrounded by gardenias, yellow roses and succulents run along the center of each table with a garland of eucalyptus leaves. I was expecting the room to be overwhelmed with baroque decorations, but the room is simple and understated.

"Hello, hello!" Belle rushes over to us and shakes Deven's hand first before shaking mine. "Good to see you both. I hope you like the arrangement. If there is anything you want me to change, I will have it taken care of right away."

Deven puts his hand on the small of my back, and we walk over to the tables to get a closer look.

"Do you like the arrangement?"

I peer up at him. "I love it. I thought it was going to be…"

"Opulent like the wedding?"

"Um, yes." My eyes dart back to the lovely table. "Everything about this wedding is grand, and tonight's rehearsal dinner is so simple…more intimate."

"As it should be." He kisses the hair on top of my head. "It's only our family here with us tonight."

"Which is a much more comfortable environment for me."

"I know it is. Look at me."

I gaze into his hypnotizing blue eyes. He cups my cheek with his hand. "I love you, and I can't wait to marry you tomorrow." He leans his forehead against mine and the tip of our noses touch. "Looking forward to you becoming Mrs. Deven Blake."

"Hmm. I love the way that sounds."

"As do I." He cocks his head slightly and his lips touch mine. At the same time, his cell phone rings.

Oh, what timing.

He pulls his phone out of his pocket to see who is trying to reach him. "Sorry, angel. I have to take this."

"Yeah. Of course."

"This is Deven," he answers and goes off towards the far end of the room.

I look around. A table with all the presents for our wedding party has been placed in the corner next to the fireplace. The click-clack sound from the heels against the hardwood floor can only mean Belle is coming towards me. She likes being in Deven's presence a lot more than being in mine, so why is she coming towards me? I have rarely had any interaction with her.

"I hope the ambiance and the décor are to your liking."

"Oh, it very much is."

"Deven wanted the tone of tonight's dinner to be more subdued."

What she doesn't know is this is my preference. There will be enough extravagance tomorrow to last a lifetime. All the lavishness is not my style at all, but this here tonight is better suited to me.

"It's just right."

"You're a very lucky lady. It's obvious he loves you very much. He will do anything for you."

And how does she know this? Did Deven say something to her or did Rodrigo? I don't feel compelled to say anything back to her and only give a nod in return.

"Everything will be perfect tomorrow. You and Deven will not be disappointed."

"We better not be." The sound of Deven's voice makes me jump. *How did I not hear him approach?*

"I have everything under control. Your wedding is going to be spectacular and will be the most talked about wedding for some time to come."

Belle is one of the best wedding planners in the country, and it's the reason why Deven hired her. She doesn't miss a beat. "Now let me go over a few things with you both," she says as she looks down at her clipboard.

~ * ~

This is a rehearsal dinner but there is no rehearsal tonight. For Deven and I, this is the time we get to spend with our family as it may be difficult to do so at the reception tomorrow night. Everyone arrives to dinner earlier than the indicated time on the invitation, and it is an opportunity for all of them to meet.

"Cari."

I spin around to see Deven with an Asian couple I don't recognize.

"I'd like to introduce you to Brad's parents. Mr. and Mrs. Wu, this is Cari."

We exchange greetings and handshakes.

"Deven has spoken so much about you," Mr. Wu tells me.

"You're so pretty." Mrs. Wu's comment makes my cheeks turn pink.

Mr. Wu slides his hands into his pant pockets. "Brad mentioned you're part Chinese."

"I am," I confirm. "My family is also here tonight."

"Oh. We'd like to meet them in a little while. We wanted to meet you first and thank you for inviting us here tonight and to the wedding."

Deven places his hand on Mr. Wu's shoulder. "Mr. Wu, it's not necessary to thank us. We're like family."

"Deven is right. We're very happy that you and Mrs. Wu are here."

"Deven told us you attended Boston University."

"Yes, I did."

"Do you miss Boston?"

"It's hard not to. There's a charm to that city, and it's so rich with history."

We get into a conversation about living in Boston versus living in New York. They're happy in Boston but also torn as they would like to be closer to Brad.

"Why don't we go introduce you now to her parents?" Deven suggests.

"Yes. We'd like that," Mrs. Wu says.

Deven and I search for Aimee and Max. We find my entire family clustered together on one side of the room. We make the introductions and they instantly hit it off. Deven and Max also exchange a few kind words. I feel optimistic that Deven may finally be coming around to liking Max.

Out of the corner of my eye, I see Kaitlin. I haven't seen her since Dalton's funeral. On the last trip to Los Angeles, I expressed to Deven that I would like for her and I to get along. It's time I make good on it. I don't want there to be any animosity between us. I tell Deven I want to speak to Kaitlyn and excuse myself. He looks at me quizzically as I leave him with my family and Brad's parents.

Kaitlin sees me coming towards her.

"It's good to see you again," I say to her.

"Yeah. Good to see you too."

"How have you been?"

"Good."

The two of us stand there as a cloud of silence hangs over us. *I thought I could do this, but the words seem to be lodged in my throat.*

"I have something I want to say," Kaitlin starts.

What could she possibly have to say? "Oh. Of course. Please, go ahead."

"I wanted to apologize to you when you and Deven came to L.A., but Deven said it wasn't the right time then. I want you to know that I'm really sorry for the trouble I've caused. I can see how much Deven adores you. You make him very happy, and I like seeing him that way."

I am taken aback by her apology. It's something I wasn't expecting to come from her.

"He makes me very happy as well."

"I see it. You two have the kind of love that makes other couples envious."

I don't know if that's true, but I hope she will someday experience such a love.

"I'm working hard to make things better…to make my life better."

Deven's made me aware she is making an effort to change. "I accept your apology, and I admire you for wanting to make the change. Just continue to stay on that path."

"I will. I promise."

Kaitlin and I spend a little more time talking and getting to know each other a little better before dinner is served.

There is no assigned seating tonight. My gregarious best friends are sitting at the next table entertaining our parents and siblings. Deven and I are at the table with a blend of some of our extended family. Deven's cousin, Madeline, chooses to sit next to me. I find her to be cheerful and friendly. Like everyone else in the family, she wants to know all the details about the proposal.

Madeline tells me about herself and her life in England as dinner is being served to us. Her eyes light up when her plate is set down in front of her. There is a two pound lobster on her plate. She thinks Deven deliberately had this as one of the choices on the menu because she loves it. That's not the reason, but I'll let her think it.

Madeline has not stopped talking throughout dinner. As we're enjoying our flambé dessert, she casually makes mention that she loathes Deven's biological mother and tells me how fortunate I am that I haven't met her yet. *If she only knew.*

Deven stands up with a wine glass in his hand. He clinks his fork against his glass to get everyone's attention. "May I have your attention please?"

The conversations in the room ceases as everyone gives him their undivided attention. Deven begins by thanking everyone for being here with us. He goes over briefly what will happen tomorrow after the ceremony. Then he shares our story about how we met and how he knew I was the one for him.

One of the many things that I love about Deven is the self-assurance he carries. It's an attribute I wish I had. He knows what he wants and goes after it with confidence and determination. And it's why he's as successful as he is.

Deven doesn't give up easily, and it's also why he has me. He knew from the beginning we belonged together. Even after I moved back to Boston, he was determined to win me back. I didn't think I could ever experience such sheer bliss, but I was wrong. Deven is everything a girl wants and more. And I'm the lucky girl who captured his heart.

~ * ~

The evening has come to an end. Rodrigo and Hunter remain with us after everyone has left. Belle and her assistant are packing up the table linens, lanterns, and the welcome sign at the entrance.

"Say good night to your bride-to-be," Rodrigo tells Deven.

Deven pulls me tight to him and kisses me. Hunter clears his throat.

"The queen needs sleep," Rodrigo says.

Deven reluctantly breaks the kiss. "Hmm. You're right. Cari does need to rest."

"I meant *me*," Rodrigo clarifies.

"Why don't you two head back to the hotel and I'll bring Cari back in a bit?"

"Absolutely not. You will end up bringing her back to your house. You're not supposed to see her until tomorrow afternoon."

"Too long."

I giggle at Deven's remark.

"You're coming with us, Cari."

"Come on, Rodrigo. Give me an hour with her."

Rodrigo cocks an eyebrow. "Not tonight. She remains a virgin tonight."

"What?!" Deven, Hunter, and I all say at once.

"No hanky panky tonight. Save it for tomorrow night."

"In case you forgot, she's not a virgin anymore," Deven reminds him in a low voice.

"She will be tonight."

I have to give in. The baby and I do need to get some sleep. "I really should go and get some rest. We have a busy day ahead of us tomorrow."

"I guess you do need to rest. I'll drive you back to the hotel then," offers Deven.

Rodrigo crosses his arms. "She'll come back to the hotel with us. You can drive yourself back to your house."

I place my palms on Deven's chest. "He's not going to let you have your way with me tonight."

"I can see that." He lets out a heavy sigh and then embraces me. "I love you, Miss Snow."

"This is the last night I will be Miss Snow."

"Okay. We love you both. Let's go, Cari." Rodrigo's patience has run out.

Deven releases me but takes hold of my hand. He lifts it and kisses it.

"See you tomorrow, Deven," Hunter says.

Rodrigo grabs my free hand and pulls me away. "Get some rest, Deven. We'll see you tomorrow."

CHAPTER THIRTY-NINE

CARI

Someone is calling my name and knocking on my door at the same time bringing me out of my peaceful sleep. *What time is it?* I look at the time on my phone. It's not even half past eight yet. There's only one person it can be. I get out of bed and open the door for Rodrigo.

"It's here. It's finally here. Today's the day!" By the sound of his voice one would think he's the bride. He is practically singing as he enters my room carrying a tray with two champagne glasses on it.

"Good morning."

"Good morning to you, señorita." He walks towards the window and puts the tray down on the table between the chairs.

I climb back onto the canopy bed. "Are those mimosas?"

He comes over with the two glasses which I take from him. He sits next to me on the bed. "Yes, but the virgin kind. Breakfast will be here shortly."

"What did you get baby and I for breakfast?"

"I ordered for you and the baby a hearty protein breakfast consisting of breakfast meats and eggs. You and the baby need as much energy as possible to make it through the day."

"Thank you. It will be a very long day. Gosh. This all feels like a dream. I'm marrying one of the world's most eligible bachelors."

"Not to mention one of the richest."

"I love *him*...not his money."

Rodrigo puts his arm around me and gives me a hug. "I know, but it's nice to know you will never have to worry about being poor either."

He's right about that. I put my head on his shoulder. "Thank you."

"For what?"

"For everything. You've always been there for me from the time we became friends. And during the melancholiest moments in my life after Grams and Gramps and the baby I lost…don't know what I would have done without your presence and constant love and support. There is no truer friend than you."

"And I will always be there for you. You're not only my best friend, but you're my sister too."

"Always."

"Don't make me cry with all this sweet stuff. Today belongs to you and Deven. A toast to you on this special day."

We both raise our glass.

"To a happy ever after. Love you."

"Love you too."

We clink the glasses and drink some of our orange juice. *Mmm*. The juice seems to quench a thirst I didn't even know I had, and I end up drinking the rest of it. It must be the baby.

"A little bit thirsty were you?"

"Yeah. I think it's the baby."

"The baby needs all the nourishment to keep growing. Would you like for me to get you more?"

"Nah. I have water."

There's another knock on the door and someone letting us know that our breakfast is here. It's time to eat and satisfy the baby's appetite first and then send birthday wishes to my soon-to-be husband.

CHAPTER FORTY

DEVEN

I barely slept last night eager for the day to move forward so that Cari and I can finally become husband and wife. I leave my bed and go out on the terrace. There is a slight chill in the air, but the sun is starting to rise. The seagulls are flying high, and the ocean is calm. It's going to be a marvelous day.

I lean back on the chaise, close my eyes, and reminisce about the first time I saw Cari. No one had ever grabbed my attention the way she did. It was an instant attraction, and the intense connection on the dance floor that night could be felt from afar. I never believed in love at first sight until I saw her. As our relationship evolved, I found myself falling deeper in love with her. She was so different from anyone I had ever dated. Everything I wanted in a partner I found in her. Our relationship is meant to be like she is meant for me. *She is my soulmate.*

The first time I made love to her is ingrained in my memory forever. She looked fucking delicious in the see through piece of fabric she had on. The memories of that night when I claimed her sexy pussy is getting me aroused. Slick, tight, and so damn perfect. Yes, that's exactly what she is - *perfect.*

I hear my name and open my eyes to see Brad standing over me. *Shit.* He probably notices my hard-on. I quickly draw my knees up to hide it.

"Good morning to you. Happy birthday."

Oh, yeah. It is my birthday. "Thanks. What time is it?"

"It's almost nine. What's the matter with your bed?"

I run my hands up and down my face. "I couldn't sleep and came out here." He can deduce the rest.

201

"Nerves? Cold feet?"

On second thought, perhaps he's *unable* to deduce the rest. "Neither. I'm just excited and can't wait to marry her today."

Brad seats himself across from me on the other chaise and stares out at the Atlantic Ocean.

"Can't believe you're getting hitched."

"Why not?"

"You must have forgotten how many different girls we had in college. I didn't think you would settle down so soon."

"I did not have half as many as you did."

"Maybe not, but then after Lilah, you just seemed to distrust women."

"Please don't bring her name up on my wedding day. She's in the past and I only want to focus on the future with my beautiful Cari."

"Sorry, bro. Hey, I'm glad you found someone you want to spend the rest of your life with. Cari is one fabulous lady."

"Yeah, she sure is, and I am going to devote the rest of my life to making her happy."

"She would have been mine had you not set eyes on her first."

"Fuck you, man."

Brad laughs. "And by year's end, you will be a daddy."

"Isn't it amazing? It's going to be a great year. Marriage, baby, company expansion."

"Yeah. Well, when I do get married, I think I'd wait a bit before having kids. I'd like to spend time with my wife first. Once we have kids, they will consume all of our time."

That's what *he* wants, but if May is the one he chooses, he better know what *she* wants.

"What if your plans don't turn out the way you want them to? What if you do end up having kids right away?"

Brad is quiet for a few seconds contemplating my questions. "Then I deal with it."

"There would be no other choice."

"Anyway, it's not about me today. It's about you. Your Mom wants to have breakfast before she and May get their hair and makeup done."

"I guess I should go on downstairs and let her make breakfast for us."

"She didn't cook."

"No?"

"She had it catered this morning. Special dual occasion."

"Well then, let's go down and celebrate."

"Good because my hunger can't wait."

CHAPTER FORTY-ONE

CARI

The past couple of hours have been nothing but a flurry of activity in my suite. The photographer kept taking pictures as the makeup artist and the hair dresser worked diligently on making me look glamorous. Everyone hired has a job to do, but the bedroom felt crowded. Eventually, I asked the photographer and the videographer to leave the room.

I stare at my reflection in the mirror completely stunned by the transformation. My hair is in an intricate loose braided updo with soft tendrils falling from the side creating a romantic look. And my makeup is perfect. I wanted neutral colors, but the makeup artist insisted on colors with a rosy tone. She said it would give me a radiant glow, and she's right.

I open the box containing my grandmother's earrings. I carefully take them out and put the beautiful earrings on. It adds a perfect touch to my look. *She would be so happy to see me wearing them today.*

The hairdresser and the makeup artist pack up their tools and leave the bedroom closing the door behind them. And now it's time to get my wedding dress on. I take off my robe and toss it on the bed. The first thing I must do before I slip into the dress is put the garter on. I sit down on the bed and put my foot through the garter pulling it high up on my thigh.

I take the dress off the hanger and step into it. The panels in the front are not loose at all, but I still prefer to have it taped to my breasts. I grab the double sided fashion tape sitting on top of the dresser. I meticulously place a piece of the tape on to secure one of the lace embroidered panels in place. *May this tape stay in place for the entire day.* I button up the dress and splay my hands on my swollen abdomen.

"Cari?"

"Come in."

Rodrigo enters and closes the door. He stops midstride. His jaw drops open and his hand goes over his heart.

"What's the matter?"

"Oh. My. God."

"What is it? Is the bump visible?" I fret it will be visible to others. I don't want anyone to suspect my condition. Deven and I agreed we will announce it to the family when we return from our honeymoon. Everyone else will know later.

"Your baby bump is not even noticeable."

"Really?"

Rodrigo nods. "Yes, really. *Damn girl!* You are the definition of sexy and exquisite!"

I feel heat rise to my cheeks. "Thank you. I hope Deven thinks so too."

"Deven is definitely going to have an erection when he sees you."

"Rodrigo."

"Cari, you always look beautiful. But today, you are really the most stunning bride ever."

I thank him and view myself in the full length mirror that is placed in the corner of the room.

"Your man may have a hard time keeping his penis in his pants until the end of the night."

"Rodrigo!"

"I may be gay, but I still know how a straight man thinks. Never ever forget that."

"Okay. I need to put double sided tape on to hold the other panel in place. After I am done, can you help me with hooking the cape onto the dress?"

"Of course," he says and reaches for the cape.

It takes only a few seconds to put the other piece of tape on. As Rodrigo hooks the left side of the cape onto the dress, there is a knock at the door.

"Who could that be?"

I shrug.

"Can you hold the other side of your cape so I can go see who it is?"

"Sure."

Rodrigo goes to answer the door and the videographer tells him someone is at the main door. Rodrigo shuts the bedroom door and returns with Max behind him. My father is quite fetching in a tuxedo.

"Wow! Cari, you look beautiful." My cheeks start to redden at my father's compliment. "Deven won't be able to take his eyes off of you."

"That's the plan. You may be a grandfather sooner than you think." Rodrigo gives my father a wink.

Why is he saying that to Max? "Rodrigo." I give him a warning stare.

"We never had the birds and the bees talk, but you're my adult daughter and I'm sure at this point in your life you know all about it."

"She sure does." Rodrigo realizes his slip and puts a couple of fingers on his lips to silence himself.

My cheeks are turning every shade of red possible. Max senses my discomfort and hugs me.

"Hold that pose." The photographer starts snapping pictures of my father and I. I cannot help rolling my eyes. *Who let him back in?*

My father pulls back and looks at me. "I missed so much in your life like your first steps and your first words. You've been so forgiving and accepting of me. Sometimes I feel like I don't deserve to be a part of your special day."

"You're my father. You do deserve to be a part of this."

"Thank you. It really is an honor."

"What happened in the past cannot be undone. We've been given an opportunity to reunite and I am very grateful for that. And I'm very happy you're here. I just wish Grams and Gramps could have been here today as well."

The sound of someone sniffling has me turn around to find Rodrigo with a tissue in his hand.

"Me too. They would have been beyond elated."

"Oh, Rodrigo." I go over to hug him fighting back my own tears. He loved my grandparents very much. "They may not physically be here, but spiritually they are."

"Yes, spiritually. If Grams was here, she would have been making a fuss over you."

"I hope I'm not interrupting anything." Hunter walks in and his hands fly to his cheeks. "Holy smokes! You are one gorgeous bride!"

I thank him and go to embrace him.

"Stand beside her so I can get a picture of the two of you," the photographer directs.

Hunter does as he's told and the photographer takes some pictures of us.

"I should get my heels on."

"I'll put them on your feet. Where are your shoes?" Rodrigo looks around the room.

I point to where I left the box yesterday. "Over in that corner."

He comes back over with the box and kneels down slipping a shoe on my right foot first. This is like the scene in Cinderella when she is trying on the glass slipper except I don't have glass slippers. I have a pair of peep toe lace Louboutin heels instead.

Hunter whistles. "Sexy lady in sexy Louboutins."

"And her man's wearing Louboutins as well," Rodrigo reveals.

"He is?" I ask.

"Oops!" Rodrigo realizes his blunder. "Guess he wanted it to be a surprise. I'm sorry to have ruined it."

Deven does own a few pairs of Louboutin shoes, but I am sure he bought a new pair for today.

"He wanted something to match you. A wedding dress was completely out of the question, so I thought maybe a pair of Christian Louboutin shoes would be adorable with the matching red soles." *I now know why he was insistent I purchase Louboutins. Leave it to Rodrigo to come up with an idea like that.*

Max nods his head. "What a good idea."

"Oh. I almost forgot." Hunter reaches inside his jacket pocket and pulls out a rectangular box. He hands it to me. "From Deven."

I open the box and my eyes nearly pop out of my socket. Inside the box lays a sparkling diamond and pearl tennis bracelet.

My father marvels at it. "Wow. That is some bracelet."

"It goes well with your earrings," Rodrigo says to me. Something tells me he might have had a hand in helping Deven pick out this gift for me.

"Deven spoils me."

Max looks over at me. "What's wrong with that?"

"You should be spoiled," Rodrigo says.

"Why don't I help you put it on?" Hunter offers.

I remove the bracelet from the box and give it to Hunter. He puts it on my left wrist. It's a little heavy, but it's an absolutely dazzling gift from the man I love the most.

CHAPTER FORTY-TWO

DEVEN

"Are you dressed yet?" May asks from the hallway.

"Just one minute," I respond back as I close the hook on my pants. I pad across to the other side of the room and open the door for my impatient sister.

"Look at you! You look so nice in your wedding tux."

"Thanks. And you look very pretty baby sis."

She rolls her eyes. "Stop calling me that. I'm not a baby. For you." She gives me a small box.

"You didn't have to get me a gift."

"I didn't. It's a gift from your beloved."

"Oh." I quickly tear off the wrapping revealing a box from Cartier. I open it to find a pair of white gold diamond cufflinks inside. "This is perfect. I can wear it today."

"I knew you would like it."

"I think it was my idea though." That's Brad and he's right. May never would have thought of cufflinks. "Cari was struggling with what to get you for a gift and asked me."

"It really is the perfect gift. Help me get them on."

"Sure thing."

I remove the first cufflink and hand it to Brad. I ask May where the photographer is as he should be in this room taking pictures of the cufflinks being put on. May leaves my room and shouts down to Leigh from the top of the steps.

"They're coming up."

"Thanks. By the way, that's a nice dress."

"Isn't this dress so pretty? Wait until you see Cari's dress."

"I can't wait. I'm looking forward to seeing her. Give me a hint of what it looks like."

"Nope. You'll just have to wait."

Leigh comes into the room with the photographer and the videographer in tow. She looks like she's about to burst into tears when she sees me in my wedding attire, and I haven't even finished putting everything on yet.

"It's just a tux," I tell her.

She smiles, but her eyes are glassy. "It's not just a tux. It's a special tuxedo on your special day, and you look so handsome. If only Dalton was alive and could see you. He'd be so happy for you and he'd be so proud of you."

He would have been. *I miss you, Dad.*

May looks up at me. "I think Dad is always with us."

"Always," Leigh concurs.

"I am happy and thankful you're all here with me today."

"I wouldn't have missed this for anything," May says. *Of course, she wouldn't.*

I turn my attention to the photographer and the videographer telling them I want them to capture the cufflinks being put on. Leigh and May back away so they can do so. Once the cufflinks are on, I get my bowtie around my neck making sure it is centered. Next on is the vest. My vest is black whereas the guys have a champagne color vest to match the color of May's dress. The photographer wants a picture of Brad and I standing together.

"Wait!" Leigh interrupts.

"What is it?" I ask with concern.

"You don't have your shoes on."

I look down. "No shot of the feet," I warn the photographer.

After a couple of pictures with Brad, I put on my shoes and my tuxedo jacket for more pictures with my best friend and my family out on the terrace. Then we head downstairs and outside to the backyard to take another set of pictures.

Brad looks at the time on his watch. "It's just about time to head on over. Are you ready?"

"I have been ready for a long time."

"Let's get married."

I give him a look.

"I meant let's get *you* married. Come on. The Rolls Royce limo is waiting for us."

CHAPTER FORTY-THREE

CARI

The final piece to my bridal ensemble is the veil. The veil I will be wearing has lace appliques on the edge and is sewn to a floral and pearl hair comb. I sit still as the hairdresser puts the comb into my hair. *In a little less than an hour, I will become Mrs. Deven Blake.* She's finished and I take one last look in the mirror when Rodrigo announces it is time to go. Hunter stands behind me holding up the bottom of my train and the delicate chapel length veil to prevent them from being damaged and filthy.

A couple of Belle's coordinators are at the hotel. One of them is in the suite with us, and the other one is downstairs in the lobby. The coordinator with us checks to make sure the corridor and the steps leading to the lobby are clear before I can leave the suite.

As I descend the staircase, I see my family in the lobby waiting with baited breath. Coming into full view, I hear the "oohs" and "aahs" and see multiple phone cameras aimed at me. I smile and wave to everyone as there is no time for hugging. The coordinator directs my family and I out to the lawn for pictures.

"Ladies and gentlemen, we are ready to take everyone over to The Breakers," the coordinator announces as soon as the photo session is finished. She leads me to the front of the hotel where a white horse drawn carriage is waiting. The outside of the carriage is beautifully adorned with bouquets of fresh flowers. I would have been fine if it was a pickup truck with bales of hay for me to sit on, but Deven wants to have a grand wedding. And money, of course, has not been an issue.

Rodrigo stands to the side of the carriage and helps me into it. Hunter hands me my train and veil once I'm settled and then steps aside to let Rodrigo get in. A crowd of onlookers start to gather outside the gates of the hotel.

Rodrigo seats himself next to me. "Ready?"

I look at the crowd and then at him. *This is it.* "Yes, I am."

He winks at me before the photographer and videographer climb aboard to take their seat across from us. Behind our carriage is another carriage for Hunter and my immediate family. Rodrigo's family, Jordan, and the photographer's assistants are in the Mercedes limo following the second carriage. The remaining Mercedes limousines are reserved for the rest of my family.

The gates open and one of the coordinators signals to the driver of our carriage to go. There are barricades set up along the route, and the police are outside the premises controlling foot and vehicular traffic. It's a little bumpy as the carriage pulls onto the road behind the police car escorting us to The Breakers. Riding in a carriage isn't as comfortable as I thought it would be. *How did people ride in these things a century ago?*

The tourists and locals stop to gawk at the ostentatious procession as the carriage travels down Bellevue Avenue. *I do not like this kind of attention.* Some of the onlookers cannot help but take pictures with their phones. I look down at my dress and start fiddling with the lace.

"Isn't this something?"

I peer up at my best friend. "I'm not used to attention like this. There are so many people staring at us."

"That's what they're supposed to do. And they're staring at the beautiful bride in this carriage. You should wave to them like the royal family does in England."

"Wave to them? I'm not royalty."

"Deven Blake is like royalty here in this country. After all, look at how extravagant this wedding is. Your wedding can rival a royal wedding."

Deven is very wealthy, but he is certainly not royalty in this country. Rodrigo waves to the crowd like he is a member of the royal family. I pull down his arm to stop him. I prefer not to have any more attention drawn to us.

It's hard to miss the heavy security presence a block away from the mansion. I admire the beautiful historic property as the carriage enters the grounds of the estate. Belle is waiting for us when the carriage stops under the porte cochère. She speaks into a headpiece giving orders. It's her show now.

The photographer and the videographer exit first to prepare to record the moment I step out of the carriage. Rodrigo gets out next and extends his hand to me. Placing my left hand in his, I cautiously step out. My train and veil fall to the ground and one of Belle's assistants runs up behind me to lift them off the ground. Belle directs the coachman to move the carriage forward to allow the second carriage and the limousines to pull under the porte cochère.

Another one of Belle's assistants rushes over to me and hands me my bouquet of white and blush pink roses. After the men have the boutonnieres affixed to their lapels and the ladies have on their corsages, we are led inside into the Great Hall.

"Whoa! This place is so cool!" I hear Harper say.

I look back to find my sister awed by the splendor of this former summer cottage. She's not the only one. Most of my family have the same reaction.

"Cari!"

I see my soon-to-be in-laws coming over. Leigh looks fabulous in a gold satin one shoulder dress with matching gold Louboutin pumps, but it's the large diamond chandelier earrings she has on that draws attention. *How many carats does she have on each ear?*

May is stunning in her dress, and her hair is styled in an updo with loose curls. Completing her look are her glittery Jimmy Choo heels. She made it very clear to me she wanted to have glittery shoes on and not "boring" fabric shoes.

"Can I have your attention please?" Belle raises her voice so that she has everyone's attention. "Those of you who are not part of the wedding party or with the photography and videography team must go outside and be seated. The rest of the group can stay right here."

There are ushers outside to take my family to the front where several rows have been reserved for them. Ken bends down and says something to Mandy. She stays close to May as Ken heads outside. Once the Great Hall is cleared of my family, Belle briefly goes over the processional order making sure to emphasize which side they need to be on when reaching the altar.

Belle takes us outside to the huge terrace where a large tent has been set up to keep us out of the sun. Belle circles Rodrigo and I to ensure everything is in place. If there is a wrinkle on our clothing she has a team ready to remove it.

Belle stands in front of me. "Cari, I have worked with many brides. All have been beautiful, but you are by far the most beautiful bride I have ever had."

Her compliment takes me by surprise and makes me blush. "Thank you, Belle."

"You're welcome." She turns to Max. "Now Max, you need to stand next to Leigh. Tisha will tell you when to go." She points to Tisha at the bottom of the steps.

"Will do." My father leans in and gives me a kiss on the cheek.

Leigh blows a kiss to me before she hooks her hand on my father's arm and walks with him down the steps to the lawn. Hunter, May, and Mandy are lined up and await their instructions to begin their walk to the altar. I can't see the altar from where I stand because huge plants have been placed on the terrace to obstruct the view. Belle fluffs my train and straightens it out.

"Are you ready sweetie?" Rodrigo asks.

Butterflies are fluttering around in my stomach. All eyes will be on me shortly. "What if I trip and fall? The baby?"

"Stop being a drama queen. That's my job. Relax. You won't fall."

"How can you be so sure?"

"You got this. You'll be fine."

I close my eyes and take in a deep breath. I release it slowly.

"You're both next. Remember to walk slow and have a huge smile on your face," Belle tells us.

Rodrigo offers me his arm. "Shall we?"

I nod and hook arms with Rodrigo. He carefully guides me down the steps. When I look up from the ground, I take notice of the transformation on the lawn. *It's breathtaking.* The combination of the expansive blue sky and vast ocean creates a picturesque scene. The aisle has a makeshift walkway installed under the runner preventing high heels from sinking into the grass. *Belle really does think of everything.* On each side of the aisle is a sea of guests, and at the end of the aisle is the altar. The altar is beautifully draped and decorated with flowers, and the ocean is its natural backdrop. *It is nothing short of magnificent.* Then my eyes hone in on a much more magnificent sight…the handsome man who is about to be my husband.

A slight tug to the back of my dress draws my attention away from Deven. Rodrigo leans in and whispers to me that Belle is obsessed with straightening my train and veil. Thankfully, it is the last time she will need to do so. She walks around us giving us one final inspection. The music changes and everyone stands. *It's time.* With one hand on Rodrigo's arm and the other holding my bouquet, we get ready to march down the aisle.

CHAPTER FORTY-FOUR

DEVEN

I am not allowed to see my bride before the ceremony. There is no "first look" for us. Both Belle and Rodrigo are determined to keep me from seeing her until the start of the ceremony. *Who made up such a ridiculous rule and why the fuck isn't it banned?*

Evelyn (one of Belle's staff) comes towards us. "The bride just arrived. The groom and the best man will follow me to the other waiting area."

May comes over and hugs me. "See you at the altar."

Leigh gives me a cheek to cheek kiss. "I'm so happy for you."

"Thank you."

I turn to Ken and we exchange a bro hug. "Not everyone can find someone as special as Cari. She's a keeper."

"Oh, I know. I'm never letting her go." I kneel down to Mandy. "You're going to do great out there. Just walk down to me when you are outside, okay?" She gives me a nod.

The four of them walk over to the other part of the massive foyer. Instead of following Evelyn, I take a few steps to the other side.

"Don't even think about it," Brad warns as he places his hand on my shoulder to keep me from wandering off.

"Think about what?"

"You want to see Cari."

"Damn right I do."

"Don't ruin it. You'll see her in a few. Come on."

Why can't he understand how badly I want to see her? I follow Brad to the Loggia where Evelyn is waiting. I look out as far as I can onto the lawn. Every seat is filled with the exception of the rows reserved for Cari's family. The photographer suggests we take more pictures. I don't want to take any more pictures right now but agree to it only to kill some time.

The priest arrives and we speak briefly. Evelyn receives word from Belle that it's time to start the ceremony. I turn my attention to the lawn again and see Owen taking his seat. Evelyn guides us outside to the terrace to begin the journey to the altar. At last.

The harpist and the pianist transition from the piece they had been playing to the overplayed musical piece at most weddings. I wanted something different, but Cari happens to love Pachelbel's "Canon in D Major." She very much wanted this selection to be played during the processional. It wasn't worth arguing over, and I let her have her way.

The priest begins the walk to the altar. Evelyn holds me back until the priest gets there and turns around. Then she gives me the go-ahead. I keep my hands to my side and smile as I walk past the guests down the very long aisle. *All I can think of right now is that I will get to see Cari soon. It's only a matter of minutes.* I reach the altar and turn to watch Brad stroll down waving to some of the guests along the way. He gives me a nod and a smile and takes his place by my side.

Leigh and Max are now coming towards us. She looks remarkable and I know Dad would agree with me if he was here today. She is such a gracious lady and a wonderful mother to both May and I. Max gives me a nod and I respectfully nod back. Leigh blows me a kiss before her and Max part to take their seats.

May has her hand on the crook of Hunter's arm as they make their way down together. When they reach the finish line, Hunter gives me a thumbs up and May winks at me before they both take their place on the other side.

The music continues to play, but Mandy hasn't appeared. I look at Ken and he shrugs his shoulders. As I turn my attention back to the aisle, there's a chorus of "aahs." Cute and coy Mandy is randomly sprinkling white and pink rose petals on the runner. It's a long walk for her and she doesn't seem to be smiling much. It must be intimidating for her with all the guests looking on. When she's a couple of feet away from me, I bend down and put my arms out. She runs into my arms and I hold her.

"I'm so proud of you. You did good," I whisper to her. I release her and point to Ken. She happily runs over to him.

I stand back up as the musicians begin to play the selected piece chosen for Cari's walk down the aisle. She didn't want the traditional "Here Comes the Bride." After listening to many songs over *many* days, she finally decided on the song "Let It Be Me."

The priest requests everyone rise from their seats. My heart starts to pound as I wait with anticipation for my beautiful bride to appear. Most of the guests have their cameras in the air ready to take pictures of her.

Oh my God. I feel as if the air has been sucked out of me. There she is, resplendent in her wedding dress with the most captivating smile on her face. I had no idea what her dress looked like, but I had thought it would be more conservative. The dress she is wearing clings well to her showing off her perfect figure. And that deep neckline is very alluring. *Cari is the sexiest bride on this planet.* The urge to run up the aisle, take her in my arms, and kiss her madly crosses my mind.

"Do remember to breathe," Brad reminds me as my eyes are glued on Cari.

My heart is overflowing with love for my angel. Her grin is as big as mine the instant she sees me. She walks down gracefully on the arm of Rodrigo as everyone takes pictures of her. I want to tell her how gorgeous she looks when she stops at the altar, but I'm incapable of speaking.

She turns and gives her bouquet to May. Then she turns back to Rodrigo and they exchange a cheek to cheek kiss. He smiles at her and takes her hand to place it in mine. I close my hand around hers. He gives me a nod and goes to his seat. Cari and I turn to face the priest.

Everything is perfect…right here, right now. The infinite sky is as blue as can be. The sun is beaming brightly. My gorgeous bride is by my side. And we are amongst our loving family and friends as they witness our union.

The priest begins the ceremony with a greeting. With this being an interfaith marriage, we had to compromise on what to include in the ceremony. The priest follows with prayers, scripture readings, and The Homily. I have the urge to tell him to speed things up. It seems like he is never going to get to the good part.

At last, the time has come to exchange rings. Brad pulls out the pouch containing our rings and gives me Cari's ring first. I take her left hand. Her engagement ring has been temporarily moved to her other hand so I can slide the wedding band on. The priest instructs me to repeat after him.

"Cari, I give you this ring as a sign of my faithful devotion. I will always love you, cherish you, and honor the vows promised to each other." I slide the diamond band onto her finger. She looks up at me with those beautiful jade eyes of hers. *How I adore her.*

Brad then hands my ring to Cari.

She takes my left hand and stares lovingly into my eyes. "Deven, I give you this ring as a sign of my faithful devotion. I will always love you, cherish you, and honor the vows promised to each other." Those words will be etched into my brain for as long as I live. She places the platinum ring on my finger.

I glance down at my left hand. *She's officially mine, and I'm officially hers.* And it feels amazing to have this ring on my finger as a symbol of Cari's love for me.

The priest says a final prayer. *Amen.* Cari and I both cannot contain the wide smiles on our faces as the priest finally pronounces us husband and wife. I wait no longer and draw her into my arms placing my lips on her heavenly lips. The kiss is not rushed. The applause and cheers force us to pull apart and smile at each other before facing the guests.

"Ready, Mrs. Blake?"

"Ready, Mr. Blake."

Cari signals to May for her bouquet. Clasping my hand with hers, we walk back up the aisle together as husband and wife.

CHAPTER FORTY-FIVE

CARI

The luxury buses are lined up in front of the mansion ready to shuttle our guests over to The Marble House for the cocktail hour. In the meantime, Belle gives us a strict schedule we have to adhere to for pictures and the tea ceremony. According to her agenda, we are due at The Elms before the guests arrive for the dinner reception which doesn't leave us with much time.

As Belle's team coordinates the bus loading, our immediate families and wedding party stay behind for pictures. One of the coordinators directs them into the ornate dining room where Deven and I have already been posing for many pictures. There are a lot of congratulations and hugging going around, and the photographer patiently lets us finish before we have to move along.

After pictures at The Breakers and along the Cliff Walk are over with, we are all ushered into limousines and taken to The Marble House. The Chinese Tea House and part of the mansion grounds have been blocked off and hidden from the guests for privacy while the traditional tea ceremony takes place. Belle had forewarned Deven and I that everyone could not be accommodated inside the tea house due to its size. We discussed this with Aimee and Max and devised a plan.

Custom requires the bride and groom to dress in the traditional Chinese garb for this ceremony, but it isn't possible with the time constraint. My grandparents go inside first as they are the matriarch and patriarch of the Lew family. Deven and I kneel down on the pillows placed in front of them as Aunt Lisa pours tea into the teacups on the tray. Aimee purchased a Chinese teapot set exclusively for this ceremony and carries the tray over to Deven and I.

I give my grandmother her cup of tea, and Deven gives my grandfather his cup. They take a sip of their tea, put the cups back on the tray, and they each hand Deven and I a red envelope. The red envelopes (also known as "lai see") contain a gift which is usually money. Deven and I had requested donations be made to our chosen charity in lieu of gifts; however, Max told us to accept the gift as it is customary to do so, and in turn we can donate the money to the charity.

Aimee and Max sit down next. Deven and I repeat the same procedure with the tea and receiving the red envelopes. This goes on a few more times with my aunts and uncles and even Leigh. Aimee and Max wanted Leigh to partake in this tradition as well.

We depart as soon as the tea ceremony is finished and arrive at The Elms as scheduled. There is a short window of time before the guests are shuttled here for the real party. My eyes sweep over the lawn. *Wow!* The expansive lawn behind the mansion has been completely altered to accommodate our wedding reception. The photographer leads the way to the sunken gardens, but Deven and I break away from the family to look inside the tent.

A huge clear structured tent has been built to contain the noise inside. Chandeliers and track lighting are suspended from the ceiling, and carpeted flooring has been laid down to blanket the ground. Inside the tent is a separate room where the Venetian Hour is to be held. The caterers are stationed in a blocked off outdoor kitchen erected exclusively for their use. There is a wide path which provides direct access between the kitchen and the tent for efficient service. But the most conspicuous things of all are the trailers surrounding the back of the tent. These are the luxury air-conditioned restroom trailers that Deven insisted on renting. Each trailer will have an attendant in each cabin to maintain its cleanliness and replenish supplies as needed. *Money really has no boundaries for this wedding.*

Belle and her team have done a phenomenal job coalescing The Gilded Age with the present. The beautifully decorated tables are reminiscent of a bygone era. They are dressed with antique white satin tablecloths and a gold lace overlay. The matching satin covered chairs have a lace bow chair sash and an antique pearl brooch pinned in the center of the bow. Each place setting has a set of delicate gold pattern plates adorned with a gold trim around the edge, and there's gold baroque flatware. But the one item on each table that's sure to grab everyone's attention is a tall chandelier centerpiece with an oversized floral arrangement of blush and ivory roses atop and strands of crystals dripping underneath. The entire set up creates quite an impression.

A huge LED dance floor occupies the center of the tent. The live band is on one side of it, and the DJ is on the other. *Deven was firm on having both a band and a DJ.* There are two large HDTV's near the dance floor and a few others placed around the tent. Three separate bars are located in the corners. And towards the back are the photo and video booths. We start to make our way there when one of the coordinators somehow tracks us down and tells us we need to be in the garden for pictures. Deven and I are exhausted from all the pictures we've taken today. We vacillate about going back outside, and finally decide to rejoin the group hoping this last photo session will not take long.

When we are at long last done with the outdoor photograph session, we head back to the mansion and gather in the dining room. Belle and her team are waiting for us along with my hairdresser and makeup artist. Belle arranged to have a table set up with finger foods and a couple of bar carts with glasses of champagne and a variety of soft drinks for us since we missed the cocktail reception.

Belle and the makeup artist go around the room giving our parents and the wedding party a quick facial refresh prior to the grand entrance. The coordinator comes over to me and takes away my bouquet. The pregnancy and the day seem to be catching up to me making me feel woozy. I grip Deven's arm.

His smile fades as a look of alarm appears on his face. He leans in and whispers, "What's wrong?"

I take a couple of breaths. "I'm feeling a bit dizzy."

He leads me to one of the chairs. "Sit down while I get you a bottle of water."

I nod and take a seat.

Rodrigo rushes to my side. "What's the matter, sweetie?" His voice is filled with concern.

"Dizzy. Deven went to get a bottle of water for me."

"How about I get you something to eat? I can ask Belle to have someone bring in a bread basket for you."

"Nah. I don't want to draw attention. I'll stick to the water. It could be dehydration causing me to feel this way."

"Possibly, but do promise me you will make time to eat tonight. Nourishment is important." He gives me a knowing look.

"Promise."

My hairdresser comes over to me and removes my hair comb and veil. She inserts the vintage gold and pearl hair comb in its place and gives the veil to the coordinator to pack away.

Deven hurries back with a bottle of sparkling water. I gratefully take the bottle and guzzle down the water in record time.

Deven's eyes are wide. "You were definitely parched."

I glance down at the empty bottle in my hand. "Yes, I think we were." I lift my head to look at him.

He kisses my cheek. I remember my cape has to be removed. I ask Deven and Rodrigo for help, and they gently unhook the cape from each side of the dress. Rodrigo takes the cape and goes to give it to the same coordinator who took my veil.

Deven rubs his hand on the back of his neck. "Wow."

"What is it?"

"I had no idea how much of your back is exposed. You're so sexy. This dress on you..." His voice fades and he's struggling for words. I reckon it's because he's aroused.

"Quiet please. I need everyone's attention," Belle says raising her voice above the noise. "We are about ready to introduce our bride and groom. Anyone who is *not* part of the grand entrance must go outside now and take their seats."

The coordinator returns the bouquet to me. Belle instructs everyone to line up in the order they are to enter. The first of our squad to be introduced will be our parents. Max will be flanked by Aimee and Leigh. Following them are my sisters, Rodrigo's parents, Rodrigo and Hunter, and May and Brad.

Mandy and Ken will precede Deven and I.

We follow Belle out to the terrace and then down the steps to the lawn where we wait. The music is blaring, and the emcee tells our guests to clap their hands as he is about to make the introductions. The DJ plays "Handclap" for their entrance, and the guests elevate the noise level with cheering and clapping as our squad is being presented.

Deven and I wait for Belle to let us know when we can make our entrance. The song playing now is Guy Sebastian's "Who's That Girl." This was the song we danced to that night at Club XTC.

Belle speaks to her coordinator through her headset and then faces us. "Get ready."

Cheering and applause erupt again when the emcee presents us as Mr. and Mrs. Deven Blake. Deven pumps his fist in the air as we walk in. A ton of flashes go off as we make our way towards the lighted dance floor where our family forms an arch for us to cross under. They clap their hands after we make it to the other end, and Deven playfully takes a bow. The emcee announces we will have our first dance.

Deven puts out his hand. "May I have this dance, Mrs. Blake?"

I love hearing my married surname. I smile at my hot husband. "You may, Mr. Blake."

I place my hand in his. Lifting my hand to his lips, he kisses it just as the band starts to play "I Knew I Loved You." He brings our clasped hands to his heart and places his other hand on the small of my back. His eyes pierce mine as he pulls me closer to him, and we move to the music.

This is heaven…just the three of us. *It's our circle of love.* Deven dips his head and kisses me affectionately. The sounds of clapping and whistling break our kiss and I blush.

"I can't kiss you like that again with all of them looking on. My cock wants to come out and play. Can't pull away from you so stay very close to me for a little while longer."

I nod and lean into him pressing my cheek against his as we continue dancing. He hums softly into my ear and as he does, the emcee invites everyone to join us on the dance floor.

CHAPTER FORTY-SIX

DEVEN

Cari decided to omit the father-daughter dance. She thought it would be more fitting to have a dance with Rodrigo instead which had my full support. *Rodrigo deserves a dance more than Max does.* Let's face it. Rodrigo has been an extremely important person in her life. He's been there for her more than her father ever has been. The connection between Cari and Rodrigo will never be broken.

For the mother-son dance, I selected the song "There You'll Be" dedicating it to both Leigh and my father. There are some children who cannot accept having a stepparent, but I certainly wasn't one of those kids. When my father met Leigh, I saw a different kind of happiness in him. It was a happiness only a partner can give. Seeing my father that way brought me great joy. I accepted Leigh with an open heart and she always treated me like I was her own biological son.

I escort her to the center of the dance floor. The flashes on the cameras go off nonstop. She's fighting back tears as we dance, and I try to make her laugh instead. May comes onto the dance floor to join us and the three of us sway to the song together.

What Leigh doesn't know yet is that I wrote a note thanking her for all she has done for me but most importantly, for being my mother. She'll find the note along with a small gift to remind her of what she means to me when she returns to Connecticut.

After our dance, it's time to get this party started. The DJ pumps up the music for the dancing crowd and invites everyone to come back onto the dance floor.

The evening is full of love, bliss, and boundless energy. Everyone appears to be enjoying themselves whether they're dancing, at the photo and video booths, interacting with the celebrities and the uber-rich, or eating and drinking. Cari and I have been going around talking to everyone. We feel blessed and happy to have so many of our family and friends here to share this special occasion with us.

As the catering team work on clearing the tables and setting up for dessert, the man of honor is called upon to make the first speech. Rodrigo strides to the dance floor and takes the microphone from the emcee. Without looking at a piece of paper, he begins to speak. He starts with a brief montage video of him and Cari together. He then speaks sweetly of Cari, how they met and how their friendship blossomed. He also recalls the moment he and Hunter first saw her with me…something she has never mentioned. *I'm going to have to inquire about that later.* When he is done with his speech, he has everyone raise their glass for a toast.

Afterwards, Brad gets up. *Yep, it's his turn to make a speech.* He has a piece of paper in his hand and I can't wait to listen to what he wrote. Unlike Rodrigo, Brad does not open with a montage of us. *Thank heavens.* He starts by joking if everyone knows who I am, and there's a roar of laughter. Then he reveals it's my birthday. *Thanks, Brad.* The band begins to play "Happy Birthday" and everyone joins him in singing to me including my Cari.

Birthday song and wishes done with, he continues on with his speech recounting our college years together and then admitting he didn't think I would marry so soon. He thought the two of us would be bachelors for a very long time making everyone in the room chuckle. He tugs at my heartstrings when he mentions my father and shares some of the memories the three of us had at BG. My father always treated Brad like a son. I attempt not to get choked up. Cari seems to sense my emotion and reaches for my hand. He wraps up his speech by saying a few wonderful things about me and then Cari making her cheeks turn slightly pink. *She's still not used to receiving compliments, but she's adorable when she blushes.* Like Rodrigo, he too asks everyone to raise their glass for a toast. Brad's speech was really perfect. It was short, funny, and heartfelt too.

~ * ~

The cake has been rolled out onto the dance floor. Belle directs Cari and I to stand next to it for the photo op first. *Great. More pictures.* All the flashes going off are starting to make me see spots and give me a headache. Belle then has me stand behind Cari to cut the cake. Cari picks up the cake knife and I place my hands over hers. We cut a slice of it and put it on the plate. Following tradition, we feed each other a small piece of the cake. The cake is then whisked away to be cut and served to our guests, but Belle has us remain where we are.

Belle hands to Cari her throwaway bouquet as the emcee calls all the single ladies up to the dance floor for the bouquet toss. My sister, of course, is one of the first to run up. Cari laughs while I shake my head knowing Brad will not be the first to run up when I throw the garter. What is shocking to me is the sight of cousin Maddie and Leigh approaching the dance floor. I'm not sure I am ready to entertain the thought of Leigh getting remarried yet.

On the count of three, Cari tosses the bouquet. Someone catches it and the floor clears. Rylee offers an awkward smile with the bouquet in her hands. I imagine Max must be less than thrilled about this.

A chair is brought to the middle of the floor for Cari to sit on. May, Hunter, and Rodrigo circle me. Hunter passes a piece of cloth to May.

"What's that?" I ask May.

She folds the cloth. "A blindfold."

WTF? I'm being blindfolded?

Rodrigo pulls out another piece of cloth.

"And what's that for?"

"To tie your hands. Surely, you didn't think this was going to be easy, did you?"

They're challenging me? Well, I'll show them how easily I can get the garter with my eyes blindfolded and hands tied.

May tells me to get on my knees and then covers my eyes with the blindfold while Rodrigo works on tying my hands behind my back. I can't see a damn thing, but I can hear the guys whistling and cheering me on. *That's right. I got this.* The best way to do this is to rely on my nose. I lean forward and the tip of my nose taps something hard like a bone or maybe her knee. There's laughter.

"You need to go under my dress," Cari whispers to me.

Yes, I will definitely do so. I feel something go over my head. It must be her dress meaning no one can see where my mouth is. *I like this game.* I glide my nose up one of her legs. The tip of my nose feels something. It's the garter. Since I can't see exactly how far away I am from her delectable pussy, I tease her by licking around the garter. Her leg twitches from the sensation. *Excellent.* Gripping the garter with my teeth, I slowly drag it down her leg. I emerge with the garter in my mouth. My hands are untied and the blindfold is removed. I look at my gorgeous bride and her face is fire engine red. I give her a chaste kiss and stand up.

The single guys come onto the dance floor, and Brad is in no hurry to join them. *I knew it.* I wave the garter in the air earning loud roars from the guys. Turning my back to them, I count to five before tossing the flimsy thing. I swivel around to see who caught the garter, and it's Brayden! Max doesn't seem too happy an older guy caught the garter that will be placed on Rylee's leg. Meanwhile, Brad looks relieved and I know it's because he's not ready to make a permanent commitment. Will he ever be ready?

~ * ~

The Venetian Hour opens to our guests signaling the night is winding down. An hour and a half later, the emcee announces the final dance of the evening. The guests (some drunk and some not) flock to the dance floor one last time. Everyone is dancing and singing along to "Livin' On A Prayer" which also happens to be one of my favorite songs. Cari and I join the dance crowd as this special day comes to an end.

CHAPTER FORTY-SEVEN

DEVEN

It's official. We're married. She belongs to me forever. After a very long day, Cari and I return to the hotel together. With her hand in mine, we stroll up to the gated private entrance which leads to our room. As tradition calls, I sweep her up in my arms and carry her over the threshold. Once we're inside, I set her down on her feet gently. She gasps when she sees the canopy bed decorated with two interlocking hearts made of fresh red rose petals. At the foot of the bed is a table with a bottle of champagne chilling in a bucket and two glasses.

"How beautiful," she reacts to the hearts.

"I disagree. You're much more beautiful."

I turn her to face me and lay my hand on her cheek. She circles her arms around my neck, and our mouths collide with urgency. I have been aching all day for her, and now I finally have her to myself. My cock is not being shy at all as my hands figure out how her dress comes off. Sensing I am encountering trouble with this, she pulls away from our kiss to remove what looks to be tape off of her breasts before unbuttoning her dress. Sliding her arms out of the dress, it falls to the floor. *Sweet Jesus. She has no panties on.* She smiles at me with lascivious intent.

I swiftly lose my tux and boxers as I gaze at the stunning naked beauty in front of me. My cock thanks me for freeing it from the confinement it was in. Looking at my stiff cock, Cari licks her upper lip with her tongue. *Holy fuck. That is so hot.*

My desire for her leaves me no choice but to throw back the covers ruining the rose petal hearts in the process. I lift Cari off the ground and sit her down on the bed. She lies on her back and spreads her legs. *Oh, good girl. I love my exclusive access to her.* Standing at the edge of the bed, I stare hungrily at her delicate and glistening pussy. *Mine forever and ever.*

I dip my head between her thighs and drag my tongue up and down and across her bare snatch. *She's so damn wet.* I suck on her delicate folds savoring her juices. *Mmm. I love eating her pussy.*

"Oh, Deven," she calls my name as her body writhes.

"Hmm?" It comes out like a hum as I am consumed with lapping at her pussy.

"Need. You. Inside." Her breathing is ragged.

Oh, her wish is my command. I withdraw my mouth and join her in bed. I lie down beside her and roll her onto me. She lowers her head and caresses my lips with her tongue. *Damn.* I lift my head slightly and crush my mouth to hers. *She's intoxicating.* When our lips finally part from the passionate kiss, she sits up and locks my thighs in place with her knees. *She's so fucking sexy. I want to mouth fuck her and fuck her pussy at the same time.* The tightness of her pussy drives me wild as she sinks over my rigid cock. She reaches out for my hands and holds them as she rides me. I watch her tits bounce as she moves up and down on me, riding me like a pro.

I have the need to burst inside her right now. *I'm so close to doing so.* Pulling her down to me and holding her tightly, I roll us over so I am on top of her. I am careful not to press my entire body on her and shift my weight onto my elbows instead.

The moonlight shines through the glass terrace doors providing some light. I make out my angel's face. Dipping my head, I kiss her softly and lovingly this time as she runs her fingers up and down my back. Then I slither down to her tits and suck on them, one at a time while my fingers simultaneously rub her erogenous zone. *Fuck. She's practically dripping wet and it makes me want to devour her pussy again.* She grips the sheets as her body squirms from pleasure. *I love her reaction.*

After I have my fill of her tits, I push deep inside her and keep my dick buried there. A few drops of my cum seep into her. I pull my dick out and slam back into her warm pussy loving the sound of her whimpering as I do. I torment her by pushing the tip of my cock in and out of her entrance, but

I'm also tormenting myself. It's difficult to refrain from exploding inside her.

Her hands frame my face holding it in place so she can look deep into my eyes. "I love you so much, Deven."

"I love you so much more, Cari. Always will." My love for her is unfathomable.

I need her now. My entire body and cock are rock hard as I pound into her. *Her pussy is so accommodating.* I plunge deep into her and can no longer hold back. *Boom!* I burst and there it goes…all of my semen flowing into her. I am confident I would have impregnated her tonight had I not already planted my seed in her. We both gasp for air. My arms feel like jelly and can barely hold me up as I wait for my dick to go limp.

I roll myself off of her and draw her close to me. Our bodies are damp with our blended sweat. *She smells good.* I fucking love the scent of her after we have sex. *Sex with her will always be over the moon.* We lay together in silence. The combination of the lack of sleep, the busy day, the booze, and the earth shattering sex with my wife have all finally gotten to me. Sleep wins.

CHAPTER FORTY-EIGHT

DEVEN

A cool light breeze brings me out of my slumber. *Why is there a breeze coming into the room when the windows and doors are closed?* I roll over to my side and open my eyes to find the bed empty. I notice the door is open. Getting out of bed, I go to search for Cari.

I stop under the doorframe when I see the back of her, and I suck in my breath. I gawk at my extremely sexy wife as she stands outside on the terrace in a short white robe gazing into the night sky illuminated by the moon. I quietly step back into the room to get my phone. Turning off the flash, I take a couple of pictures. This image of her will be embedded in my mind as long as it never deteriorates but should I fall into the hands of Alzheimer's like my father did, there will always be this picture from our first night as a married couple.

Carilyn Jade Blake is my wife. I love knowing she is *at last* my wife. "You are indeed a dream come true, Mrs. Blake."

She turns around and licks her lips at the sight of my nakedness and obvious erection. *Like what you see don't you, baby?* I bet she's blushing. She comes towards me, tugs me to her, and kisses me. My hands reach under her robe and cup her smooth ass.

She kisses my face. I really like when she takes control. She stops and steps back. Reaching for the belt on her robe, she unties it, and takes off the robe. *Fuck me.* She takes my hand and guides me back inside.

There is one temptation that I will never be able to resist and that's Cari. She has me take a seat in one of the chairs facing the fireplace and goes to turn the fireplace on. *How ironic as I don't feel cold at all.* She comes back and

233

kneels down in front of me spreading my legs apart. *Ooh. Is she going to do what I think?* She squeezes my balls and takes my hard cock in her mouth. I gasp. *What a fucking amazing feeling. Why has she never performed oral sex on me before? Please don't stop.* She gives good head, and she needs to suck on my cock a lot more. *This is not going to be a one-time experience.*

I watch as her head moves up and down on my dick while her mouth and tongue expertly lubricates it. *It's so erotic.* I relish this intimate connection. I want to very much come in her mouth so she can taste it, but she's pregnant. *Ugh!* I throw my head back and close my eyes. *Exercise control, Blake.* Opening my eyes, I stare at the ceiling attempting to control the urge.

Her mouth releases my cock and I look down to find her peering up at me. "Does it not feel good to you?"

How can she even ask that? "Oh, angel. Never second guess anything you do to me. That was so fucking amazing. It felt so damn incredible. I don't know why you stopped."

"I'm not sure what else to do. I've never done this before."

My angel needs to feel much more confident about her sexual skills, and I will make sure she does.

"You could have fooled me. Come here."

She sits on my lap resting her head on my shoulder and snuggles up to me. I wrap my arms around her. She yawns and I realize how much more tired she must be now that she is carrying our child.

"It's been quite a day."

"Hmm…" Her response is faint.

I will not jeopardize her or the baby's health. "Let's get some sleep."

She nods. I lift her in my arms and carry her back to bed.

CHAPTER FORTY-NINE

DEVEN

After brunch with the family, we depart with Jordan on my private jet for a two week long honeymoon on our private island. It will be a couple of weeks of nothing but relaxation, rest, sex, fun, and more sex.

Midway through the flight, Cari expresses she feels queasy. She gets up from her seat and rushes to the restroom. I go after her. The restroom door is unlocked. I open it to find her with a bag over her mouth and her forehead damp with sweat.

I'm concerned. "What's wrong?"

She shakes her head. Just when I think she is about to tell me, she throws up into the bag. Her face is pale, and she's quivering. She pulls the bag away from her face disposing of it in the trash and rinses her mouth. Feeling helpless, all I can do is stand there and hold her hair up and away from her face.

"It's a case of morning sickness."

"I see. Is there anything you can take to stop it?"

Her smile is weak. "It doesn't work like that."

"I don't like to see you suffer."

"I'm not suffering. It's really nothing I can't handle. All that matters is that the baby is fine."

I look down at my watch. "There's still another hour before we land. Why don't you lie down?"

I take her hand and bring her into the bedroom. She lies down and falls asleep almost immediately. I kiss her forehead and cover her with a light blanket. Then I close each window shade and sit in the chair across from the bed not wanting to leave her side in case she has to throw up again. I have to educate myself on this pregnancy and make a mental note to order some books about it so I know what to expect.

The Rolls Royce is ready and waiting when we arrive on the island. We're greeted by Wyeth. He and Jordan collect our bags and place it in the trunk as we get in the car. Cari still looks pale, but for now, her morning sickness has subsided. She puts her head on my shoulder.

When we get to the house, I carry her over the threshold. She doesn't think I need to do it twice. I don't agree with her, but I'll keep it to myself. Wyeth and Jordan bring our bags up to our room while I go into the kitchen to grab a couple of bottles of water.

Cari sits on the barstool at the kitchen counter.

"Do you feel well enough to take a walk on the beach?"

"I do."

"Wyeth can have the chef make us something to eat first and then -"

She puts her hand up to stop me from continuing. "No food for me yet. You have lunch and I'll go unpack."

"I'll help you unpack."

"I can handle the unpacking." She slides off the barstool and goes upstairs.

Wyeth enters the kitchen and I inform him Cari will not be joining me for lunch. I request for a hearty Cobb salad and have him tell the chef to make a little extra in case Cari is up to eating later. I lean against the door to the terrace and reflect back to the evening I had proposed to Cari. It was one of the best nights ever in my life.

~ * ~

Cari and I stroll hand in hand along the beach. The heat from the blazing sun propels us to go into the ocean water to cool off. After frolicking in the water for a bit, we head back to land. In the midst of our way back to the cabana, I stop to appreciate my beautiful and sexy pregnant wife. Her body is gradually changing as the baby continues to grow, but she will always be beautiful to me.

It isn't long before I untie her bikini top and free her tits. Her bikini bottom comes off next. My hands leisurely slide down her silky smooth skin along the curves of her magnificent body. When my hands reach her waist, I drop to my knees and kiss the tiny bump that is our child. I pull back to look up at her and our eyes lock. She gets down on her knees and meets me at eye level. Cradling her face, I move to kiss her. The kiss becomes fervent. I remove my swim trunks and lay her down on the wet sand as the gentle waves lap onto the beach. *Sex on the beach is one of my favorite activities here.* I hover over her aligning myself and ready to let the throes of passion consume us.

"I love you, Mr. Blake."

"I love you, Mrs. Blake."

I will never tire of hearing her say she loves me nor will I ever tire of saying it to her. She has my heart, my life…all of me. *She is my destiny.*

CHAPTER FIFTY

CARI

The sound of the waves awakens me and I open my eyes to see dusk settling in. We both fell asleep after the round of glorious lovemaking we had. I reach for the remote control and turn on the flameless candles inside the lanterns surrounding our cabana. I look over at my husband. *My husband. My man.* He's so attractive even when he's asleep.

I try not to wake him as I go to search for my bikini. We have to head back and shower before dinner. *Where is my bikini?* It's nowhere in the cabana. I walk back towards the ocean and find it on the sand along with Deven's swim shorts. I retrieve our swimwear and put mine back on. Deven is up as I near the cabana.

"Found this." I toss his swim shorts to him.

"I don't need them."

My eyebrows arch. "Do you plan on going into the house naked?"

"Do you really want to go back in? I can have Wyeth set up dinner for us here on the beach."

"I want to take a shower before dinner. The baby and I are hungry."

"Then we definitely need to feed the two of you, but first, I want to start with an appetizer. Come to me, angel."

I do as he requests and go to him. He undoes my bikini bottom. *Oh, well.* He brings his fingers to my clit and gently rubs it. Then I feel his warm tongue teasing me there. He licks and sucks on it with ardor. I throw my head back from the intense pleasure it gives me.

The desire between us is potent. My thighs are tingling and I want him to make love to me again. *Goodness. What has gotten into me? I want him so much.*

All I want to do is constantly have sex with him. He somehow manages to guess my thoughts and pulls me down onto him. I part my legs to straddle him as he works quickly to undo my bikini top. He strokes my taut nipples with his thumbs stirring my arousal which is just about to boil over. The need to have him in me is urgent.

He pushes inside me, and I gyrate my hips causing him to groan. I like to hear him groan when I ride him. It makes me feel good and powerful to know I can do that to him. His hip suddenly bucks striking deep into my core. I cry out his name. He does this a couple of more times before he steadily lowers his hips. Wrapping his legs around mine, he flips me over onto my back keeping our connection intact. Every inch of him is submerged deep inside me. *I feel as if I am the most desirable woman in the world.* He pushes back the hair from my face and draws me in for a passionate kiss.

The love he has for me is immense and palpable as we rock together in perfect rhythm. His tempo changes and he rocks faster. *Ooh...ooh...ooh.* He slams into me and has me seeing stars as I soar up into the galaxy. *Oh. My. God.* He keeps at it until we come together. My body clenches as a wave of orgasm washes over me. He shudders and then lets his warm fluid stream into me.

He looks very deep into my eyes. It's so deep it feels like he's staring into my soul. "You're amazing and perfect in every way. There's no one like you."

I shake my head. "You're the one that's amazing and perfect."

He kisses me and then holds me tight in his arms. This god of hotness owns me completely...mind, body, heart, and soul.

~ * ~

Upon arriving back at the house, Deven tells Wyeth we will have dinner in a half hour. He also informs Wyeth that he and the staff can retire for the evening once dinner is ready. I haven't seen Jordan since returning to the house and question Deven on his whereabouts.

"Where did Jordan go?"

"I gave him some time off. I actually owe him a few days."

"Just a few?"

"He's not going to have much to do here the next two weeks; therefore, it's going to be a vacation for him."

I want to roll my eyes at his comment because being here is really not a vacation of any sorts. There isn't much to see or do on the island. We head on upstairs to shower before dinner.

When we come back downstairs, our covered dinners are on the kitchen island. Deven pulls out the bar stool for me. Once Deven is seated, we take off the plate covers. We are treated to a delicious dinner of grilled snapper with pineapple mango salsa accompanied by grilled vegetables.

Deven stares at my empty plate. "Seems you and the baby were starving."

I'm embarrassed for finishing my meal so quickly. "We were."

His eyes shift to my slight bulge. "Let's make sure you try not to skip any more meals."

"Yes, sir."

He finishes his dinner and we do the dishes rather than running them through the dishwasher. We sit in the living room after cleaning up and check our social media accounts to find many pictures from our wedding already posted. It's the first time we have seen any of the pictures. We begin to scroll through them. Now that the spectacle is over, I can truly appreciate the effort Belle, her team, and Rodrigo put in.

My memory drifts back to the ceremony yesterday. Deven held my attention the minute I saw him at the altar waiting for me. He looked extraordinarily handsome in his three piece tuxedo sporting the widest smile I had ever seen on his gorgeous face. My love for him was spilling over as we stood under the altar listening to the priest, making promises to each other, and patiently waiting for the priest to officially pronounce us husband and wife. What made the moment even more meaningful was knowing our baby took part in our special day.

Deven is everything to me. He's caring, gorgeous, loving, loyal, smart, influential, and strong. My love for him is deep and intense, and I will dedicate myself to always keeping him happy.

Not all of us grow up with the perfect family of a mother, a father, and siblings. Not all of us are lucky enough to know our biological parents. Some

240

of us grow up to love and some of us to hate. As for me, I have been blessed. I never got to know my mother, but I did finally get to know my father. I was raised and showered with love by my doting grandparents. I survived an abusive relationship. I graduated with the highest honors. And I eventually fell in love. Love and happiness always prevails. I am married to the most incredible guy in the universe and come December, we will have our own little family. Ultimately, I have my happy ever after.

Love at first sight isn't reserved for fairy tales. It's real, and Deven and I are proof that it can happen. Deven is my world, and I am his. We're going to have a blissful life together. *He is my destiny.*

The End

Or is it?

Books by R.C. Stern

Fate + Chance = Love (The Blake Family Series Book 1)

Simple + Complicated = Impossible (The Blake Family Series Book 2)

Our Hearts + Our Journey = Our Destiny (The Blake Family Series Book 3)

There's more to come.

The Blake Family Series carries on with Mayleen and Brad's story in the next installment!

Acknowledgements

I would like to begin by giving thanks to God first. The journey to complete this book has been long and at times, grueling. There were days I thought I would never finish writing this story, but through prayer and faith, I got it done.

To my AIH: never forgotten.

To my fabulous readers: thank you, thank you, thank you for your continued support and for giving Cari and Deven the opportunity to share their story with you. They're not gone. They'll still have a place in the upcoming books. Stay tuned! *"Reading gives us someplace to go when we have to stay where we are." - Mason Cooley*

To my brother: the words "thank you" are not enough to express the gratitude I have for you. I can always count on you. Love you. *"Brothers and sisters are special. They fight. They make up. They laugh. They cry. They're far from perfect. But when you really need them, they have your back." – Helen Barry*

To my sons: you both are definitely the best part of me…the best part of my life. I am so very lucky to be your mother. Love you both. *"There has never been, nor will there ever be, anything quite so special as the love between a mother and a son." – Author Unknown*

To BC: you are a blessing. Thank you for your encouragement and feedback. *"Anything is possible when you have the right people there to support you." – Misty Copeland*

To my wonderful friends: a huge shout out to all of you for your constant support. *"Friends are the sunshine of life."* - *John Hay*

To my musketeers: your support has meant a lot to me through the course of writing this third book. Thank you. *"The greatest gift of life is friendship, and I have received it."* – *Hubert H. Humphrey*

To my gracious friend: thank you for all the encouraging words. *"Many people will walk in and out of your life, but only true friends will leave footprints in your heart."* – *Eleanor Roosevelt*

To my bookish friend: thank you for your positive words and boosts especially when I encountered writer's block. *"A sweet friendship refreshes the soul."* – *Proverbs 27:9*

A special thank you to my dearest friend: you have been my number one cheerleader from the very beginning and continue to be. You gave me motivation when I needed it most. You believed that I could get this book done. Thank you for reading what I sent to you, giving me your opinion, and bearing with me as I contemplated the many possible titles for this book. Most of all, thank you for being your wonderful self, and constantly being there for me. *"I have learned that friendship isn't about who you've known the longest, it's about who came and never left your side."* – *Yolanda Hadid*

And last but not least, to my friend who has made an impact on my life: you knew from the beginning what this book meant to me and you stuck by my side through it all. From the bottom of my heart, thank you very much for everything. *"It's unbelievable how you can affect someone else so deeply and never know."* - *Susane Colasanti*

Connect with R.C. Stern

Facebook: www.facebook.com/authorrcstern

Goodreads: www.goodreads.com/R_C_Stern

Instagram: authorrcstern

Pinterest: www.pinterest.com/authorrcstern

TikTok: @authorrcstern

Twitter: www.twitter.com/author_rcstern

www.ingramcontent.com/pod-product-compliance
Lightning Source LLC
Chambersburg PA
CBHW060151180626
46813CB00007B/2696